HOLES IN THE WALL

JC RYAN

BOOKS

By JC Ryan

Rex Dalton K9 Thrillers

The Fulcrum

The Power of Three

Unchained

Sideswiped

The Inca Con

The French Girl

Duty of Care

Donna Teresa

Under the Pope's Windows

The Shanghai Strain

The Delphi Technique

Holes in the Wall

The Abyss

Unearthed

Remorseless

The Message

Dedicated to my good friend Mitch Pender, a military dog trainer, for giving me the idea for this series and guiding me through the intricate and amazing capabilities and psychology of those majestic four-legged soldiers.

Mitch has a lifetime of experience and an exceptional depth of knowledge as a military dog handler and trainer.

I am deeply indebted to my friend, co-author, co-conspirator, and mentor, David Lee, who, with his in-depth understanding of Hong Kong and China, came up with the idea for this novel and tirelessly assisted me in developing the outline and advising and supporting me throughout the entire writing process.

Vinci Books

vinci-books.com

Published by Vinci Books Ltd in 2025

1

Major Characters

Rex Dalton: Former black operations specialist working for CRC.

Catia: Married to Rex. Former Mossad mission support specialist.

Digger: A black Dutch Shepherd. Former military dog. Rex and Catia's companion.

Josh Farley: Black operations specialist working for CRC. Friend of Rex, Catia, and Digger.

Marissa: Married to Josh. Black operations specialist working for CRC. Friend of Rex, Catia, and Digger.

John Brandt: CEO of CRC (Crisis Response Consultancy), a private military contractor specializing in black operations on behalf of their clients such as the CIA and other US security agencies.

Christelle Proll: former deputy director of the DGSE, the French equivalent of the American CIA. Engaged to John Brandt.

Chris McArdle: Second in command of CRC.

Declan Spencer: John Brandt's best friend. Former Navy SEAL commander, now captain of the luxury yacht, the *TOMATS*.

Greg Wade: Team leader of CRC's small but highly skilled group of IT specialists.

Rehka Gyan: IT expert. Greg's love interest.

Howard Lawrence: Director of the CIA.

Martin Richardson: Deputy director in charge of CIA operations.

Yasmin Burke: CIA disguising expert.

Ollie Campbell: A CIA field agent during the Cold War and friend of John Brandt.

Jordyn Lancaster: the senior senator from New York, chairperson of the Senate Committee on Foreign Relations.

Sun Jia: the cleaner.

Sun Yan: Sun Jia's son and computer expert working for Unit 61398, part of the Information Operations and Information Warfare, the cyberwarfare division of the People's Liberation Army (PLA).

Ming and Lei: Sun Yan's wife and daughter.

General Lang Jianhong: Commander of the People's Liberation Army (PLA) Ground Force.

General Dai Min: a senior general in the PLA (People's Liberation Army) in charge of China's nuclear arsenal.

General Jin Ping: in charge of Information Operations and Information Warfare, the cyberwarfare division of the PLA.

Li Lingxin: Former President of the PRC (People's Republic of China).

Liao Qigang: New President of the PRC (People's Republic of China).

Tao Huan: Chairman of the Central Military Commission, the head of the military.

TOMATS: a luxury yacht the name derived from the first letters of Ernest Hemingway's classic short novel, The Old Man and the Sea.

About Holes In The Wall

The PRC's economy is operating at eighty-five percent of capacity. The biggest challenge for manufacturing companies across China is demand, not supply. The national debt is five trillion US dollars. The Chinese economy is a house of cards.

Then the President of the People's Republic of China dies while in office. A heart attack is what the official statement said.

Eight months later, an office cleaner steals candy from a bowl on a general's desk. After that, nothing would ever be the same.

Prologue

Beijing, China

Present time

Every weeknight at 10:00 p.m., the buzzer on the door from the rear alley sounded, and one of the guards would let the cleaner in. They called her *Lǎo fù rén*; it meant old woman. Her real name was Sun Jia. She wasn't old; she was in her early fifties, 54 to be exact. But the privations of life had manifested in her features: dull eyes, deep lines on her face, hunching shoulders, and silver-gray hair. When she laughed, which was not often, gaps could be seen where teeth used to be when she was younger. In China, dental problems were considered a minor health concern, and dental care education all but non-existent.

Pushing a trolley with cloths, bottles with liquid cleaner, a bucket, dusters, brooms, and a vacuum cleaner, she reached the office of General Lang Jianhong, Commander of the People's Liberation Army (PLA) Ground Force. His was one of seven offices she cleaned every weeknight. General Lang's office was the most prestigious of them all; that's why she always started with his.

She had no husband; he left her thirty-four years ago when she told him she was pregnant. Her son worked for the government—something to do with computers. She didn't understand anything about computers, but Sun Yan was the pride of her life. He was married and had one child, a four-year-old girl, Lei, Jia's only grandchild, and the delight of her life. Once a month, on a Sunday morning early, she would make the one-hour train ride to visit her family and spend the day with them. On the other Sundays, she attended church in the morning.

She had always taken pride in her proletarian job, which was the best she could get with her basic education. Serving one of the top generals in the PLA and his staff, even if it was only to clean their offices five times a week, late at night when they'd all gone home, was an honor not bestowed on many.

That was until she met General Lang, once, about seven months ago, when he came into the office late one night to get some documents from his wall safe. He was extremely rude to her, ordering her to wait outside with a barrage of invectives. And when he came out of the office, he told her to spray air freshener in there when she was done to get rid of her disgusting body odor lingering inside.

His words were humiliating, degrading. Jia was dirt poor and uneducated, but she had dignity. She never neglected personal hygiene. Her mother would not have used the words 'cleanliness is next to godliness', but she definitely understood the principle and taught it to Jia from an early age.

That was the day when Jia's respect for the revered general and the joy of her job took a nosedive. But, she didn't have another job to go to. She needed the money; the little financial support her son could afford to give her was not enough to keep body and soul together if she didn't earn an income of her own. Even then, she had barely enough.

Though the joy of her job was gone, there was one thing she still relished: sitting in General Lang's luscious leather swivel chair behind his desk every night and eating one candy from the big hand-painted ceramic bowl sitting on top of the general's impossibly large desk. She knew what she was doing was not only a sin; she was also living dangerously—the general could have counted the candy. But this was her payback for his incivility.

She always took two candies; one she ate, and one she kept for her granddaughter. Tonight, she studied the variety of candy bars and noticed one she had never seen before. It was red, rectangular, about half an inch wide by two inches long, and a quarter of an inch thick. She took it out of the bowl. It had no wrapping. It felt like plastic. She turned it around carefully; she had never seen any candy like that. She licked it—no sweet taste. *Maybe Lei would like it.*

She put it in the top pocket of her overall jacket and retrieved her favorite, a *pinyin*, white rabbit, milk candy wrapped in printed waxed paper. She removed the wrapper and put it in the same pocket as the plastic candy. She put the *pinyin* in her mouth, leaned back in the chair, closed her eyes, and allowed the sweet sensation to fill her mouth and thoughts.

Manhattan, New York, USA

Present time

Josh and Marissa Farley arrived in New York shortly after midday in their rental car. They had a dinner date with Marissa's best friend from university and her husband that night. The next day they'd visit the Statue of Liberty and a few other sites around the city, and on Sunday morning, they would be off to Martha's Vineyard, Massachusetts, for seven days. They'd never been to Martha's Vineyard and wanted to see for themselves what all the fuss was about.

The Farleys had reservations at the four-star One Tree Hill hotel in Manhattan, less than half a mile from Wall Street. They checked in, dropped their luggage in their room, and went out for lunch. Afterward, they returned to the hotel and had a nap, then showered and got ready to meet Marissa's friend and her husband for dinner at their home on Long Island.

Josh fastened his seatbelt, looked at Marissa to see if she was ready, and turned the key in the ignition. His head started spinning. He looked at Marissa; her mouth was open as if she was taking a deep breath. Her image blurred, and then, darkness.

Unknown location

Present time

The pounding headache was the first sign that he was alive. Next was the thundering disconsonant noises filling his ears and then the filthy smell that filled his nostrils, roiling his stomach.

Josh remained still and tried to reconstruct, but all he remembered was starting the car, feeling dizzy, seeing Marissa gasping for air, and then, darkness. He was on a bed, his hands and feet tied to the frame. He was completely naked. His mouth was covered with duct tape, his head covered in a hood—the source of the nauseating odor threatening to rid his stomach of his lunch. *They must have dipped the hood in a cesspool.*

Over the hood was a set of earphones strapped tightly over his ears blasting the sounds of fire alarms, police sirens, breaking glass, crying babies, and screaming people into his brain. With no amount of shaking and wiggling of his head, was he able to get rid of the earphones pumping out the cacophonous sounds.

He pulled on the restraints holding his arms and legs down, but they wouldn't budge.

"Marissa!"

No answer.

He had no idea where he was or what time it was. What he did know was that he and Marissa had been abducted. And both of them were going to die—after they'd been tortured for information. Who their abductors were, what information they wanted, he didn't know, not yet. For now, the abductors were softening him up with the age-old psychological routine of sleep deprivation, starvation, and disorientation.

What are they doing to Marissa?

"Marissa!" he shouted again—it was useless; his voice was muffled by the duct tape and the stinking hood and the unhinging noise in his ears.

Then, all of a sudden, the noise stopped, and Josh heard the screams of a woman in his ears. He jerked on the restraints and twisted; it was as futile as before.

"Marissa!"

A Chinese-accented computerized voice came over the earphones, "That was your sexy wife, Josh. She's entertaining the men next door. That black, laced lingerie of hers got them... how shall I put it... worked up."

The Hadean noises resumed.

Part I

EIGHT MONTHS IN THE MAKING

Chapter One

TEN MARSHALS TO SEE YOU

Beijing, China

Eight months ago

Zhongnanhai, literally translated as 'Central and Southern Seas,' is the former imperial garden in the Imperial City of Beijing next to the Forbidden City. It is the central headquarters for the Communist Party of China and the State Council, China's central government, and the office of the President of the People's Republic of China. Zhongnanhai is China's version of America's White House.

In his office at Zhongnanhai, Li Lingxin, President of the PRC (People's Republic of China), was at his desk. The past three hours had been the worst of his life, and it was about to get worse as it dawned on him that his hourglass had run empty. It began with a call from the President of the United States three hours ago.

For the past two years, Li had a task force working on

a weapons-grade virus, which he and his co-conspirators were hours away from unleashing on the world. He had grand visions of how an unsuspecting world would descend into utter chaos as their economies collapsed and civil unrest ripped their countries apart. In the utter chaos, China would have emerged as a knight in shining armor to save them from the devastation of the virus and total economic ruin. Within twelve to eighteen months, China would have been the most powerful nation on earth. He, Li Lingxin, would have been the most powerful man on earth, the supreme leader. Chairman Mao's hundred-year plan to make China the world leader by 2049 would have been achieved in 70 years—30 years ahead of time.

But three hours ago, that call from the President of the United States had turned the dream into a nightmare. General Yuan Lee, the man in charge of China's biological warfare program, under whose leadership the deadly virus had been developed, had betrayed him and defected to America. How it happened without the Ministry of State Security's (MSS) knowledge was a conundrum he didn't have the time to solve. But when he saw the traitor sitting next to the President of the United States, it felt like a bullet had hit him in the stomach—it was just a matter of time before he would bleed out and die.

Two and a half hours after that fateful call, he had signed the last executive order and had been staring at his own letter of resignation for the past half hour when there was a knock on the door. His aide entered and told him that there were ten marshals in the reception area, demanding to see him immediately. He said nothing, only nodded slightly, and sighed softly.

The marshals filed into his office, formed a semicircle in

front of his desk, and stared at him. No word was said, not even a greeting. Everyone knew what this was about.

The last person to enter was one of the president's guards. He also said nothing; he didn't salute either. He walked to the president's desk, unholstered his 9mm NP-22 pistol, a clone of the German-made Sig Sauer P226. He removed the magazine, checked that one round was chambered, pocketed the magazine, and placed the gun with the one round in it on the president's desk, within reach of his right hand. He turned and left the room in the same manner he entered, neither saying a word nor saluting.

Exactly one hour and five minutes later, the lonely guard outside the president's office door jolted when he heard a single gunshot on the other side of the door. He took a step toward the door but then remembered the marshals' instructions and remained at his post.

Less than a minute later, the door opened, and one of the marshals appeared in the anteroom pushing the president's office chair. The president's body was slumped in the chair. His face and upper body were covered with his own jacket.

The guard came to attention. There were no other guards.

The marshal said, "Your shift is over. You can go now. We'll take care of this."

The guard saluted, made a half-turn, and left.

It was Li's wish that his body should not lie in state, nor be embalmed for posterity like Chairman Mao's or some of history's most infamous and controversial leaders. It was his wish to be cremated and his ashes scattered over the South China Sea.

Seven days later, the late president's wishes were honored in a massive, glamorous state funeral. The world was told that President Li had suffered a fatal heart attack. Only a few people knew different.

By 6:00 a.m., the vice president of China, President Li's other advisors, and co-conspirators were all in custody, and the haggling to elect a new president was in progress.

Beijing, China

The three most powerful offices in China were: the president, the general secretary of the Communist Party of China, and the chairman of the Central Military Commission, the head of the military.

Li Lingxin held all three offices. That had to change. One man with all that power was not good.

On paper, the Communist Party Congress (CPC) determined who would lead the 1.39 billion people of China. The CPC delegates elected the Central Committee of about 200 members. The Central Committee, in turn, elected the 24-member Politburo, and they selected the seven-member Politburo Standing Committee, China's top decision-making body.

Under the People's Republic of China (PRC) constitution, the president was supposed to be mostly a ceremonial office with limited power. But Li Lingxin changed that. He managed to remove the term limits to his presidency, which was always two terms for his predecessors. He had also centralized much of the institutional power by taking personal charge of economic and social reforms, military restructuring and modernization, and the internet.

However, what very few people outside the Communist Party's inner circles knew was that the president and anyone else in the top three positions was actually beholden to the marshals. There were seventeen of them after General Yuan's defection. They were generals of the People's Liberation Army (PLA) who was not controlled by, nor were they part of the PRC government. They were part of the Chinese Communist Party (CCP).

Li Lingxin came to power with the support of eleven of the eighteen marshals at the time. Not a significant margin; if two generals changed allegiance, Li would have been in trouble. And that's precisely what happened now—ten of the marshals wanted him out.

Chapter Two

PRESIDENT HESITANT

Beijing, China

Eight months ago

A meeting of the Politburo was to be held on the third day to elect a new president, four days before Li's state funeral.

In the lead-up to the Politburo meeting, behind the scenes, it was a raucous affair. Candidates were identified by the marshals. The candidates had very little involvement in the process. They made no speeches, ran no campaigns; in fact, they didn't even know they were in the run; they would merely be told by the marshals once their deliberations were over.

After much horse-trading and wheeling and dealing, three candidates had risen to the top. Tao Huan had seven marshals in support, Zhuan Zexi had six, and Liao Qigang had four. Liao had been considered an outsider all along.

Still, when all had been said and done, Liao's marshals were the kingmakers.

In the aftermath of Li's failed attempt to elevate China to world leader status, the international community had to be appeased. Zhuan Zexi and Tao Huan were hardliners, hawks. Zhuan much more so than Tao. It was not what the country needed now. Liao was a moderate, a dove, and highly regarded by the international community because of his free-market initiatives. Policies that the world believed would eventually lead China to a western-style democracy with a free market economy.

Tao Huan's marshals made a compromise; they would throw their weight behind Liao Qigang to become President and General Secretary in exchange for Tao Huan becoming Chairman of the Central Military Commission, the head of the military. And to make sure Zhuan Zexi would not become a problem in the future, he was given a choice, mayor of Shanghai or early retirement on a full pension. Zhuan, could not have been happy, but in a politically correct gesture, for the Party's sake and unity within, he chose retirement. A prescient choice, he would later come to realize.

By midday on the second day, Liao, unaware that he was even in the run for the presidency, had the support of ten marshals and was informed of their decision.

However, Liao told them he had no desire to be president. His reluctance stemmed from the fact that he knew what was going on in China's economy, just like the late Li Lingxin did, which was the *raison d'être* for his plan to unleash the virus across the globe.

By definition, Liao was not a pure communist. He was an economic liberal in that sense. But very few people understood that Liao's liberal fiscal policies were not to subvert the Party and turn China into a capitalist state; it was to let Western politicians and business leaders think China was advancing toward democracy and capitalism. But all along, Liao's only intent was to acquire foreign capital, technology, and other resources to modernize China and *strengthen* the Communist Party. Mao's communism didn't exist anymore. It had morphed into socialism with a Chinese flavor, a euphemism for economic policies appearing to be capitalistic and free market-orientated, but in reality, it was a totalitarian, top-down structure with rigid rules and social restrictions.

China's economic policies, to which Liao had contributed a great deal over the past two decades, had lifted the country from obscurity to the second most powerful economy in the world in three decades. China was now the top nation globally in terms of manufacturing output and the percentage of its national output generated by its manufacturing sector. China's total GDP in 1980 was less than $90 billion in current dollar value. Today, it was over $12 trillion. China had double-digit year-on-year economic growth. The west was smiling; China was on the way to democracy, a new player in the international market, the answer to many of their own economic problems caused by expensive labor and overbearing labor unions. The world had never seen such immense economic growth in such a short time.

Notwithstanding three decades of spectacular economic growth, the Chinese economy was on the verge of collapse. It was like looking at an intricate pattern of dominoes on a large table before the first domino would fall over and set off a cascade of toppling pieces until all the pieces were down. Only one had to fall. And there were already a few that were shaking violently.

Liao's reluctance was quickly defeated when the marshals reminded him about loyalty to the Party. "Was it not for the Party, you would've been a peasant pig farmer somewhere in the countryside," the lead marshal, General Lang, told him.

Liao's grandfather was with Mao Tse Tung on the Long March. An eight-thousand-mile strategic retreat by the Red Army of the Communist Party of China to evade the Kuomintang (Chinese Nationalist Party) army. Only ten percent of those who started the arduous march completed it. The Long March was the beginning of Mao Tse Tung's ascension to power and sealed the personal prestige of Mao and his supporters as the new leaders of the Party for decades to come. They were considered heroes and appointed to leadership positions and assured a well-heeled future.

Liao's father, the son of a high-ranking Maoist who had fought in the revolution, was a party man and member of the Politburo.

Liao was born into privilege, grew up in Beijing, went to a prestigious private school in France where he mixed with and befriended the children of Chinese Communist Party members, the children of party officials and marshals and generals. That was where he met Tao Huan, who had now been selected as Chairman of the Central Military Commission.

After school, Liao studied economics at the University of Cambridge in England and earned a Ph.D. before returning to China to take up a role in government as was preordained for the children of the privileged class.

If there was one thing Liao had learned early in life, it was that one never refused the Party. All power came from the Party. The Party was your life. The Party took care of you from the cradle to the grave. The Party made you what you were. If you wanted power, you belonged to the Party, and when the Party needed you, you never refused. If Liao had a religion, it was the Party.

He had no choice; he had to accept.

General Dai Min, a senior general in the PLA in charge of China's nuclear arsenal, finally put a stop to Liao's objections when he said, "The dire economic situation you have described to us is partly your fault, Liao. So, get over to Zhongnanhai and fix it and lead this country to greatness. You'll become the most powerful man on earth. You have our support. Get on with it. And don't disappoint us."

At the end of the discussion, General Lang Jianhong told Liao that he and Tao would get an induction the next night after their confirmation by the Politburo.

Tao didn't have much to say during this meeting; he was happy to take up the role offered to him without any quibbling, as it befitted a loyal Party member.

The next day, the Politburo 'elected' Liao Qigang as the new President of the People's Republic of China and Tao Huan as Chairman of the Central Military Commission, the head of the military. The day after, they would start their tenures.

The palace revolution was complete.

In whispered tones, in the inner circles of Communist China's hallways of power, Liao would often be referred to as President Hesitant.

Chapter Three

THE INDUCTION

Beijing, China

Eight months ago

It was late-night, past ten, when General Lang Jianhong opened the door to the secured meeting room in Zhongnan-hai's basement and let Liao in to meet the rest of the marshals who supported him. General Tao Huan was already seated at the conference table.

General Lang was the leader of the group and did most of the talking. It quickly became clear this was not an induc-tion in the true sense of the word; it was a military order group—Liao and Tao were there to get their orders.

"You have four and a half years left until the next Congress, but, as you know, that means nothing," Lang said. "Congress does not elect the paramount leaders; we do. We're the trustees of our country's safety, security, and future. We can and will 'retire' you whenever we deem it necessary."

There was no ambiguity in Lang's statement. Liao and Tao understood what he meant and nodded in silence.

"I'll tell you what Li Lingxin did and why he's gone." Lang told them about the virus Li was about to unleash in the world. Liao knew all about it though he never supported Li in the endeavor. To Tao, it was news.

"Not that we disagreed with the idea of world control; after all, that's the hundred-year plan," Lang said. "But Li was wrong with his method and timing. And he never consulted with us."

The latter was probably the main reason for his downfall, Liao thought.

"China is not prepared for the backlash from the world. The inevitable war that would have followed would have destroyed our country. We couldn't let him carry on with it. The one mistake we made was to allow Li Lingxin too much power. We won't make that mistake again. Henceforth you should regard us as the trustees of the political power of China. We're your mentors and protectors."

Liao and Tao didn't have to be geniuses to understand the message. It was crystal clear—henceforth, they were the puppets of the marshals.

General Dai said, "The reason we have deeply troubling economic issues, Liao, is partly due to you and your liberal economic policies. What else did you expect when you infected our country with the disease of capitalism? But it has gone so far it can't be reversed. We have to go ahead, but slow it down. We've taken three steps forward. It's time to take two steps back and get our plans in place. You brought the economic policies in; you have to manage them now."

Liao was wondering where and when the marshals became so educated in economic matters that they felt confident to advise him on it. But he knew better than to comment.

The meeting continued for another hour or so before General Lang concluded, "We will give you a few weeks to get your feet under your tables, and then we'll start to create a new plan to achieve the hundred-year plan. We're thirty years away from 2049, but if done properly, we can achieve the goal much earlier."

Liao let out his breath quietly as he and Tao left the room. *At least I have a chance to survive the first few months.*

Chapter Four

FIRST DAY IN OFFICE

Beijing, China

Eight months ago

On the fourth day after Li Lingxin's demise, Liao Qigang, the new President of the People's Republic of China, walked into the office where he, as Minister of Commerce, had visited so many times in the past to brief President Li on economic matters.

Though he had a full contingent of staff at his beck and call, he didn't expect any welcome cards or a guard of honor to cheer him on and wish him good fortune as he started his new job. He checked the desktop and then the drawers; there was no letter from his predecessor. He was not surprised; President Li had probably not been given time to write one.

It made him grin humorlessly when he thought about the anecdote of the three letters. A new president arrived in his office for the first day and found three sealed envelopes on his desk left by his predecessor. The envelopes were numbered one to three. On each envelope was a hand-written message. On the first, it said, "Open this one when you encounter your first problem," and so forth on the second and third envelopes.

Three months later, the new president had his first real problem. He opened the first envelope, and the letter inside contained one line, "Blame it on me."

Six months later, the second envelope had to be opened because of another crisis, and the message inside was another one-liner, "Announce a restructure."

A year later, the third and final envelope had to be opened, and the one-line message was, "Time for you to write three letters."

The thing was, Liao's predecessor had already been blamed, in secret. In public, the man was a deity. No one would dare to criticize him; it would reflect badly on the Party. As for the second option, the restructuring had already taken place. Liao had been dealt a hand of cards; he had to play with what he had.

Liao looked around and noticed the only new feature since his last visit—the bullet hole in the wall behind the chair where the former president sat. He started to wonder why it had not been fixed when it dawned on him—*it's a message for me.*

Liao was the man who kept Li Lingxin abreast of the economic state of affairs. China was heading over the edge of an economic cliff into a canyon of oblivion. The late President Li understood it, and the virus was his plan to stop the economic decline and make China the greatest nation on earth. Li came within a hairbreadth of achieving it, was it not for the betrayal by General Yuan Lee, which was one of the things that had to be unraveled. How did it happen, and who was responsible? He had summoned the Minister of State Security to his office for the first meeting of the day.

The second urgent matter was Li Lingxin's virus. For that, he had summoned the director-general of the CCDC (Chinese Center for Disease Control) to his office for the second meeting of the day.

The third and most important of all was the plan to make China the world leader that he and Tao had been ordered to develop and implement under the auspices of the ten marshals, the Trustees. For that, he and Tao had scheduled a meeting that would last the rest of the day.

Liao sighed. He was wondering if he should write the three letters now and put his head in the path of a bullet and decorate the wall with another hole as a message for his successor. But he had never held a gun in his hands; he was more than likely to make a big mess of it. Maybe poison? But he had six to eight months. Maybe there was a way out? He would know when he had met with the second-most powerful man in China, General Tao Huan, Chairman of the Central Military Commission, the head of the military.

Chapter Five

MAKE AN EXAMPLE OF THEM

Beijing, China

Eight months ago

But first, the matter of the traitor, General Yuan Lee.

Xuan Bai was the Minister in charge of the Ministry of State Security (MSS), China's intelligence, security, and secret police agency responsible for counterintelligence, foreign intelligence, and political security. They have been described as one of the most secretive and brutal intelligence organizations in the world.

Xuan had no illusions that this was going to be a friendly meet and greet with the new president. The fact that he was the president's first visitor on his first day in office was an indication of the importance of the meeting. It could only be one matter. How did General Yuan defect without the MSS knowing about it? In China, it was not only the rank-and-file citizens who were kept under watch by the state's vast surveillance apparatus. Senior officials had their watchers too. But in Yuan's case, his department had slipped up, grossly.

Xuan didn't know much about the man who came out of nowhere and became president. As Minister of State Security, he and President Liao, former Minister of Commerce, knew each other, but they very seldom had the need for each other's company; therefore, he didn't know the man personally as well as he would have liked to.

When he stepped into the president's office, he was still reeling from the humiliation inflicted on the MSS by General Yuan's defection. He knew the Americans were behind it, but he had no answer for the obvious question awaiting him inside the president's office. "How is it possible that your department, with its vast resources and technology, didn't even have a whiff of it?"

But Xuan had no way of knowing that seven of the marshals who supported the new president were, in actual fact, involved in the whole affair. He would've been infuriated to know that the marshals had collaborated with his archenemy, the CIA, in the process.

President Liao didn't know about it either.

The bottom line was, four days after the defection was discovered and President Li had died in this very office, Xuan Bai still had no idea how the Americans did it.

As far as Xuan was concerned, this meeting had only one of two outcomes; he would be arrested and disappeared; that was the most likely scenario. Or he would be asked to resign; that would be a best-case scenario.

Xuan's initial assessment of Liao was that he seemed to be an even-keeled soft-spoken man, not one given to outbursts of rage. It sounded, Xuan didn't recognize any hidden messages, as if the President merely wanted to know what progress had been made to unravel the mystery. All Xuan could tell him was that they were working on it.

Liao seemed to accept it, but then there was a slight, almost imperceptible change in his demeanor. He looked Xuan straight in the eyes and said in a measured tone, "I want you to leave no stone unturned to find out how it happened and who was responsible. And then I want you to make an example of them."

"Yes, Mr. President." Xuan felt a cold chill run down his spine as he looked into the president's dark penetrating eyes. They reminded him of the eyes of a snake. He adjusted his initial assessment of Liao from an even-keeled person to an extremely dangerous person.

Xuan was relieved when he walked out of the meeting, knowing he'd just been given another lease on life. But the message in those spine-chilling eyes was unmistakable— make this happen, and don't make a mess of it.

The moment Xuan was back behind his desk, he asked his secretary to get hold of the senior MSS agent in Shanghai, Ren Shi, the man in charge of the Yuan Lee investigation.

Beijing, China

Eight months ago

The next meeting was about Li Lingxin's virus still raging in Shanghai—it had to be stopped.

The Chinese Center for Disease Control and Prevention (CCDC) is an agency of the National Health Commission, based in Beijing. Their task is to develop and apply disease prevention and control (especially infectious diseases) to improve and protect the public health and safety of the citizens of the PRC.

Liao instructed the director-general of the CCDC to take all necessary measures to contain and eradicate the virus. Even so, they had to keep it as a weapon in their biological arsenal. Therefore, scientists had to find a cure and vaccine for it.

The director-general understood his orders and undertook to make it happen. And he kept his promise. Within days, he had put all areas where the disease was raging into draconian lockdowns and enforced them with the help of the police and military. Within weeks the number of infected went down, and three months later, the virus was gone.

Chapter Six

THE STATE OF THE NATION

Beijing, China

Eight months ago

Shortly after the director-general of the CCDC had left, Liao's secretary told him General Tao Huan had arrived for their meeting.

Tao entered, took a seat, and accepted a cup of tea from the secretary. He must have noticed the bullet hole in the wall but didn't comment. They didn't have to say it; they knew they were in it together—if the one failed, so would the other. And that could very well mean two more bullet holes in the wall.

Liao and Tao were never close friends during their school and university years or thereafter; neither were they enemies. Liao was an economist, and Tao, a militarist. They had different interests, expertise, and world views. Even so, they had a common loyalty to the Party and the realization that the buck had been passed to them, and it stopped with them.

Logically that should have made them friends, allies at least, but it didn't—friends and allies could trust each other; they couldn't. For self-preservation, it was best to assume that they were appointed as each other's watchers. That's how things were done in the PRC. A person was given a job, then two more were assigned to make sure the job got done, and a third person was assigned to watch the watchers. Everyone knew they were being watched.

Liao told Tao what was going on in the economy but remained careful not to criticize anyone in the process. Tao was not uninformed about the economic problems; he just didn't understand it as well as Liao did.

But Liao was used to it. He had to explain economic principles to many people many times; most noteworthy were fellow ministers and his predecessor. International economic matters were a complicated subject at the best of times. And sometimes, Liao thought, those who said economists couldn't even tell what happened in the past, let alone predict the future, were right. Notwithstanding, some things were very easy to understand: if you spend more than you earn, you will be in trouble very soon. Simple as that.

Besides the deficits, there was the US-China trade war that had been gaining rapid momentum. The US imported $539.5bn in goods from China in 2018 and sold to China $120.3bn in return. The difference between those two numbers—$419.2bn—was the trade deficit, and that was the reason for the US-China trade war. It was one of the major factors impacting the country's economy.

"Not only that," Liao said, "we have to be honest with ourselves and admit that some of our business practices, such as our state-sponsored intellectual property theft, currency manipulation, and fentanyl production, are also to blame for the growing antagonism among our trading partners.

"Those factors together with a global economic downturn and pervasive austerity measures implemented by governments across the world are the reasons China is rapidly losing its glitter as an investment haven. Our trading partners are taking punitive measures against us for our shady business practices by withdrawing business from us. The economy is now operating at eighty-five percent of capacity. The biggest challenge for manufacturing companies across China had become demand, not supply."

"A bleak picture indeed," Tao sighed.

Liao nodded. "All that needs to happen now to take us back to the dark ages is the eruption of the volcano in the Ching Hai Province or the Three Gorges Dam in the Yangtze River Valley to break."

For years, scientists have been warning about China's volcanoes. There are no less than fifteen of them varying in size and in various states of activity. Some of them are posing imminent threats; others are dormant. In the highlands of the Ching Hai Province is a volcano that has been dormant for more than 450,000 years. But lately, geologists have been raising alarm that this one was overdue for an eruption. Some thought the geologists were fearmongering; others believed them and were worried. The devastation caused by such an event would be immeasurable. More than half a billion people would die, and large parts of the country would become uninhabitable for a very long time.

But the most real threat was the Three Gorges Dam.

Throughout its history, China had tried to tame its rivers. But they were not always successful. The 3,400-mile Yellow River was the second-longest in China and was known as 'China's Sorrow' because of the floods that had devastated communities along its banks in the past. Discounting famines and pandemics, the 1931 central China floods were deemed the deadliest natural disaster of the 20th century. More than 140,000 people drowned, and no less than 3.7 million died in the nine months that followed.

The Three Gorges Dam got its name from its location near three scenic gorges along the Yangtze River. When the construction of the dam was completed in 2008, it was 202 yards tall and 2,525 yards wide. It had 34 power generators producing 22,500 megawatts—the world's largest hydroelectric facility. Apart from the electricity generated, the dam also served as a pivotal part of the flood-control system for the Yangtze basin protecting cities such as Wuhan and Nanjing.

The Three Gorges Dam, although the biggest, was only one of several dams along the Yangtze. The network of dams had to hold and release water in a coordinated fashion to ensure that downstream reservoirs and overflow lakes were not overwhelmed all at once. The biggest threat was massive rainstorms that could devastate the entire system. Such a calamity would decimate major urban centers downstream and kill and displace millions. Transportation links and supply chains would be disrupted. Widespread disease and the death of millions more would follow. The physical damage would be massive, and the loss of life staggering—politically and economically, it would be the 'perfect storm' for any president.

Tao was shaking his head when Liao finished. "For now, let's hope that we'll be spared those natural disasters. Let's talk about something we can control; the economy. What has to be done to get it back on track?"

Liao said, "Earn more and spend less. In other words, austerity measures. Severe austerity measures. It will take time for those to take effect, and it's going to hurt the people. They will suffer, they're going to be unhappy, and unrest will be rife. It's going to get awfully bad before it might get better, if ever."

"How much will Hong Kong, Macau, and Taiwan contribute if we controlled them?" Tao wanted to know.

"Well, all of them have a much higher per capita income than we have on the mainland. In theory, if they were fully incorporated into China, we would share in their wealth. But then you have to keep in mind that they have only a fraction of the number of citizens we have. The increase in income our citizens would see would be insignificant. There would, however, be other benefits to our economy, which could make a bigger dent in our economic problems. Be that as it may, it's not as easy as just annexing those areas; there are international political and economic repercussions to consider."

"Agreed," said Tao. "But if we're able to limit international interference, it might be a profitable venture?"

"Yes, absolutely, but on the proviso that our trading partners don't inflict more economic damage through boycotts than the profit we stand to make."

"How about the untapped fish, oil, and gas resources in the South China Sea around the Spratlys?" Tao asked.

"We're not going to fish ourselves out of our fiscal troubles," Liao said with a wan smile. "But the oil and gas could make a significant difference. However, to tap into those sources, we'll have to control the South China Sea, at least the area around the Spratly Islands. Is that possible?"

"We can if we control the Straits of Malacca, Sunda, and Lombok."

"I don't know how you're going to do that, but I can tell you what we're going to need is a distraction. We need to get the people's minds off their suffering and focus them on external threats and opportunities."

Tao, as a militarist, believed in the words of Chairman Mao, 'Political power grows from the barrel of a gun'—military power. Not parade ground displays such as the October 1 National Day Parade held in Tiananmen Square in Beijing every year. No, he wanted China to be the dominant military power in the world. The Americans and NATO allies had been fighting wars since WWII while China had been training. It was time to give the world a real demonstration of the PLA's real military power.

For the next few hours, Tao educated Liao on what China had been doing for decades to increase its military power. The PLA consisted of five professional service branches: The Ground Force, Navy, Air Force, Rocket Force, and the Strategic Support Force. With 2.8 million soldiers, China had the largest military in the world. The United States was second. The only other countries with more than one million active-duty troops were Russia, India, and North Korea—all of them China's neighbors.

The Global Firepower ranking used 50 different measurements, including military might, financial information, logistical capacity, and geography, to determine a country's PowerIndex ('PwrIndx') score. The Chinese military was ranked third in the world, holding a military power index rating of 0.067 (0.0000 being perfect). The USA had a rating of 0.062, and Russia a rating of 0.064. In other words, despite their overwhelming numbers, China still ranked third in terms of firepower.

"But no one ever mentions the sixth branch, the Cyber Force," Tao said. "At cyber warfare, we're decades ahead of anyone else. If we had more time, I'd tell you in much more detail about how important cyber warfare has become in our time. For now, suffice it to say that cyberspace is the frontline of modern warfare, and we're the world leader."

Liao frowned.

Tao explained. "When you disable the enemy's cyber capability, the war is more or less over. Their electric grid and communications systems will be down. Their fighter jets, bombers, and drones won't fly—those that get off the ground will end up smashing into the side of a mountain or into the ocean. Their satellites will be out of commission, and their ships will drift around in the sea rudderless and blind—sitting ducks for us to pick off at will.

"That's how we can outmaneuver them—win the cyber battle, and the rest will tumble like dominoes."

"I guess we have to add to those forces also our Economic Force," Liao said. "Although I'm the first to admit, our economic warfare capability has diminished greatly. Still, it is a force that our enemies cannot ignore because so many of them are very much dependent on us to keep their economies afloat."

"But maybe with the right plan, over time, we can rebuild it. For the past three decades, we've been winning the global economic war. We have to get back on top again," said Tao. "I don't know about you, but I got the impression the Trustees already have a high-level plan which they will communicate to us in the months to come?"

"Yes, I got the same feeling. Even so, we have to take into account the world has slowly but surely been waking up to the fact that there is indeed a global economic war going on. They're not so gullible anymore," Liao said.

Chapter Seven

TO DEAL WITH REALITY

Washington, D.C., USA

Eight months ago

Liao and Tao would have been surprised to know that twelve time zones away, in Washington D.C., the President of the United States was in conclave with his advisors. The main talking-point on their agenda was China's new leaders.

The President of the United States and his advisors could only speculate about what had happened behind the scenes during the selection process; nevertheless, the outcome was a big surprise. Groups of analysts in the intelligence community made it their business to study high-ranking politicians and government officials across the world. China was no exception—the analysts knew all about Tao Huan, Zhuan Zexi, and others. A few of them even had bets on who the next president of China was going to be—Liao Qigang didn't feature on any of their lists.

After opening the meeting, the president asked, "Does anyone believe Li Lingxin died of a heart attack?"

No one did.

The president smiled. "Good. I feel a lot better now. I know I'm regarded as the most powerful man on earth, but giving someone on the other side of the world a fatal heart attack over a video connection is probably not within my powers."

When the laughing subsided, the president continued. "Am I the only one who was surprised about the election of Liao Qigang?"

Tia Chapman, Director of National Intelligence (DNI), smiled. "No, Mr. President, it was a big surprise across the board. But once we got over it, it made sense that, given the circumstances, they decided to go with a moderate rather than one of the hardliners such as Zhuan Zexi or any of the other hawks. Tao is also a military man and hawkish but probably less so than any of the other choices they had."

"I think it's also of significance that they've decided to break the hold Li Lingxin had on the country by holding the three most powerful positions; president, the general secretary, and the chairman of the Central Military Commission," the Secretary of State said.

"So, what can we expect from the Liao-Tao duo?" the president asked.

Tia Chapman said, "Liao is an economist. Looking at his track record, one could easily conclude that he will be different than other Chinese presidents. After all, he's the brains behind the Special Economic Zones (SEZ), areas in China where free market-oriented economic policies and flexible governmental measures are in operation instead of the 'planned,' as in totally government-controlled, economic activities elsewhere in the country. The SEZs are attractive to foreign and domestic businesses because trade is conducted without the interference of the Chinese central government, and it offers attractive tax and business incentives to entice foreign investment and technology.

"But that would be a mistake. Although Liao might be a pro-business communist, he's a communist no less. His economic policies are there to strengthen the Chinese Communist Party and nothing else—they won't become capitalists under him. My bet is they're already planning their next move as we speak. Remember, they all subscribe to Mao's hundred-year plan; they won't give up on their dream of a world under Chinese communist rule."

Hayden Price, White House Chief of Staff, nodded. "And that's one of their major advantages over us; they make five-year, ten-year, hundred-year plans and execute them while we can only bargain on four-year plans, the time between election cycles."

Over the next half an hour, discussing Li's virus threat and the factors giving rise to it, they concluded that a lot had gone wrong over a long period when previous administrations got on the China bandwagon without understanding the Chinese Communist Party's mindset. The CCP had no intention to evolve into democracy and capitalism. Their SEZs were not the beginning of capitalism. They were only a way to generate income for the CCP to execute their world domination strategy and get the world to pay for it.

"Much of it can be blamed on our mistaken belief that everyone in the world wants to be like us," said Lauren Woods, the Secretary of State. "Not everyone wants to be like us. China wants to be communists, not capitalists. And they want to bring their brand of communism to the world. Lately, it has become obvious that the CCP believes they have an obligation. In fact, they claim it is their right to rule the world."

Stanley Newton, the Trade Advisor, added, "When we and the rest of the Western world allowed China into the World Trade Organization in 2001, no one really expected the outcomes we see today. With the wisdom of hindsight, it is probably safe to say it was a mistake to let them in the door without laying down the rules first. We should've insisted that they were allowed to join on the condition that we play on a level playing field. In other words, no currency manipulation, equal labor laws, and other acceptable free-market principles. We thought the Chinese were impressed by our technology and manufacturing prowess and wanted to learn from us. They were, and they did, but not enough to abandon communism.

"China has cheap labor, and their labor unions are a joke, Mr. President. Some say their 2008 Labor Contract Law permits collective bargaining similar to those in Western countries. But those who say that ignore the fact that the only unions they allow are those affiliated with the All-China Federation of Trade Unions, the Communist Party's official union.

"They manipulate their currency, and they subsidize their manufacturing, so much so, they have an unfair advantage over every competitor. From across the world, companies outsource their manufacturing to China, and we're the biggest culprit.

"I can go on. The bottom line is, Mr. President, the Chinese pulled the wool over the eyes of Western politicians and business leaders, having them believe China was advancing toward democracy and capitalism. The truth is they've acquired our money, technology, and other resources to modernize China—communist China, that is.

"For more than three decades, the West has pumped hundreds of billions into China's state-owned businesses. We've equipped them with almost everything they need to match us, technologically, economically, and militarily.

"Not only did China benefit from the demand for their manufacturing services, but they also excelled at the theft of intellectual property. To the tune of six hundred billion per year from us alone. Globally, that figure would probably approach one trillion dollars. They stole and copied from us and built an entire economy on our innovations. I don't think for one moment they're going to cease and desist."

"But their economy is in the tank at the moment, is it not?" the president said.

Blake Gordon, the Secretary of the Treasury, said, "Yes, Mr. President, over the past few years, their economy has contracted by almost twenty percent; they're in the doldrums. Their exports are dwindling fast. Officially, its government debt is more than five trillion US dollars. Standard and Poor estimates there is also an additional five-point-eight trillion undeclared debt. The declared debt alone equates to more than forty-eight percent of their GDP. More than twenty-five percent of all loans are nonperforming in Chinese banks. The Chinese economy is a house of cards at the moment. They'll have to deal with it, or they'll face disaster. That's probably part of the reason they elected an economist as president and not a military hawk."

"Agreed," said the president. "They *are*, indeed, facing economic problems, and they're worried about it. And they've just given us a demonstration of how they intend to deal with it. That virus was, as far as I'm concerned, only the first salvo—thank God they missed, but I'm of the opinion they're reloading their guns, so to speak."

The DNI nodded. "I agree, Mr. President. They might be a bit embarrassed that we caught them red-handed before they could unleash the virus, but that's not going to change their obsession to achieve Mao Tse Tung's ideal of a communist-controlled planet by 2049.

"Think about the BRI, Belt and Road Initiative, formerly known as One Belt One Road or OBOR, the Chinese world infrastructure plan to build roads, rail and shipping lanes which would connect almost seventy percent of the world's population and give access to more than half of the world's GDP. A modern-day silk route, but with a slight difference; they would build it for the countries they could persuade to take part in the initiative and loan them the money. Those are 'debt traps' that would shackle those countries to China, which would seize strategic assets as compensation for defaulted loans and contracts. Thus, China gets control of it all.

"And let's not forget their continued illicit production of the deadly opioid, fentanyl. They've promised to stop. They lied and continued. They are killing forty-five thousand Americans per year. They won't stop; it's a moneyspinner for them—more than a hundred billion dollars annually."

The President said, "If there is a lesson to be learned from this virus bullet we've dodged, it is that we've reached a crossroads with China. We agree that we can't trust them, and by all accounts, Liao is not going to be much different from his predecessor. The question is, what do we do to assure we're not caught off-guard again?"

The DNI said, "Mr. President, the biggest chink in our armor is the lack of intelligence. China destroyed our intel-ligence networks, which left us clueless about the virus threat. It was an act of God that we became aware of it and happened to have highly skilled assets in Hong Kong at the time to solve the problem in the nick of time. The only reason Li Lingxin had a 'heart attack' was because he was caught red-handed by outsiders, which, if allowed to continue, would've plunged them into a war with the entire world. Their goal is to isolate and destroy the US, and then the rest would topple easily. China was not ready for a global war, but they are betting on themselves in a one-on-one confrontation with the USA. As I said before, I think they're already back at the drawing board planning the next offensive."

The DCI, Howard Lawrence, said, "The Chinese military leaders all but worship their ancient military genius Sun Tzu who said, 'All warfare is based on deception. Hence, when we are able to attack, we must seem unable; when using our forces, we must appear inactive; when we are near, we must make the enemy believe we are far away; when far away, we must make him believe we are near.'

"We know the PRC breached our walls a long time ago. They're near. The intelligence war waged against us by China is growing in aggressiveness and skillfulness. As China advances economically and technologically, its spy activities are becoming more sophisticated, the tools at their disposal are more powerful, and their espionage operations are intensifying against not only our own intelligence services but also cyberattacks against U.S. government databases and companies. They're stealing trade secrets from the private sector, using venture-capital investment to acquire sensitive technology, and targeting universities and research institutions.

"But, and I'm sad to say, only a handful of our political leaders are prepared to heed our warnings when we tell them just how near the enemy is and how perilous the situation is. Let alone getting them to support us when we ask for their help to address the problem through legislation."

The president grinned. "Politicians, in general, are not known for their ability to deal with reality, unless, of course, they're about to lose an election. Nevertheless, I want the DNI, the Chairman of the Joint Chiefs of Staff, the Director of National Intelligence, the National Security Advisor, the Homeland Security Advisor, and the Director of the CIA to establish a workgroup. Your brief is to assess our situation, our readiness to heed another attempt by China to destroy us. Identify the shortcomings and tell me what we need to do to address them. Call in the help of other agencies, even our allies—the PRC is not only a threat to the US; they're a threat to the free world."

Chapter Eight

IT WAS PERSONAL

Shanghai, China

Eight months ago

To Ren Shi, the lead investigator, personally appointed and briefed by the Minister of the MSS, the defection of General Yuan was humiliating and painful, and it was personal. He would not rest until he found the traitor and killed him and those who helped him.

But first, he had to figure out how they did it. It took him and a team of MSS agents ten days from the time they had learned about the defection to discover how it happened but not who was responsible.

Ren had been relieved of all other duties and sent to Beijing to report directly to Minister Xuan Bai. Xuan told him that the orders for this mission came directly from President Liao. Xuan gave Ren all the background information and stressed the importance of absolute secrecy. Ren had to report to him, Xuan, only.

Ren learned that Yuan's defection was all about the virus that was raging in Shanghai. Yuan was the general in charge of China's biological weapons program, and under his supervision, the virus had been manufactured in a lab as a bioweapon. Xuan also told him about the attempts to stop the information from reaching the outside world and the MSS's failure to do so.

After his briefing, Ren knew all about Dr. Zheng Xuefeng, another traitor and defector now living in the lap of luxury in the United States. Zheng was the former CEO of Zexian Biomed, a biotech company located in Shanghai. Ren also knew about Dr. Benjamin Yatsir, a former employee of Zexian Biomed, a Jew, and a medical microbiologist and virologist. Yatsir was the man who told a school friend about the virus. The MSS knew about Yatsir's contact with his friend, arrested and interrogated him, and learned who the school friend was. Her name was Dora Frankel, the sister of David Sarlin, the CEO of HK Securities, one of the richest people in Hong Kong. The MSS had sent one of the Hong Kong-based triads, Sun Yee On, after her, but they had failed to kill her.

Ren was like a bloodhound on a trail. Ten days after the defection, he knew how Yuan got to America and how his impostor got to Hong Kong. He knew about the American couple who was ostensibly from Texas and the American woman with a diplomatic passport. Whether they played a role in the general's escape or not, he could only guess. For now, he decided, the man to track down was the one who pretended to be General Yuan and flew to Hong Kong, on a Chinese military plane, in the general's uniform. *Can you believe it? A Chinese military plane. The man's audacity seems to be boundless.*

The Shanghai Waldorf Astoria hotel's CCTV footage supplied him with good images of every suspect. The faces of the Texan couple and the woman with the diplomatic passport were undisguised. The old Italian and his wife's photos were high quality but useless because of the professional job done with their disguises. It was anyone's guess what they really looked like.

But Ren also realized that the Americans must have had help from the inside to pull off the defection of Yuan Lee. And although his brief was to find and kill Yuan and the people who helped him defect, he was sure it was also part of his job to expose everyone on the inside who was involved. He had no doubt there were insiders.

After figuring out how they did it, Ren got on the first flight from Shanghai to Hong Kong. He had a few leads.

The first stop in Hong Kong was the police commissioner and then the prison where Tian Song-li, the leader of SYO, Sun Yee On, the Chinese triad (mafia) group operating out of Hong Kong, was kept. On a promise that he would be released if he cooperated, Tian told Ren everything he knew.

Tian told him he had orders from an MSS agent to capture or kill Dora Frankel, but it turned into a complete mess. *Fortunately, the idiot in charge of that mission had disappeared.*

Even so, after his talk with the Police Commissioner and Tian, Ren knew the Matz's and David Sarlin were involved, and that was a bit of a dilemma. Those families were on the MSS's hands-off list. Not that the MSS would never touch them but to do so required presidential authorization. Which, obviously, the disappeared MSS agent in charge of the botched operation must have had from the late president.

Interesting, Ren Shi thought. *Did President Li Lingxin actually approve the killing of Dora Frankel? Maybe, but my orders are to find Yuan and his accomplices, not dwell on the oddness of presidential orders. Especially not an icon such as Li Lingxin.*

Ren also learned that the rescuers of the abducted women were on a yacht named the *TOMATS* that was anchored at the jetty on Matz Island until the day before Yuan was spirited out of Shanghai. Through the international S-AIS (Satellite Automatic Identification System), keeping track of the ship's position, course, and speed, Ren's IT team had quickly tracked the yacht down; it was now in the Red Sea en route to the Cote d'Azur, France. It was registered in Malta under a company name, which was owned by no less than five other companies, which, in turn, were owned by a labyrinth of other companies that were owned by trusts and more companies. It was a dead end. The owners of that yacht had no desire to let anyone find out who the real owner was. But having the name of the yacht and being able to track it was good enough for now.

When Ren showed them the photos he had copied from the CCTV footage, Tian and his men had no problem recognizing the faces of the Texans but didn't recognize Yasmin Burke. They also didn't recognize the old Italian couple, but the big black dog looked familiar. There was a big black dog like that one with the people who rescued the women who they abducted.

Ren had tasked his IT team to track the Texans down.

A week later, the team admitted defeat. The images of the Texans, Joshua and Marissa Elizabeth Crawford, did not show up in any of their vast facial recognition databases. Through the resources provided by the Cyber Force, the MSS IT team had access to almost all of the American government networks and databases, but the Crawfords were not in them. So, they obviously used fake names when they were in Shanghai—no surprises there.

Even so, to Ren, the lack of photos and information were significant—the Crawfords' or whatever their real surname was, had been scrubbed from all government systems. And that meant they were involved in secret operations. They could be working for the CIA or any of the sixteen security agencies in the USA or the vast number of private military contractors working for said agencies.

The next target was the woman with a diplomatic passport, Yasmin Burke. If he could get hold of her, she might be able to tell him if she were involved, and if so, she would know who her co-conspirators were and where to find them. She might even be able to tell them where to find Yuan Lee. And, who knows, maybe she'd know who the insiders were.

Chapter Nine

FINDING YASMIN BURKE

Langley, Virginia, USA

Seven months ago

Ren Shi had decided it would be easier to find Yasmin Burke. He was right. Like the Texan couple, her image was also nowhere to be found in the government databases. However, working on the presumption that the name on her passport was real and that she could be working for one of America's security agencies, hence her absence in the databases, he instructed his IT people to scour open sources.

In the lexicon of the intelligence community, it was known as OSINT, Open Source Intelligence, the collection and analysis of information gathered from public sources such as Facebook, Twitter, LinkedIn, YouTube, Instagram, Pinterest, and many others.

There were even free websites that specialized in finding matching images. TinEye was one of them. It was a reverse image search engine developed by a company based in Toronto, Canada. It was the first image search engine on the web to use image identification technology rather than keywords, metadata, or watermarks. Google, Yahoo, Bing, Pinterest, and many more websites also had image search features. Targeting information could be collected on virtually anyone, anywhere, with a computer or a smartphone and a little time.

Yasmin Burke didn't have a social media presence, not unexpected. If she worked for a security agency, she would've been prohibited from having one. But no matter how careful she or her employer was to hide her identity, there was not much they could do to stop her friends and family from talking about her on social media and post pictures of them with her. It was simply a matter of feeding her image to the vast social media databases, ask it to find all matches, sit back, and wait for the results. It was like unwrapping a birthday present.

And Ren's IT team had access to an MSS-developed system that was much more sophisticated and had access to much more data than TinEye and others. MSS had been using this system to collect IDENTINT, identity intelligence, about high-value targets such as government employees, politicians, military personnel, and other targets of interest.

It took Ren's IT team only a few minutes to come up with a number of photo matches for Yasmin Burke from the social media websites of friends and family. From there, it was easy to establish that she lived in Falls Church, Virginia, less than eight miles from the CIA headquarters in Langley.

Ren placed a tick in the employer box. She worked for the CIA.

Hacking into local authorities' street surveillance

cameras, he was able to put ticks in the physical address and vehicle boxes. He was now able to put a physical surveillance team on to track her movements and study her routines.

A week later, he instructed a team to place GPS trackers on her car and break into her house and bug it. While they were in her house, they accessed her personal laptop and cloned the hard drive. Now they had access to all her personal information, including all her financial records. They installed a piece of software on her laptop, which would make them privy to all her future online activities. That afternoon after work, when she entered her home, her phone and tablet automatically synced with her laptop, and she was none the wiser. The same spyware installed on her laptop was now living happily on those devices as well. Apart from the ability to listen to her phone calls, the spyware on her phone mimicked the phone entering a powered down state while it was still transmitting. In other words, to her, it would have looked as if her phone was switched off after she'd powered it down—it was not—they could listen to all conversations taking place up to three yards from the phone. From that point onward, Yasmin Burke's life was an open book to them.

In his daily report to Minister Xuan Bai, Ren was finally able to inform him about the breakthrough.

In his reply, the minister cautioned Xuan to be very careful. "You're operating on foreign soil. Take all precautions to ensure nothing points back to the PRC government. For now, all I want you to do is observe and report."

Ren suspected that meant the final orders to act would be coming from higher up, the President. The most desirable scenario would've been to get all of his suspects, including Yuan Lee, in one go and get rid of them before they could warn each other. But that was highly unlikely as Yuan Lee would have been in protective custody.

For months after tracking her down and putting electronic surveillance tabs on her, they listened to her talking on her phone, talking to herself, talking to friends and colleagues; they were even privy to the breakup with her boyfriend. They were waiting and watching for a breakthrough, which they knew would come.

Chapter Ten

OPERATION MIDDLE KINGDOM

Beijing, China

Six months ago

Two months after taking office, Liao and Tao attended the first planning meeting with the Trustees. It was a whole-day affair taking place in a secured room at Zhongnanhai.

General Lang Jianhong chaired the meeting. He started the session by giving their plan a name, Operation Zhōng Guó, translated as Operation Middle Kingdom.

The English names for countries didn't always correspond with what the inhabitants called their homeland. For instance, Greece was known as 'Hellas' to the Greeks, and Egypt was known as 'Misr' to the Egyptians. Similarly, China's official name was Zhōng Guó, meaning the middle or central country. It was said that the name originated in ancient times when the people believed that their country was the center of the civilized world surrounded by barbarians. The origin of the name China was unclear; some believed it came from the Sanskrit word 'Chinasthana,' meaning the country to the East of India. Others believed it derived from the Qin (pronounced 'Chin') Kingdom.

The Trustees believed their ancient ancestors to have been clairvoyant to call their country the Middle Kingdom —thousands of years later, with the fulfillment of Chairman Mao's 100-year plan, their country would indeed be the center of it all.

Lang continued and laid out the broad strokes of the plan to which they would add the details over the course of their future meetings. Then they asked Liao to give them a detailed description of the economic issues facing the country.

It was a bleak picture, they agreed. The question was what to do about it? Liao repeated the discussion he had with Tao on his first day in office. It boiled down to spend less and earn more.

To spend less meant that the government had to introduce severe austerity measures. There were not many objections to Liao's proposals. And they agreed, the citizens were going to suffer, and they were going to be unhappy. But there were no alternatives. Civil disobedience had to be dealt with harshly.

However, on the topic of civil disobedience, the trustees had two headaches. The first was called the Tuidang movement. Tuidang meant 'Quit the Party.' They were a peaceful grassroots resistance movement that had been growing in leaps and bounds since its birth in 2004. By 2018 they had more than 321 million members and counting, who had renounced the oaths they had made to the Communist Party. According to their website, their mission was: To investigate and document the atrocities communism has perpetrated against humanity. To assist all ethnic Chinese worldwide to renounce communist indoctrination and culture. To provide a means for all ethnic Chinese to withdraw from the Chinese Communist Party, Young Pioneers, and the Communist Youth League. To help the Chinese people take their first steps toward individual liberty and to help them adjust to living in a free society. And to coordinate the global Tuidang movement.

Some human-rights experts believed the movement had the ability to peacefully disintegrate the Chinese Communist Party. Lech Walesa, former Polish President, called them "History's Tsunami."

To be sure, the Tuidang was a thorn in the flesh of the PRC government and getting more irritating by the day as renunciations came in droves from people of all walks of life in the Chinese society, from top military personnel and government officials to villagers and students.

The second pounding headache was religion. Karl Marx's statement, 'Religion is the opium of the people', was often quoted in discussions about religion. But less attention was given to the full context of that statement, which was, 'Religion is the sigh of the oppressed creature, the heart of a heartless world, and the soul of soulless conditions. It is the opium of the people.'

Marx believed that religion was similar to administering opium to sick or injured people. It reduced their suffering and gave them pleasant illusions. But he believed religion to be harmful to his revolutionary goals because it prevented people from seeing the class structure and oppression; thus, religion prevented the socialist revolution.

With the establishment of the People's Republic of China under Mao Tse Tung in 1949 came an era of wide-scale religious repression. In keeping with its Marxist roots, the CCP declared itself atheist. After Mao, greater freedoms were granted, and the state eventually recognized five official religions: Buddhism, Christianity, Daoism, Islam, and Protestantism. The practice of any other faith was formally prohibited.

The activities of the state-sanctioned religions were regulated by the State Administration for Religious Affairs (SARA), who controlled all aspects of religious life, including leadership appointments, selection of clergy, and interpretation of doctrine. All religious leaders had to undergo training to learn how to adapt their religion's doctrine to government and CCP thinking.

Notwithstanding the official recognition of the five religions, they were not treated equally. The Uyghurs of the Muslim faith could testify to that. More than one million of them had been interned in eighty-five secret internment camps without trial in Northwest China since 2017.

The Christians (Catholics and Protestants) were also feeling the squeeze as if in the grips of a boa constrictor. Christianity was the fastest-growing religion in China. In 2010 they were estimated to number between 68 and 130 million, predicted to reach 247 million by 2030. Strangely, China was the world's largest producer of Bibles, printing its 150 millionth Bible in 2016 for both domestic and international markets. And it was becoming obvious the CCP didn't like it at all as Christians experienced growing repression. According to Open Doors, a U.S.-based Christian nonprofit that tracks the persecution of Christians worldwide, China ranked as the tenth most difficult and dangerous country in which to practice Christianity.

Harassment and detention of Christian believers, blocking entry to sites of worship, interrupting gatherings, dismantling crosses, demolishing churches, disbanding congregations, placing facial recognition systems in churches, and calls for rewriting the Bible to conform to CCP dogma were becoming commonplace as the CCP singled out religious groups as potential threats to national security, social harmony, and core interests. "Religion became a weapon in the hands of dissidents for inciting the masses and creating political disturbances," declared Ye Xiaowen, former SARA director.

The twelve men in the room agreed; faith-based organizations were one of the most serious threats to the Communist party. As much of a worry as the Tuidang.

Their only course of action was to put the MSS and law enforcement agencies across the country on notice to prepare themselves to deal with any form of dissidence rapidly and ruthlessly. They had the names of all Tuidang members, domestic and international, as well as Muslims and Christians, or so they believed.

It was time to break for lunch.

Chapter Eleven

CREATE DISTRACTIONS

Beijing, China

Six months ago

When the twelve were back in their seats around the conference table, after lunch, Lang started. "We have to make America believe we're inactive while we're active—make them believe we are far away. To accomplish that, we'll create distractions. There are many options; let's discuss them."

Tao said, "I can think of several international incidents that would take the Americans' attention away from us. For instance, North Korea could start testing its missiles again. We know that the West has kind of accepted that North Korea is a nuclear power. The thing that worries them most now is that North Korea might develop long-range missiles to deliver their nukes to American soil.

"Another distractor could be if India and Pakistan are

pushed into another conflict. After all, they have been in conflict since 1947. A few well-executed false flag operations should see them at each other's throats very quickly.

"The Middle East—there is so much potential for conflict, we could pick and choose which one to foment. The region could be the next frontline, where we can challenge American dominion. But to start with, I suggest we look at Iran. China and Iran both have global and regional ambitions, and we both have belligerent relationships with America. The enemy of my enemy is my friend. Let's make a pact with them, a strategic partnership in trade, politics, culture, and security. It's a win-win for both of us. We will have access to Iran's oil and gas, and they will get out of the stranglehold of international sanctions—"

General Dai Min smiled. "That would certainly ruffle the Americans' feathers."

Tao added, "And those of Israel and the Sunni Muslim world. There is potential for creating similar diversions in South America and in the countries Russia has been eyeing for some time, such as Ukraine, Estonia, Lithuania, and Latvia. And, last but not least, let's not forget Turkey's dream of re-establishing the Ottoman Empire."

General Wan Huang of the PLA Air Force cleared his throat. "Okay, it's clear, international opportunities abound. I'd like to look at America itself. The presidential election is about eighteen months away. They're already campaigning, the battle lines have been drawn, and the knives are out. Every candidate is looking for dirt on opponents. Let's give it to them—manufacture it if necessary. Combining international crises with internal strife will keep the Americans too busy to worry about what we're doing.

"We've got many sympathizers in both houses of their congress. We've even got a few informers among them. It's time to use them. There are many more we can target for recruitment.

"We know in election years they are extremely risk-averse and would do anything to avoid bad press, let alone get into a war. A mere allegation of sexual misconduct is enough to disqualify a candidate immediately—with or without any substantiation. So are accusations of corruption, nepotism, racism, and sexism."

General Jin Ping was rubbing his hands in excitement. "We could make their lives a living hell."

Jin was in charge of Information Operations and Information Warfare. In other words, the cyber warfare division of the PLA, which was organized into three groups: Military network warfare forces, network warfare specialists in the MSS and the Ministry of Public Security (MPS), and Non-governmental cyber forces. The latter was their offshore IT specialists, citizens of countries such as India, Pakistan, Iran, Russia, Ukraine, former Eastern Bloc countries, even the US. Many of them, in fact, most of them, didn't even know they were working for the PRC government. Jin used front companies with no apparent links to China to hide their true identity when outsourcing offshore.

One of the units under Jin's command was the mysterious Unit 61398. US intelligence agencies often referred to Unit 61398 by names such as: Advanced Persistent Threat 1 (APT1), the Comment group, and Byzantine Candor. Designations cybersecurity firms give to state sponsored hacking groups and criminal cybergangs.

Unit 61398 had a large server farm in operation and a little over a thousand staff. Since 2006 they've systematically stolen hundreds of terabytes of data from at least 141 organizations, 115 of them in the US, across 20 industries worldwide.

Despite the fact that the Chinese government had never acknowledged the existence of Unit 61398 and strongly denied that the country's military has ever supported any hacker activities, General Jin was a happy and confident man. The PRC's electronic warfare and cyber espionage forces had been expanding rapidly in numbers and capabilities in recent years. China produced more than four million STEM (science, technology, engineering, and mathematics) graduates every year, and Jin got the pick of the crop. But that was not all; thousands of STEM students in the United States were Chinese nationals, and some of them were spying on their US employers. Jin's cadres had stolen more than $300 billion worth of intellectual property, including the blueprints of advanced American weapons systems.

General Jin Ping had ample reason to stick feathers in his cap. In 2015, his hackers penetrated the United States Office of Personnel Management (OPM) and stole the personal records of 18 million people—everybody who has worked for, tried to work for, or *was* working for the United States government.

From 2014 to 2015, Jin's cyberforce was responsible for the infamous Anthem data breach, the biggest single compromise of healthcare data in history—the health records of 112 million people.

Equifax was an American multinational consumer credit reporting agency, one of the three largest consumer credit reporting agencies in the world. They collected and aggregated information on over 800 million individual consumers and more than 88 million businesses worldwide. Jin's cybertroops breached Equifax's firewalls and stole the personal and financial data of 147 million people.

But hacking was not all Jin's troops did. They were also masters at social media manipulation, and that was what

General Jin had in mind to help him create turmoil in American politics.

The information gathered by Jin's people came in very handy in the honey trapping and kompromat operations of the PRC's intelligence agencies. Honey trapping is the practice of using romantic or sexual relationships for interpersonal, political, or monetary purposes. Kompromat, short for 'compromising material,' is a specialty of the Russians and other post-Soviet states, which PRC's intelligence agencies had adopted. It is the practice of collecting, even manufacturing, damaging information about targets such as politicians, business people, or other public figures to create negative publicity or to use for blackmail and extortion.

Next up was Vice-Admiral Deng Jie, the commander of the People's Liberation Army Navy (PLAN). He steered the conversation to the high seas, suggesting that large-scale, well-planned, well-timed naval exercises in the Atlantic and Pacific oceans would cause major diversions. He also suggested a series of black operations against large cargo ships disguised as terrorist and pirate attacks.

Worldwide, ninety percent of non-bulk cargo is transported by container ships in TEUs (twenty-foot equivalent units). Modern container ships, rivaling crude oil tankers and bulk carriers in size, are able to carry more than 21,000 TEUs. There are an estimated 785 million TEUs in use at any given time. Sinking a few of them in strategic places at critical points in time would, without doubt, cause major distractions.

It was past midnight when the twelve men wrapped up the planning session. They were excited and energized by the prospects of Operation MK.

Chapter Twelve

WHEN IN ROME

Rome, Italy

Five months ago

After leaving Hong Kong in a hurry after the defection of General Yuan Lee, Declan Spencer, the captain of the *TOMATS*, had sailed the yacht back to Europe. There they spent a few weeks on the French Riviera (Cote d'Azure), the south coast of Spain, Corsica, and Sardinia before going back to Rome, the *TOMATS*'s base port.

Since the launching of the *TOMATS* under its current name, about three years before, the yacht had served as CRC's mobile mission control center for several major missions around Europe and once in Hong Kong.

The *TOMATS*, the name derived from the first letters of Ernest Hemingway's classic short novel, *The Old Man and the Sea*, was a luxury superyacht that Rex had appropriated from a Saudi Arabian prince, Mutaib bin Faisal bin Saud, an international black-market arms dealer and human trafficker.

The *TOMATS* had three decks, was equipped for ocean travel with ultra-modern stabilization technology, advanced communications equipment, a helipad, and every nod to comfort that one could imagine. It had a range of six-thousand nautical miles, a top speed of seventeen knots, and a cruise speed of fifteen. It was powered by two Caterpillar diesel engines producing close to five-thousand horsepower.

Apart from the very comfortable lodgings for the seventeen crew members, including the captain, there were accommodations for fourteen guests in seven luxurious staterooms. There was a hot tub, sauna, Turkish bath, infinity pool, gym, dining room, and several lounges. One of the lounges had been repurposed to house the sophisticated electronics gear and computer equipment that could be concealed when necessary. Another was turned into a secured communications room. Inside the latter was, among others, an impenetrable encrypted satellite video system, the latest technology in communications.

It was while the *TOMATS* was in Rome that Brandt, Spencer, and Rex had a discussion about the role the yacht had played in CRC missions over the past few years and what role it could play in the future. They were in agreement; the *TOMATS*, although never intended to be instrumental in covert operations, nevertheless turned out to be an ideal mobile mission control center. And, of course, the presence of a contingent of Special Forces crew members had turned out to come in very handy on all of the missions so far.

Spencer said, "Thus far, the *TOMATS* has only been targeted by the bad actors once—in Hong Kong. But it would be unwise to think it wouldn't happen again. I think we should look at upgrading her security and communications systems. I have a few features in mind, but we'll need DARPA for that."

DARPA is the acronym for Defense Advanced Research Projects Agency. They were the research and development agency of the United States Department of Defense responsible for the development of emerging technologies for use by the military. During its existence, DARPA had been responsible for some of the most radical technological inventions in history. The internet, various computing technologies, global positioning satellites, stealth technology, unmanned aerial vehicles (drones), micro-electro-mechanical systems (MEMS), and many others were all credited to them. Although the US military was their original customer, the agency's inventions have played a major role in creating a multitude of multibillion-dollar private industries.

"Okay, I'll have a chat with Martin," said Brandt. Martin Richardson was the deputy director in charge of CIA operations. He and Brandt were good friends.

"While you're at it," Rex said, "we might as well upgrade our agents' equipment as well. See what you can get from them and the CIA's technical division in terms of surveillance, communications, and protective gear for operators."

"You mean like James Bond's car and pen and watch and stuff like that?" Spencer chuckled.

"Yeah, that kind of stuff." Rex smiled. "As well as mini drones, tracking and listening devices, personal GPS tracking devices, the latest in body armor, and such."

A month after the conversation between Brandt, Spencer, and Rex about the technology upgrades to the *TOMATS*, the yacht was in a shipyard in La Spezia about two hundred and forty miles north of Rome. A team of US

Navy shipbuilders and technicians, all with the necessary security clearances, was hard at work on the upgrades.

The modifications to the yacht, Spencer was told, would take four to six weeks. He welcomed the downtime and spent all of it in Rome with his Italian love interest, Simona Bellucci.

Simona was formerly known as Sophia Maiorani from Naples. Rex and Catia had known Simona for quite a few years. Catia met her the night Rex had saved her from the Camorra in Naples and delivered her to the doorstep of a Mossad safe house close to the Jewish Quarters in Rome in 2011. Catia was responsible for creating a new life, a new face, and a new identity for her, in order to hide her from the Camorra. However, four years later, in August 2015, the Camorra had tracked her down, and in an enigmatic confluence of events, Rex and Digger turned up at the right place at the right time to rescue Catia and Simona from a team of Camorra thugs trying to apprehend them.

To protect them, Rex took Catia and Simona to the *TOMATS*, at anchor in the Port of Civitavecchia not far from Rome, Italy. That's where Spencer met her.

Catia was the first one to note the vibes between Simona and Spencer. There was an eighteen-year age gap between them, but that didn't stop them from enjoying each other's company. Since that time, Simona had been Spencer's guest on the *TOMATS* whenever they got the opportunity.

Everyone at CRC who had met Simona liked her. She was a friendly and outgoing type, and she was a beautiful woman with bob-style wavy auburn hair and brown eyes.

While waiting for the upgrades to the *TOMATS* to be completed, on a Friday morning, while Simona had gone out to get her hair done, Spencer took a taxi to a nearby piazza. There was a jewelry shop that had caught his eye a few days before when he and Simona went there for lunch. He had been thinking about this day for far more than a year, and today was the day when he was going over to action. *When in Rome, do as the Romans do.* He told himself.

An hour later, he left the jewelry shop with a very big smile on his face and an engagement ring in a dainty little jewelry box in his pocket. He and Simona had a dinner date at La Pergola on Via Alberto Cadlolo, the renowned luxury hotel restaurant with panoramic views of the Eternal City from the roof.

When they met in 2015, Simona's English was not perfect, but orders of magnitude better than Spencer's Italian, which consisted of only a few words; please, thank you, yes, and no. But the two of them had made a conscious effort to learn each other's mother tongue, and now Spencer was ready to ask the big question in Italian.

Spencer had picked the ideal venue. The ambiance was perfect, the food was exquisite, and Spencer's companion was stunning. If Simona suspected what was about to happen, she didn't give any indication, but then Spencer had to wonder why she had insisted on getting her hair done that morning when she had it done less than a week ago.

With their dessert in front of them, Spencer looked at Simona, opened his mouth, and then, instead of saying the words he'd been practicing for days, he started stuttering.

Simona put on the most beautiful smile Spencer had ever seen and said, "Is there something you want to tell me, Declan?"

That's when he knew she knew. "Ah... I..." He felt like an idiot, a seventy-something-year-old idiot, no less. "Will you marry me?" *That must have been the most unromantic proposal ever.*

Simona started laughing, and Spencer's courage sunk to the floor, but only until he saw Simona's head bobbing up and down and tears streaming down her face. Spencer was too stunned and too clumsy to know what to do, so he just stared at her, waiting.

Finally, she managed to regain enough composure to say, "Yes, Declan, yes. I will marry you."

By the time they had been served their espressos, Declan and Simona had decided that they'd been waiting long enough; they were going to get married the next weekend. Just enough time for their friends to come to Italy.

When they were back at Simona's apartment, they were on the phone with Spencer's best friend, John Brandt, and his fiancée, Christelle Proll. The next call was to Rex and Catia, who were in Rome, their home when they were not on the *TOMATS*.

The next Saturday, all their friends were in Italy. John and Christelle, Rex, Catia, and Digger, Josh and Marissa, and, of course, Declan's first mate, Billy Walton, a retired US Navy Commander, ten in all. The wedding ceremony and reception were held at a historic country house among the vineyards of Tuscany.

Simona had resigned from her job at the museum in Rome to take up the job of supply and administration officer of the *TOMATS*.

Chapter Thirteen

THE GREAT WALL OF CHINA

Beijing, China

Four months ago

The construction of the 13,170 mile-long Great Wall of China, a major tourist attraction, started in the 7th century BC and continued until the time of the Ming Dynasty, 1368 to 1644 AD. It was a series of fortifications protecting the historical northern borders of ancient Chinese states and Imperial China against enemies from the Eurasian Steppe.

China also had another great wall. At 3,000 miles, this wall was not known to many; in fact, the authorities kept its existence a secret. It was known as the Underground Great Wall of China, consisting of a labyrinth of tunnels used by the PRC to store and transport mobile intercontinental ballistic missiles. Western intelligence sources didn't know much about the tunnels but had obtained information indicating that the tunnels were reinforced with a special type of steel, invented by Chinese scientists, that would withstand attacks by bunker-buster bombs and nuclear weapons.

It was inside one of these underground facilities on the outskirts of Beijing where several divisions of General Jin Ping's special cyberespionage units toiled 24/7.

When Jin entered the facility housing the SM (Social Media) Unit this morning, as always, it struck him how quiet the place was. There were almost 300 people at work on computers in rows upon rows of desks. Most of the workers had two screens, some even had three, yet the loudest noise rising up from the acre of open-plan office space was the clicking sound of keyboards.

Their operation was set up like a production line in a factory. At the beginning of the line were the harvesters, Unit 61398. They were located in the same underground facility, in an area adjoining the SM Unit. They collected the data and dumped it on the servers of the first analysis team. The analysts used algorithms and eyeballs to filter out the targets they deemed to be worthwhile pursuing. The list of targets was passed on to the SE (Social Engineering) Unit.

They had team members who were fluent in English and whatever languages their targets spoke, and they were highly skilled in social engineering. In the context of information security, social engineering meant they were masters of deception, able to manipulate individuals into divulging confidential or personal information. To that end, they had received extensive training in the psychology of human behavior, among other skills.

They had their own social media accounts. In fact, every team member had multiple accounts—all of them fake, complete with photos, friends, likes, and comments. Which account they used depended on their target's profile. To an

American friend, they were American, to a British friend British, French to the French, etcetera. They used a network of global proxy servers and fake IP addresses to hide their true location and make them appear to be in or near the country of their target.

The harvest from the United States Office of Personnel Management (OPM) produced by Unit 61398 was a treasure trove. They had the names of 18 million people working for the US government, including military and security agencies, in the past and present, even those who applied to work for them. Using their data mining tools, the SE team built complete profiles of where those people worked and lived and every bit of personal information they could get. It was mindboggling to see how much of that kind of information was readily available on social media.

They were using sophisticated algorithms to scan social media mentions of their targets, looking for keywords indicating exploitable vulnerabilities. Yes, people and their friends talked on social media about their own and their friends' money problems, loneliness, marital or relationship problems, asshole managers, infidelity, sexual harassment, sexual deviances, identity crises, and humanity's favorite pastime, they gossiped—the list was endless. And so were the opportunities to take advantage of their gullibility.

The key was trust. Building trust was a multi-stepped process. Sometimes it took a few days, sometimes months, sometimes longer. Make contact, befriend, listen, help, and sympathize. They used every known psychological trick in the book, and some not even in the books, to get into the hearts and minds of their targets. It was their job to make their targets think of them not as a stranger but as a close friend in whom they could confide their innermost feelings and secrets. Not a small feat to achieve without ever meeting face-to-face, but the SE team was good and spectacularly successful. It was nothing short of mindblowing to see what information people were giving out once trust had been established.

Not everyone succumbed to the charms of the SE team, most didn't, but it was a numbers game. Snaring one in a hundred was considered an excellent ratio, but one in a thousand would have been equally impressive. It depended on the quality of the information the target provided.

Although it was not one of General Jin's conquests, it was an example he often quoted to his operators. A lowly corporal with a gender identity crisis in the US Army, then known as Bradley Manning, later Chelsea Manning, became an intelligence analyst and stole nearly 750,000 classified, or unclassified but sensitive, military and diplomatic documents and handed it to Wikileaks. That was one disgruntled employee. The OPM data breach alone gave them 18 million potential Chelsea Mannings. They had millions more and counting thanks to the prolific hacking efforts of Unit 61398.

No real person had a real social media account with no friends, and oftentimes the target's friends were better sources of information than the target itself.

Frequently, targets were identified that warranted personal attention. Those names were passed on to the MSS and other intelligence agencies for action by their recruiters and enforcers, who used different tactics ranging from very subtle to extremely brutal to get what they wanted. A case in point was the bit of juicy gossip by a friend of one of Senator Lancaster's staffers gossiping about the senator's relationship with one of her staffers, Jason Crawley. It was that bit of information that caught the SE team's attention, which they passed on to the MSS.

Similarly, one of the SE team got an alert when the algorithm picked up a few keywords in a Facebook post from a friend of one of their targets who had thus far not responded to any of their advances, playing hard to get, so to speak. The target was Jack Ross, the young CEO of a small but very successful tech company in Sunnyvale, Silicon Valley, known as Penultimate Pty Ltd. He and his business partner and a team of 'white hat' or 'ethical hackers' as they were known, hired their services out to the IT departments of financial and medical institutions, retail chains, manufacturers, and others. Their job was to attempt to break into their clients' networks and hack their websites, and soon they'd built a reputation as the best 'white hat' hackers in Silicon Valley. Their business grew by leaps and bounds, and soon government agencies with top-secret networks came knocking on their door.

The SE team had long suspected that Penultimate did work for the US government but couldn't get confirmation until they saw the Facebook post by a friend of Jack's. Ross was one of those targets that required the personal attention of MSS agents and was duly passed on to them for action.

Another group in the SM Unit specialized in the manipulation of social media. Their specialty was to influence what was reported by the traditional news outlets. In the old days, before the internet and social media, the newspapers, radio, and TV decided what was important enough to publish. These days the traditional media published what was trending on Google, Facebook, Twitter, and others. In theory, it was much easier to get it right that way; after all, if it were trending on the internet, that's what their audiences wanted to hear. Right? Well, not entirely, because it was possible to make a topic trend artificially.

Few people understand what is going on behind the

scenes of their social media platforms. They believe social media platforms feed them only the posts from the accounts they follow. That's not true; the platforms use algorithms to curate information from other accounts and present it to users based on their likes, votes, shares, and comments. For instance, a post is shown to some users, and based on their reaction, i.e., if they liked it or voted for it or shared it or commented on it –positively or negatively–it will be highlighted to others. And the more they do it, the wider it was posted. Lies and extreme content generate more reactions than the mundane and therefore spread faster and wider.

But who is doing all this liking, voting, sharing, and commenting? Oftentimes it's no one; it's an army of accounts called bots controlled by hackers. Researchers estimate that, at times, more than half of the social media conversations going on about newsworthy topics are conducted by bots. These bots are so good at mimicking real humans they're indistinguishable. All that is needed to make a topic trend is to tell the bots what topic has to get their attention, sit back, and watch it happen.

Across all social media platforms, the number of duplicate and fake accounts is estimated to be in the order of 1.3 billion. From time to time, social media companies would announce that they've disabled millions of accounts, but it seems they're fighting a losing battle. Statista.com reported in 2019 that sixteen percent of Facebook's 2.8 billion accounts were fake or duplicates, equating to an astounding 448 million accounts.

The SM team had a few hundred million of those fake accounts across various social media platforms. It enabled them to pick topics that they would like to play up. Whether it was true or not didn't matter; all that was required for the mainstream media to pick it up was a few million 'people' expressing outrage, interest, and excitement. Thus the SM team was able to control the narrative of whatever topics they chose. They had the ability to destroy or make reputations at will. Causing distractions was as easy as pushing a few buttons.

Chapter Fourteen

THE SENIOR SENATOR FROM NEW YORK

Washington, D.C., USA

Three months ago

The United States Senate was often described as home to a hundred presidents in waiting. The aspiring presidents fell into one of three groups; freshman senators, second-term senators, and senior senators. Jordyn Lancaster, the senior senator from New York, was in the latter group. Those who were most likely to have their eyes on the White House.

She was two inches short of six feet, had unflawed features, and an athletic body. She was fifty-four but looked thirty, the result of CrossFit five times a week, a low-carb diet, Botox, weekly visits to the best hairstylists in D.C., and good genes. Her deep-blue eyes were sharp and piercing, and her blonde hair was cut in a voguish bob that dropped to her strong jawline. It was not arrogance that she radiated;

it was confidence—the absolute conviction that the world around her had been organized exactly the way she wanted it. It bestowed on her a graceful *sang-froid* that made her peers pale by comparison.

Jordyn Lancaster was beautiful—very beautiful—in the same way an iceberg was beautiful. And equally forbidding. Her smile could be as cold as it was seductive. She struck a stately figure—the epitome of elegance and possessing a razor-sharp mind, a lethal combination of attributes she had put to good use in the cutthroat world she coinhabited with other swamp-dwellers in the place known as Washington D.C.

She came from old money; her grandfather made a fortune in the oil industry, her father was a real estate mogul, and she inherited it all. As a Harvard Law School graduate, she was welcomed into New York state politics fresh out of university. By the age of thirty-three, she took her seat in the US Senate and was now in her third six-year term. She had all the money she wanted; what she craved now was power—the kind of power only a president had. She had enough support among her constituents back home and in the House and Senate to throw her hat in the ring for the upcoming presidential election. And, of course, being one of the media-darlings didn't hurt at all. She knew she might not secure her party's nomination for the top spot at the National Convention but getting the tap to be the vice president of whoever was going to be nominated as the party's candidate would bring her within a heartbeat of the Oval Office. After all, over the years, fourteen vice presidents had fulfilled their ambition by becoming president. Eight of them succeeded to the office on the death of the president they served.

Senator Jordyn Lancaster was a formidable opponent; her colleagues on both sides of the aisle knew that all too well. Although no one would dare to call her by her nickname to her face, she knew what it was. Bomber was a play on her surname in reference to the Lancaster heavy bombers used by the British during the Second World War. But the nickname that started off in jest proved to be an apt name for two more reasons; one was her beauty, and the other, the manner in which she dealt with adversaries, which usually was as subtle as a bomb dropped from a Lancaster heavy bomber. She liked the name but never encouraged anyone to use it.

The media loved her because she was well-spoken, livened up their audiences with her alluring beauty, and hated the current president with a passion. Of course, the media often spoke of her stately comportment and sunshiny nature—"exactly the type of personality the American people deserved in times like these."

However, there were not many people in D.C., the locale of the highest concentration of friendly-looking weasels on the planet, who knew that Senator Lancaster was a consummate actor. She was once married to a man of Italian descent, they had a big Italian wedding, and five years later, a big American divorce. A skeleton in her cupboard was a brief visit to the dark side of the fence of decorum when she had an alleged, but only in whispered tones, fling with one of her staffers, Jason Crawly, twenty years her junior, a few years ago. She had no worries that it might get to the ears of the press during the current or future campaigns—the #MeToo movement was for women who were aggrieved about the sexual indiscretions of their male bosses. That she had a near-nymphomaniacal proclivity for bedding men half her age, only three people knew; she, her ex, and Jason Crawly. Her ex was under a gag order, and Jason Crawley was still working for her in exchange for his silence. She had, however, also covered her bases just in case Crawley got it in his head to speak out about her abuse of power to get him into her bed by keeping a few sexual harassment claims made against him by junior staffers on file. Of course, Crawley knew the claims were bogus, but he also knew equally well that nothing destroyed careers as quickly as sexual harassment allegations, substantiated or not.

Lancaster was the chairperson of the Senate Committee on Foreign Relations, tasked with leading foreign-policy legislation, funding foreign aid programs, as well as arms sales to and training for allied countries. Her committee was also responsible for the confirmation hearings for high-level positions in the Department of State. It was her position on this podium that put her and the president at loggerheads on a perpetual basis. But she was clever enough to pick the battles she wanted to fight. Among them was the battle about relations with China. The president started the trade war with them and made no bones about the fact that he firmly believed they were a threat to national security. Lancaster, on the contrary, was advocating for better relations and open trade agreements with the world's second most powerful nation. And Beijing loved her for it but wouldn't make a move to support her until they could control her.

Senator Lancaster was a powerful woman; the MSS understood that. They also understood that senators and representatives were regularly privy to top-secret information, and by virtue of their positions under the US Constitution, were deemed trustworthy to do so. Therefore they were not subjected to security clearance checks. They only had to swear an oath of secrecy at the beginning of each term. That's why the MSS had dedicated a team of analysts and undercover agents to study the life and habits of Senator Jordyn Lancaster.

Chapter Fifteen

A COMPROMISED PROJECT

San Francisco, USA

Two months ago

It was 5:00 a.m. in San Francisco when the driver of the garbage truck turned into the alley. The driver and his assistant didn't notice anything unusual. It was the same row of dumpsters in a long alley they had to empty every morning. When they got to the third dumpster, they noticed something unusual—the human arm dangling out of it. If the container were not filled to the brim as it were, they wouldn't have seen the body. It would've landed with all the other garbage in the back of the truck, eventually on the garbage dump where the body might have been found or not.

It was not the first time they'd seen bodies in dumpsters in Downtown San Francisco. It was one of the most dangerous neighborhoods in the city.

There was a process to follow when a body was discovered. Stay on-site. Phone the police. Phone the office to let them know to send another truck, for they would be kept on the scene until the police told them they could go, which would take hours. They followed the protocol.

They didn't remove the body; they only raised the half-open lid further to get a better look at the body to which the arm was attached. The sight nauseated them instantly. A male, Caucasian, they both thought, but he was so messed up they could've been mistaken. He was completely naked.

Then the police arrived and confirmed what the truck driver and his assistant already knew—the man was dead. The police duly cordoned the area off with crime scene tape and waited for the homicide detective and the medical examiner to arrive. When the ME arrived, the body was hauled out of the dumpster and transported to the morgue.

Two hours later, the truck driver's and assistant's contact details were noted, and they were free to go. The detective's work had started. Who was this man, and who had tortured him to death?

Menlo Park was the city located at the eastern edge of San Mateo County within the San Francisco Bay Area. It was said that Menlo Park was where one would find the highest number of educated people in California, if not all of the United States. Nearly seventy percent of residents over the age of 25 held a bachelor's degree or higher. The city of 32,026 inhabitants was home to the corporate headquarters of Facebook and where Google and Round Table Pizza were founded. And a small but very successful software development company, Brexico, their mainstay was the development of a missile guidance system as part of a joint venture between the United States and Australia to develop hypersonic cruise missiles in a bid to counter China and Russia, who were in the process of developing similar weapons.

Brexico's lead developer was Sebastian Barnes. A fact that only came to the attention of the FBI four days after his body was discovered in the dumpster in the alley in Downtown San Francisco.

Barnes had a top-secret clearance, though, such a clearance didn't mean the bearer would not give up secrets under torture, which, by looking at the photos provided by the coroner, was exactly what had happened to the poor man.

A brilliant thirty-five-year-old software engineer with a wife and a three-year-old son had been killed, and the hypersonic cruise missile project had been compromised. Two years of meticulous work had been rendered all but useless.

Chapter Sixteen

JWICS

Las Vegas, Nevada, USA

One month ago

Zac Macmillian was destined for greatness; that's what his parents and teachers told him. From his father, a professor in chemical engineering, and his mother, a heart surgeon, he inherited the brains to fulfill his destiny, whatever it was going to be. He grew up in the lap of luxury; whatever he wanted, his parents gave him; toys, computers, smart-phones, stashes of pocket money, his own car on his sixteenth birthday. All Zac had to do was say, "I want..." and he got it. The only thing Zac didn't get from his parents was attention and recognition—the demands of their profes-sional careers didn't allow them to spend quality time with their only child. Subconsciously they tried to make up for it by never saying no to any of his whims.

In search of the great destiny prophesied over him, Zac

only doubted what it was going to be until he got his first computer. He was mesmerized. By the age of eight, he wrote his first lines of computer code. By the age of twelve, in 1995, commercial use of the Internet had grown substantially, and the first wave of internet startups, Amazon, eBay, and the predecessor to Craigslist, began operations. By then, Zac was earning more than just pocket money from building websites for friends and family. He was the go-to person for all computer-related questions to everyone who knew him.

According to the Guinness Book of World Records, in June 1994, the ten-year-old American boy Michael Kearney was the youngest person ever to obtain a college degree. A record that was still standing when Zac attained his degree in computer science from Santa Clara University in the year that he turned fourteen.

If the exceptional achievement was not enough to convince him of his destiny in information technology, there were the symbolic indicators—his date of birth, January 1, 1983, generally considered to be the official birthday of the internet. And the fact that he was born in San Jose, California, the largest city in the global center for high technology and innovation known as Silicon Valley.

Zac 'knew' he was the right man, in the right place, at the right time, and he was a genius.

He was not the stereotypical nerd with thick glasses, a puny body, and pale skin from lack of sunlight. Zac was five foot ten, with an athletic build, lascivious dark hair, and deep brown eyes. He didn't like to participate in team sports or any sport for that matter, or group activities, but he did spend an hour a day in the gym and ran five miles every morning before breakfast.

But as he grew up, it became apparent that Zac was

awkward. It was only many years later when psychologists would diagnose him with histrionic personality disorder (HPD). A disorder characterized by constant attention-seeking behavior and extreme emotionality. Usually, people with this kind of disorder become uncomfortable and emotional when they are not the center of attention. People who had experienced Zac's tantrums used pejoratives such as erratic, crazy, rude, temperamental, volatile, and such to describe his behavior. Zac had many acquaintances but no real friends. Friendships were short, and romantic relationships never lasted more than a few weeks. He found it challenging to get a job and impossible to hold it down for more than a few months when he had one. Managers and coworkers alike found it impossible to work with a person who wanted to be in the limelight all the time and threw tantrums when he wasn't.

But somewhere, Zac had to find an outlet for his genius, and that's how he landed in the belly of the beast, the Darknet, home of everything illicit and inappropriate, the online home of criminals and hackers, the burglars of cyberspace. The only drawback of the Darknet was that everything was done anonymously, and anonymity was the last thing Zac wanted. He had to quench his insatiable thirst for attention and admiration; therefore, he started attending hacker conventions all over the world.

Zac was twenty-eight when he made his grand entry on the world stage of hackers at DEF CON. Held annually in Las Vegas, Nevada, DEF CON was the most prestigious and largest hacker convention in the world. He was given a low-key half-hour slot among the world's most notorious hackers to make his presentation. Notwithstanding, by the end of his presentation, during which he had hacked an

ATM in less than ten minutes with his iPhone, he was a celebrity. Zac was on cloud nine.

Within a few years, he had hacked every computer device known to man, including pacemakers, insulin pumps, garage door openers, corporate and government networks, and databases. He had become one of the most sought-after speakers at these hacker cons as they were known. The obscene amounts of money he earned from what he considered mundane jobs for clients who wanted access to other people's computers, smartphones and tablet PCs, businesses' computer networks and datastores, electronic vaults of financial institutions, and suchlike gave him no measure of satisfaction, though. But it funded his bohemian lifestyle.

Zac was too intent on getting himself in the limelight and staying there to spare a moment to consider who attended these def cons. Even if he did, it was probably not going to bother him to know in his audiences were computer security professionals, journalists, lawyers, federal government employees, security researchers, students, and representatives of spy agencies from across the world. Politics were of no interest to him—too crowded by other attention-seekers. On the topics of patriotism and national security, he spent no time at all. He never questioned the ethicality of his contracts; he had abandoned any thoughts about that when he started operating on the Darknet.

It was at the 2014 DEF CON where Zac met who he thought was his first real friend in life, Michael Feng, a data analyst from Hong Kong.

Michael approached him in the bar a few hours after Zac had given his much-anticipated presentation about the vulnerabilities of social media platforms. Michael's approach was timed perfectly—when the rush of admirers who crowded around him to congratulate him had dwindled to the point where Zac was alone, Michael appeared.

"Zac, may I call you that?" Michael said.

"Yep, that's my name."

"I can't begin to tell you what an honor and privilege it was to listen to your presentation and to now meet the legend, Zac Macmillan, in person. My name is Michael Feng. Will you please allow me to buy you a drink?"

Zac nodded and held up his almost empty beer glass, "Heineken."

Michael waved the server over and said, "One Bud and one Heineken. The Bud is for me, and the Heineken for my friend Mr. Zac Macmillan, the world's foremost computer security prodigy."

The server smiled and offered her hand. "I've heard all about you, Mr. Macmillan. It's an honor. I will be your server tonight. You only have to raise a finger when you need me."

When she returned with their drinks, she placed new coasters under their glasses. Zac's had her telephone number written on it.

And that's how it started. Throughout the night until the wee hours of the morning, Michael bought the drinks. And, although Zac switched to diet coke after his fourth Heineken, Michael plied him with something much more intoxicating than alcohol—attention. To any savvy observer, it would've been clear Michael had planned it all in advance and was executing his plan with precision as he introduced Zac to a constant stream of admirers. Among them, two good-looking girls who were starstruck from the moment they were introduced. As the night went on and drinks flowed, the girls became more and more vocal about how ready, willing, and able they were for a frolic between the sheets with the great Zac Macmillan. After all, that's what Michael paid them good money for—to make Zac feel like a king. It worked; Zac was smitten by his hero-worshipping new friends.

Zac had no way of knowing that his new friend's real name was Kang Xun, an undercover agent for the MSS. Kang was extremely happy about how things were turning out. It took him two years to research and study Zac Macmillan with the help of psychologists to find the chink in the man's armor, his HPD. Zac was driven by one thing only, attention. The more he got, the happier he was.

Zac's first contract for Michael's employer, Datacube Group LTD, a front company for the MSS's technology division, a fact that Zac didn't know, earned him the tidy sum of $150,000. It was not a big job; it took him three weeks to break into the Anthem data stores. Michael was so impressed with the speed and quality of the work; he 'persuaded' his employer to pay Zac a $50,000 bonus. "That's what friends are for," Michael said.

After this initial success, Michael provided Zac with a constant stream of hacking jobs, none of them as big or nearly as exciting as the Anthem job. But in late 2015, Zac got the job to penetrate the databases of the United States Office of Personnel Management (OPM). It was an exciting job, not because of the half a million-dollar payday but because it was the first real technical challenge posed to him in years.

In 2017 he earned another $150,000 in a little over four months when he breached the security of the data warehouses of Equifax.

But Michael had a big one in mind; the MSS had been

drooling about it for years. They'd thrown vast amounts of money and hacking resources from all over the world at it, but they came off frustrated from every attempt and decided to give the job to Kang Xun, one of their best agents. His orders were clear. "If you have any doubt that Zac might not take the job, don't offer it to him. We don't want him running to the FBI."

Kang knew they had nothing to worry about. The jobs Zac had done for them before were enough to earn him a lengthy stint in the slammer. But he doubted it would be necessary to resort to blackmail, he just had to push the right buttons at the right time, and Zac would jump at the opportunity.

Even so, Michael heeded the warning, and over the course of the four days of DEF CON, he pushed all of Zac's HPD buttons, more so than on any of the previous occasions. He dangled the carrot in front of Zac in vague terms. "My employers have a new job, a big one, undoubtedly the biggest, most important one ever. They have a few contractors in mind. I've been telling them you're the best of the best, and you should get the job, but you know what idiots bosses can sometimes be."

"Tell me about the job."

"I can't, not yet. Leave it to me. I'm sure I'll be able to talk sense into their heads."

Zac was hooked.

Michael knew it but was not ready to reel him in yet. He had to drive him to the edge of a histrionic fit but not on the first night.

On the last night, Michael played his pieces like a chess master. Slowly, over the course of the night, their server became busier and more distant. Then the stream of admirers dried up, and there were no sexy starry-eyed girls. Michael's usual flood of praises had become a trickle.

By eleven that night, Zac was getting bored. This was the first time since he'd met Michael that he found himself in a wilderness of attention deficiency when in his friend's company. But then, just when he was about to throw one of his tantrums and go to bed, Michael got a call and excused himself.

Three minutes later, he came back with a very big smile on his face. "I told you I'd talk sense into their heads. The job is yours if you want it."

"Of course I want it."

"It's going to be the most exciting job you've ever done. The contract price is—"

"Yeah, yeah, that's all fine. What's it you want me to do?"

"Datacube has put two and a half million aside for the job—"

"Stop the bullshit. Tell me what you want."

"Zac, this one is dangerous, high risk. Many have tried and failed. Some are in jail, and some have disappeared. You can't discuss it with anyone but me, ever. There can be no link to Datacube or me whatsoever."

Zac raised an eyebrow. "JWICS?"

JWICS (Joint Worldwide Intelligence Communication System), pronounced Jay-Wicks, is the US Department of Defense's secure intranet system containing top-secret and sensitive compartmented information.

Michael nodded and raised his beer in a toast.

"How much time do I have?"

"Twelve months."

Zac grinned as he raised his glass and clinked it with Michael's.

Michael didn't think it was necessary to tell Zac that Datacube, aka the MSS, was actually hedging their bets— they were already working on another source who could give them access to JWICS.

A few minutes later, two very beautiful hookers joined them.

Part II

_____

26 DAYS TO CHANGE THE COURSE OF HISTORY

Chapter Seventeen

MEETING ZHÌ ZHĚ

Lingui County, China

Day 1

Eight months after Liao and Tao took office, the Operation Middle Kingdom plan was nearing completion.

Although during their many planning meetings over the past eight months, Liao got the distinct impression that the marshals had at their beck and call the services of a very experienced and shrewd advisor, he made no mention of it. But when General Lang told him and Tao it was time to meet someone very important, Zhì Zhĕ, the Wise Man, Liao immediately knew he was the source of their profound insights into matters of state he'd been wondering about. According to Lang, this man was the reincarnation of the legendary General Sun Tzu, the brilliant military strategist and author of The Art of War who lived more than 2500 years ago (born circa 544 BC).

Zhì Zhĕ lived in a secluded spot up in the mountains, 1,200 miles south of Beijing, in the picturesque Yulong River area in Lingui County. His luxurious residence was accessible only by foot or helicopter. Present in the opulent study of the Wise Man was Liao and Tao, as well as Generals Lang and Dai.

Liao didn't believe in reincarnation, but Zhì Zhĕ certainly looked the part of a re-embodied being. He didn't seem to be a day younger than 2,500 years; even his clothes and demeanor testified to his purported age and wisdom. Even so, there were three things that didn't fit the Sun Tzu picture. The first was the man's voice; not only did it sound familiar, but it also sounded much, much younger than Liao would've imagined the voice of a person of two and a half millennia would sound like. The second was the array of TV screens on the wall of the study, tuned into newscasts from around the world. The third was Zhì Zhĕ's proficiency with a computer, not a skill that Liao would've expected Sun Tzu to have had in his day.

The only other person at the residence Liao got a fleeting glimpse of was a woman who seemed to be of the same age as Zhì Zhĕ, maybe his wife.

The five men spent the day working through the final details of the plan and schedule. Zhì Zhĕ, obviously a devoted student of Sun Tzu, imparted much advice taken directly from the latter's teachings, among them:

"In war, the victorious strategist only seeks battle after the victory has been won."

"Make your way by unexpected routes and attack unguarded spots."

"Military tactics are like water. For water, in its natural course, runs away from high places and hastens downwards.

So, in war, the way is to avoid what is strong and strike at what is weak."

And, of course, no discussion about Sun Tzu's teachings could be done justice without reference to the role of deception in war.

"All warfare is based on deception. Hence, when we are able to attack, we must seem unable; when using our forces, we must appear inactive; when we are near, we must make the enemy believe we are far away; when far away, we must make him believe we are near."

"All fighting depends on misdirection."

"The whole secret lies in confusing the enemy so that he cannot fathom our real intent."

By the end of the day, before the four visitors boarded the helicopter, Zhì Zhě handed each of them a small red USB drive. It contained a complete blueprint for the implementation of the plan. It was written in the minutest detail, including the public speeches Liao, Tao, and other senior party members had to make and when.

Liao was hard-pressed not to ask the obvious question; who is Zhì Zhě? He was not entirely surprised to note that Tao didn't seem curious at all. After all, he was a militarist like the marshals. Nevertheless, although he was supposed to be the most powerful man in China, Liao knew that was only on paper; the marshals waved the scepter, and they would decide when he needed to know what.

Chapter Eighteen

ONE DOWN FIVE TO GO

Virginia, USA

Day 1

Yasmin Burke was forty-one, single, and good-looking. She lived in a one-bedroom townhouse in Falls Church about eight miles from CIA headquarters in Langley, Virginia, where she worked as a disguising expert.

She was wholly unaware that she had been the target of a professional surveillance team. She had no idea that they had been in her house, bugged every room, even the bathroom and toilet. Neither did she know that they had installed eavesdropping software on her mobile phone, personal laptop, and tablet PC.

It was Thursday; she had spent the last two days training two people, Josh and Marissa Farley, in the latest disguising techniques. She met them on a mission in China about eight months ago when she helped them smuggle a senior Chinese general, Yuan Lee, out of Shanghai. Her contribution to that mission earned her the honor of meeting the President of the United States, in person, in the Oval Office. But she had no idea who the Farleys worked for and knew better than to ask.

Usually, on Fridays, she treated herself to lunch with colleagues at the in-house cafeteria known as ADR 1. Amid the CIA headquarters' passageways were three dining rooms with the unimaginative names: ADR 1, ADR 2, and DDR. ADR was the acronym for Agency Dining Room and DDR for Director's Dining Room. ADR 1 served about ninety people a day, ADR 2 had seating for around fifty, DDR was exclusively for the DCI—Director of Central Intelligence—and guests. Dining in ADR 2 and DDR was by invitation only, while ADR 1 catered for staffers. In any other setting, ADR 1 would have been a regular café replete with tablecloths, wicker chairs, a seasonal menu, a staff of waiters, and a view over the treetops to the Potomac River.

Whether the chefs were members of the other CIA—Culinary Institute of America—or not, they were all subjected to extensive reference checks. Even so, the chefs and waiters wore badges that read 'Escort Required' because none of them had clearance to handle classified documents. Therefore, they had to be escorted anywhere outside the cafeteria. There were no modern-day equivalents of courtiers who tasted the king's food for poison, but the chefs were not allowed to use open flames to prepare the food—the appliances were electric.

This Thursday, the last day of the course, Yasmin invited the Farleys for lunch in ADR 1, her treat. They paid for lunch the day before at Mclean Family Restaurant.

The Farleys told her they were going to spend the night at a friend's place in D.C., and the next morning they'd drive to New York, where they planned to stay for two days. On Sunday, they would go to Martha's Vineyard for a week.

Yasmin was looking forward to a long weekend with her siblings, who had planned a surprise visit to their parents in Harrisburg, Pennsylvania, on the occasion of their 45th wedding anniversary.

When the clock struck five that afternoon, Yasmin shoved her personal belongings into her handbag, cleared her desk, and left the building.

She drove straight to her townhouse, parked inside her lockup garage, closed the door behind her with the remote, and entered the house through the internal door. Within half an hour, she had her bags packed and was back in her car. She fastened the seatbelt, started the engine, and was about to open the garage door when she was overcome by a sudden spell of dizziness.

She took a deep breath; everything went dark.

Virginia, USA

Day 1

Eventually, Ren Shi and his team's tedious efforts were rewarded.

One of Ren's surveillance team, while on watch duty on Wednesday, drove past the Mclean Family Restaurant on Chain Bridge Road, less than two miles from the CIA's headquarters, when he saw Yasmin Burke in the company of a couple who immediately piqued his interest. He had been looking at pictures of that couple's faces at least once a day for more than four months. It was the Texans, Joshua and Marissa Elizabeth Crawford. He found parking and watched the three as they entered the restaurant frequented not only by political, government, and media celebrities but also CIA personnel and retirees. The vehicle they exited was not Yasmin's; he assumed it was the Crawford's. He phoned Ren immediately. Less than twenty minutes later, Ren had joined him in his vehicle from where they were watching the front door, waiting for Ms. Burke and the Crawfords to make their appearance after finishing lunch.

When the targets appeared outside, Ren took a number of photos, which he immediately uploaded for his IT team to make comparisons with the photos in their database to assure those were the Texans. He received confirmation before the targets reached the CIA headquarters. This was an exciting new development, but not enough to make a move yet.

Thanks to Yasmin's compromised cellphone, Ren already knew about her plans to take the Friday off from work to visit her parents for their 45th wedding anniversary over the weekend. What he needed now was more information about the Crawfords' plans, but listening to their conversation over lunch didn't provide him with anything actionable other than that the Crawfords were on a two-day course at CIA headquarters. With the registration number of the vehicle provided by Ren, his IT team quickly established that it was a rental belonging to a D.C.-based company. Hacking into the company's vehicle tracking system, they were able to track the vehicle from now on. All they had to do now was keep watching and listening and waiting for an opportunity to present itself.

They didn't have to wait long. The very next day, Thursday, during their lunch break, when Yasmin and the Farleys talked about their weekend plans, Ren was listening to the audio feed from her mobile phone and got the last piece of information he needed—the Crawfords' plans for the weekend.

The opportunity came so fast; it almost caught Ren on the wrong foot. But he knew he had to act. They were still busy with their lunch in ADR1 when Ren contacted Minister Xuan Bai and told him what he had learned and his plan. Within the hour, Xuan phoned back and gave Ren the green light. "Approved at the highest level," he said. Of course, the approval was accompanied by the caution not to make a mess of things. Ren had no illusions about the hidden meaning of the Minister's warning—fail, and you're dead.

By 5:35 p.m., Yasmin Burke's limp body was tied to one of her own kitchen chairs. While she was upstairs packing her stuff for the weekend, Ren had entered her garage and placed a small container loaded with an aerosolized cocktail of carfentanil and remifentanil, derivatives of fentanyl, below the driver's seat. The container was rigged to release the gas the moment she sat down in the seat.

The gas had knocked her out before she could start the car.

Experts believed that it was this combination of carfentanil and remifentanil that Russian Special Forces used to knock out the terrorists during the Moscow theater hostage crisis on 23 October 2002.

Virginia, USA

Day 1

Yasmin heard the groan and realized it came from her own throat. Her sense of self returned slowly, like a computer booting up. She opened her eyes, but it remained dark. Her head was covered in a hood. Her head was throbbing. She tried to speak, but her throat and mouth were too dry; only a raspy sound escaped. She pushed her tongue forward to lick her lips, but it was blocked. She tried to move but couldn't; her arms and legs were strapped to a chair. She felt claustrophobic, struggling for breath, the side effects of the chemicals she had inhaled.

She felt someone pull the hood from her head and squinted against the explosion of bright light. Slowly she recognized her surroundings; she was in her own kitchen, strapped to her own kitchen chair with duct tape. In front of her stood a ski-masked man of medium height, dressed in faded jeans, a faded black t-shirt, a black leather jacket, and dark blue sneakers. Two steps to her right, she noticed another man similarly clad, about six inches taller than the one in front of her. Both men were wearing black nitrile gloves.

Whether this was a mugging or about her work didn't really matter; she was in grave danger. If a mugging, she might survive. If about her work, probably not. She was not a trained agent. Even if she were, she knew no one, not even the best agent, could withstand prolonged torturing— everyone had a breaking point.

The man in front of her, as if he were reading her

mind, said, "This could be long and painful, or quick and painless." He spoke English with a Chinese accent.

Yasmin didn't make a reply; she nodded slightly. Tears started dribbling down her cheeks. She asked, "What do you want?" But the duct tape wrapped around her mouth muffled the words to meaningless sounds.

The man produced a small notebook and pencil from the inside pocket of his jacket. He nodded to his companion, who took a pocketknife out and cut the duct tape restraints from her left arm.

She was left-handed, but how did they know?

"I ask the questions; you write the answers. Right?"

Yasmin nodded.

He showed her two pictures on his cellphone and asked, "What are their real names?"

Yasmin started writing.

Virginia, USA

Day 1

Ren learned that the Crawfords were actually Josh and Marissa Farley, and the couple who had posed as an old Italian couple in Shanghai eight months ago was Rex and Catia Dalton and their dog, Digger. She had no idea who the Daltons and Farleys worked for; it could have been the CIA or any of the USA's legion of security agencies or the military or private contractors—she didn't have the clearance to know that kind of information. She also had no idea where they were stationed. Notwithstanding, she was able to give Ren a fairly detailed description and drawings of what the Daltons looked like without disguises.

She remembered the president spoke to Rex Dalton a few hours before the mission in Shanghai started. And she was invited to the White House to meet the president after the mission. But she hadn't seen any of them since that day except, of course, meeting the Farleys again the day before when they reported for training.

She had no idea what happened to General Yuan Lee since his arrival in the USA; she could only guess that he would be in protective custody somewhere or in the FBI's witness protection program.

She also told Ren about the *TOMATS*, a luxury yacht, on which she'd spent about twelve hours in Hong Kong before flying to Beijing and then to Shanghai. But she knew nothing more about the yacht, neither who the owner was nor anything about the crew.

A little over two hours after Yasmin Burke regained consciousness, the interrogation was over. Ren injected six milligrams of fentanyl—fifty to a hundred times more potent than morphine—into a vein on her right arm. Two milligrams was a lethal dose.

One down, five to go—Yuan, the Farleys, and the Daltons—piece of cake.

Chapter Nineteen

IN THE CANDY BOWL

Beijing, China

Day 2

It was almost 4:00 p.m. on Friday when General Lang Jianhong finally turned his undivided attention to the plan on the USB drive Zhì Zhě gave him the day before.

He plugged the device into one of the USB ports on his laptop and browsed to the drive. He entered the twelve-character password provided by Zhì Zhě, written down on a piece of paper. Before he started reading, he pressed the intercom button on his desk and told his secretary that he didn't want to be disturbed.

Within minutes he'd lost track of time as he studied the documents and added comments.

It was after 6:00 p.m. when he became aware of the time and retrieved an unopened bottle of Lagavulin 16-Year-Old Islay single malt scotch whiskey and a tumbler from his liquor cabinet. He dropped a few ice cubes from the ice bucket in the mini-fridge into the tumbler and poured a generous measure of the whiskey over it.

In English-speaking countries, the people would've said, 'prost,' or 'cheers,' and it was customary to toast everyone at the table whenever anyone called a toast. And if you didn't look directly into their eyes when toasting, you might be sentenced to seven years of bad sex. In China, the people said, *gan bey*, meaning bottoms up. Lang wasn't worried about a seven-year sentence; he had a wife and two mistresses, and whenever he got tired of them, he had a choice of hookers. He said, "Gan bey. To the fulfillment of the hundred-year plan thirty years ahead of time," and took a big gulp.

By 9:00 p.m., General Lang's head was spinning, not from reading, but from the half bottle of whiskey in his system. He shook his head a few times and looked at his watch; the numbers were all double and swinging, impossible to read. He sighed. "I'll continue this tomorrow."

He was too intoxicated to realize it took him almost five minutes to accomplish the simple tasks of saving and closing the document, retrieving the USB drive, and shutting his computer down. When he got up from his chair, he was unsteady on his feet. With the USB drive in hand, he staggered to the wall safe to lock it away, but when he finally arrived at the safe, he couldn't remember the combination to the lock. He tried to say the numbers out loud but was slurring so much he couldn't understand himself. Finally, he gave up, stumbled back to his desk, and plopped back in his chair.

He started to unbutton the side pocket of his tunic to put the USB drive in it, but then his eyes caught the big hand-painted ceramic bowl filled to the brim with candy, and all of a sudden, he had a craving for something sweet. He forgot what he was busy doing and reached for the candy and didn't realize he had dropped the USB drive in the bowl when he picked up one of the sweets and placed it in his mouth.

Chewing on the sweet treat, he pushed the intercom button and started telling his secretary to let his driver know to come and pick him up, but then, somewhere in his foggy brain, a synapse fired, and he realized she had left.

With an unsteady hand, he picked up his cellphone, swiped the screen, and tried to enter the four-digit unlock key—six attempts later, he got it right. It required three attempts to hit the telephone icon and two attempts to hit the speed dial for his driver.

It was 9:45 p.m. when the driver helped the very drunk General Lang out of his office to his waiting car.

Fifteen minutes later, at precisely 10:00 p.m., as always on weeknights, the buzzer on the door from the rear alley sounded, and one of the guards let Sun Jia, the cleaner, in.

Chapter Twenty

A HOLIDAY ON THE RANCH

The Ranch, Arizona, USA

Day 2

By 9:00 a.m., Rex had already put in two hours in Brandt's office with Chris McArdle, CRC's second in command, taking care of various administrative tasks. Brandt was recovering from brain surgery he had six weeks before. In the middle of a critical mission to stop a lunatic who was responsible for a series of terror attacks in European cities as part of a plot to revive the Ottoman Empire, Brandt was diagnosed with an aggressive but benign brain tumor and had to undergo emergency surgery. Rex was appointed as the acting CEO and would continue in the role until Brandt was fit to resume his duties. In fact, Rex agreed to continue until after Brandt's wedding, three weeks hence.

John Brandt and Christelle Proll, former deputy director of the DGSE, the French equivalent of the American CIA, had worked on a few joint missions in their younger days during the Cold War. There was a romantic spark between them back then, but the Atlantic Ocean and work had put an end to it. They caught up again in 2015 when they had to work together on Operation Badr to prevent a group of fanatics from starting Armageddon. The old flame was rekindled, and less than a year later, they were engaged. Christelle had retired two months ago.

The Ranch, as they called it, was a 20,000-acre property in Yavapai County, in the western part of Arizona. It was about thirty-two miles due north of Bagdad, a copper mining town with a population of about 1,800 residents about 126 miles from Phoenix. The nearest real town was Kingman, some 20 miles away.

The Ranch had been in the Brandt family for four generations. He had turned it from a cattle farm into CRC's headquarters and training facility. The place was secluded, pristine, and beautiful. The air was clean, the spring water fresh, and the climate perfect. With arrays of solar panels, a few wind generators, and banks of Tesla batteries, the Ranch was self-sufficient in electricity. The homestead consisted of three beautifully remodeled homes and two barns converted into offices, a mission control center called the Ops Center, a communications center called the Cyber Room, and a lecture room. They kept a few cows for milk, free-range chickens, turkeys, and a herd of horses. There were also three helipads and a landing strip long enough for most small jets to take off and land, including CRC's Dassault Falcon 2000 DX private jet.

About two miles away from the homestead, in a beautiful valley, was the CRC training compound, with sleeping quarters for the recruits, various in-house and open-air shooting ranges, obstacle courses, a gym, and other facilities.

CRC had four missions in progress across the globe, which Rex and McArdle kept an eye on. All of them were of the observe-and-report kind; in other words, surveillance and information gathering—no door kicking and shooting.

With the technology upgrades Rex had requested at the time when he, Brandt, and Spencer talked about the upgrades to the *TOMATS* a few months ago, CRC field agents got, among others, personal GPS trackers, the latest in battlefield first-aid kits, mini surveillance drones, laser-directed listening devices, Molar Mics, and other covert ops paraphernalia.

The Molar Mic was an exciting new development in the field of communications for covert operators. Developed by Sonitus Technologies, the device consisted of a mouthpiece, equipped with a waterproof microphone, custom-built to fit the teeth of the operator. Once in place, the wearer can speak normally. The mouthpiece translated incoming audio into vibrations on the teeth that traveled through the bones in the jaw and skull to the inner ear, which translated them into sounds, making it feel as if the sounds were coming from within the person's own head. It was a strange sensation that took some getting used to. Nevertheless, the tactical benefits of being able to communicate in this manner were enormous.

On the wall in Brandt's office was a big screen with green dots representing the CRC agents' physical locations across the world. Apart from a secured satellite phone, every agent wore a miniature GPS tracking device on their person. They were no bigger than a quarter, hidden somewhere on them, i.e., the seams of clothes, heels of shoes, belt buckles, etcetera. They wore those devices wherever they went, whether they were working or not.

The trackers had a two-week battery life and communicated directly through satellite. If the green dot on the screen turned red, it meant one of three things: the device lost contact with the satellite, in which case it would come back online in a short while, or the device's battery was dead, and the bearer would feel a few short vibrations and a message would go to their mobile phones, or the device had been damaged which could be for several reasons including deliberately. Whatever the reason, when the light went from green to red, it was time to pay attention. An alert would immediately be raised in the Cyber Room and the Old Man's office.

The two green dots told Rex that the Farleys had arrived in New York as planned. The rest of the dots representing CRC agents across the globe were all green as well. He finished the last bit of coffee in his mug and told McArdle he was going to see if the Old Man felt up for a walk.

Walking over to the main house where John and Christelle lived, Rex thought about how Catia took to life on the Ranch like a fish to water. She was born and bred in Rome —a denizen of the concrete jungle. He was amazed at how quickly she fell in love with the wide-open spaces, the animals, and the people. Within a few weeks, she was a proficient horse rider, and it was near impossible to keep her off the quad bikes. Both of them were motorbike enthusiasts. The best time of the day was when she and Rex went out on horseback, sometimes watching the sunrise or sunset. A few times, they went camping overnight, barbecuing their food on an open fire, and lay in each other's arms, looking at the star-filled heavens until the early morning hours. For them, the time on the Ranch had been one long exhilarating vacation.

Rex found Catia and Christelle at the kitchen table in the main house discussing wedding plans. They told him John was out with Digger and Cupcake. Rex knew better than to get involved in wedding planning. He politely declined the ladies' offer of espresso and cake, saying, "Thanks, I just had coffee. I'll go and see how the Old Man is getting on with Cupcake's training. Or rather, how Cupcake and Digger are getting on with his training."

Chapter Twenty-One

THE OLD MAN'S TRAINING

The Ranch, Arizona, USA

Day 2

About half a mile from the house, next to a pond, Rex and Catia had constructed a makeshift obstacle course consisting of a few ladders, timber walls, fences of various heights, and tunnels made from old metal containers. That was where Rex headed when he left the house.

Cupcake was a four-month-old, short-haired, brindle-colored Dutch Shepherd pup, a present to John from Rex and Catia when he got out of the hospital. "Cupcake," Catia had said the day when she gave John the leash, "Your first grandchild."

John's jaw had dropped, and Christelle had wiped a tear away. It was love at first sight for John, Christelle, and Cupcake. And to demonstrate how much she liked the new members of her pack, the first chance Cupcake got, she went straight for John's slippers under the bed.

Christelle was enamored by the little bundle of playfulness and absolutely loved the name Cupcake. John and Cupcake had become inseparable.

But John and Digger didn't have such a friendly start when they met the first time. Digger was a big black Dutch Shepherd, Rex's and Catia's dog. Rex inherited him from his friend, Trevor Madigan, a former SAS operative from Australia, who'd been killed in an ambush in Afghanistan in 2014. Digger, an Australian military dog, had been his companion since Trevor asked Rex to take care of him with his dying breath. Rex, mortally scared of dogs since he'd been attacked by one as a small child, had agreed.

Rex was a man of his word, he and Digger worked through their issues, and they'd become inseparable friends. Digger had acknowledged him as the alpha in their pack and accepted Catia into the pack from the moment he met her. Digger was Rex's 'best man' at their wedding; he brought the wedding rings in on a dainty white satin cushion balanced on his nose.

In Australia, the troops were called 'diggers,' and although way back, it could have been a derogatory term, it wasn't anymore. The Aussies loved and respected their diggers just as much as the Americans loved and respected their soldiers. The name originated from WW1 with the trench warfare—the Aussies, because of their skills as miners, were the ones who designed and dug those trenches.

Although Rex never learned to give Digger proper commands, like military dog handlers do, over the years, working as a team on many missions, they had developed a unique communications system. Some of Rex's colleagues believed that the two indeed spoke a language that only they understood. However, the truth was, it was always Rex who had learned to be very attentive to Digger's behavior.

Rex couldn't help but smile at Brandt's claim these days that Digger was one of his agents. Things had come a long way since the first time Brandt and Digger met when he insisted on calling Digger the "damn dog" and chided Rex about how stupid it was for an agent of his to go around with a dog. But John was not one who was too egotistic to admit when he was wrong and often talked about how their relationship has changed. "These days, I can relax when I know he's with the team. It's like having adult supervision when the children are out playing. And I'll never forget how Digger saved my ass when he sniffed me out among thousands of shipping containers where my abductors were trying to hide me."

Catia and Rex found John's admission amusing but agreed he was right; Digger had kept them out of serious trouble on many missions over the years.

Dutch Shepherds are known for their affectionate, obedient, reliable, loyal, alert, and trainable temperaments. They are great guard and watchdogs. They are also smart and energetic, loyal, and protective, love children, and get along with other animals. "Even with an old fart like me," John had said once.

Rex couldn't help but chuckle when he came around a tree and took in the scene. He stopped in his tracks and took a step back to hide behind the tree.

Twenty yards away, John was standing at attention, like a drill sergeant.

His troops, Cupcake and Digger, were sitting next to each other, two paces away from Brandt, tongues lolling out, their eyes were fixed on him—the canine version of parade ground rest.

"Attention."

Their ears pitched up and forward.

"Lie down."

They obeyed.

"Roll," Brandt said and gestured with his hand to the left.

Digger rolled right, but Cupcake rolled to the left into Digger. Digger growled softly as if to say, "Pay attention, kiddo, look at his hand."

Brandt sighed. "No, girl, the other way. Look at what Digger is doing. Get up."

They resumed the sitting position.

John repeated the commands, and this time Cupcake got it right. Both she and Digger got a back and ear scratch and a "good boy, good girl," from John. It was clear to Rex that John had grasped the principle that dogs worked for praise and not for food.

Rex stepped out from behind the tree, laughing. "Having fun, John?" The two dogs threw a glance at him and yelped in excitement but remained seated. They looked at John, begging him to let them go and say hi to Rex, but John held his finger up and said, "No. Stay."

They obeyed but looked crestfallen and complained loudly by raising the pitch of their voices.

Finally, he said, "*Okay*, you can go."

They broke ranks and ran to Rex, yelping and barking excitedly.

Rex dropped to his knees and welcomed them.

A few minutes later, Rex sat down next to John on the bench overlooking the water. Digger and Cupcake were sitting in front of them. They were waiting for their treats and made it known. John chuckled and took two pieces of jerky out of his pocket, showed it to them, pointed to the obstacle course, and said, "Around you go." The two of them were like arrows out of a bow.

As the two dogs navigated the course with Digger leading the way, John looked at them and said, "You know Rex, I grew up on this farm. We had dogs, and I loved them, but I never knew how clever they were. Since Cupcake's arrival, I've been reading books and watching videos about dogs, and all I've learned is how little we know about *them* and how much they know about *us*."

Rex nodded pensively. "Yep, it was that insight that Digger understands me much better than I understand him, that finally made me realize he's the best friend I ever had—clichéd, but true."

Chapter Twenty-Two

ERRATIC TRAVEL PATTERN

New York, USA / The Ranch, Arizona, USA

Day 2

It was 5:00 p.m. in Arizona, 8 p.m. in New York; Rex and Catia were busy saddling the horses when Greg Wade, the head of CRC's IT team, called Rex to the Cyber Room. Greg had a worried look on his face. The GPS tracking system had alerted him that Josh's and Marissa's trackers had been going in a loop for the past two and a half hours. The exact same route of about twelve miles had been covered five times. The satphone tracking system showed their phones had gone offline about three-quarters of an hour before the personal trackers started going on the loop.

Greg's team was a small but highly-skilled group of IT specialists. Essentially, they were computer hackers, among the best in the business. With a few keystrokes, they could create havoc, blackout a city, take control of its traffic lights, enter government and corporate databases, access the bank records of any individual and organization, break through firewalls, break encryption, and much more.

Greg's enhancements to the GPS tracking software they got from the CIA's technical division notified him of the problem. He had added features to alert him when agents' devices were not staying on preplanned routes or erratic travel patterns. A message was sent to them to check if they were okay. And that's what happened with the Farleys when Greg's program detected that their GPS devices were traveling in a loop. When they didn't respond to the 'are-you-okay' message, Greg smelled trouble and raised the alarm.

Within minutes, Brandt and Chris McArdle were in the Cyber Room. Rex had Martin Richardson, a deputy director at the CIA, on the phone, alerting him of the situation. If the Farleys had fallen into the hands of the enemy, any of them, it would be a disaster. They knew too much. They knew about some of the CIA's closest guarded secrets. They knew where the bodies were buried.

Because CRC was an off-the-books secret counterterror organization, the anonymity of the organization and its employees were critical to the success of its operations. It took less than ten minutes to decide that Rex, Catia, and Digger would go to New York and try to track them down; if they couldn't get them within the next eight hours, the FBI and NYPD would be called in.

Half an hour later, Rex had left Chris McArdle in charge. He and Catia had grabbed their go-bags and Digger's gear and raced to the landing strip to get on the CRC jet to take them to New York. It was a four-and-a-half-hour flight.

By the time the jet took off from the Ranch, Greg's team was plotting the electronic trail left by the Farleys' personal GPS trackers and mobile phones on a map of the city.

During the flight, Rex and Catia were in video contact with McArdle and Brandt in the CRC Ops Center.

Trying to figure out who could've abducted the Farleys and why was impossible. CRC agents were not in the hospitality industry—they made enemies when they executed their missions. And the Farleys had been on many missions over the years. The enemies could be terrorist groups from the Middle East, Turkish radicals, Chinese, organized crime groups—there was no shortage of enemies queuing up to kill CRC agents.

The why would probably be answered the moment they knew the who. And then the million-dollar question, how did the abductors know where the Farleys would be? As for their intent with the Farleys, there could be little doubt. They would be tortured for information and killed.

In short, the three-member rescue team was running against the clock. The time they had would depend on how long the Farleys could hold out under torture. Both were trained to withstand heavy-handed interrogations, but everyone had a limit and would eventually break. Exacerbating the situation was the fact that the two of them were married; the abductors would certainly exploit that.

In the meantime, Greg's team had confirmed that the GPS devices had been attached to a bus traveling the same route over and over around Jersey City.

Greg's team hacked into the car rental company's computer system in D.C., where the Farleys rented their car. They checked the GPS tracker on the car and found it inside the One Tree Hill Hotel's basement parking in Manhattan.

They hacked into the hotel's CCTV and saw the Farleys

checking in, going to their room, and then nothing else. The Farleys, according to the CCTV footage, must still be in their room, but a telephone call to the hotel quickly established they were not. When the CCTV recordings were studied carefully, they found there were fifteen minutes when the CCTV didn't work.

The information from the tracking devices and the GPS on their satphones told Greg that the Farleys had left their room during those fifteen minutes and went down to the basement parking. The parking area's CCTV footage showed a white Ford Transit Courier delivery van parked three bays away from their car before the cameras went out. The vehicle was missing after the cameras came back online fifteen minutes later. By this time, the Farleys' satphones had gone offline, but their personal GPS trackers were still active.

They checked the footage from the street surveillance cameras outside the hotel for the fifteen-minute period when the CCTV system malfunctioned, looking at every car that came out of the hotel's parking lot. One of the four vehicles exiting during that time was the white Ford Transit Courier, and the personal GPS trackers showed they were in that vehicle.

By now, they had little doubt that the Farleys had been abducted, and the abductors were professionals. Nevertheless, the CCTV and GPS information gave them the location and time of the abduction.

Following the trail left by Josh's and Marissa's personal GPS trackers, they quickly established that the Farleys were transported to a public parking garage in Jersey City, eight miles from the One Tree Hill hotel in Manhattan.

Greg's system told them that the Farleys were relieved of

their personal GPS trackers in this garage, where they were attached to a public bus.

They looked at the CCTV footage of the parking garage in Jersey City and were not surprised to learn that the cameras were off for more than an hour between 6:00 p.m. and 7:00 p.m. They looked at the footage of the street surveillance cameras, but this was a public parking garage; cars were queuing to get in and out. There were more than a hundred cars to check. They did so but couldn't spot the white Ford Transit Courier among those leaving the parking garage.

The Daltons arrived at the Farleys' hotel at 1:30 a.m., more than nine hours after the abduction. Their friends could be halfway to the other side of the world. But that meant the abductors had to get them out of the country without being noticed, not impossible, but definitely not easy.

The problem was they were fresh out of leads.

Chapter Twenty-Three

RARING TO INFLICT PAIN

New York, USA

Day 2

Ren and two of his men had rushed to New York the night before, after interrogating and killing Yasmin Burke. Along the way, they had made a short detour off the I-95 onto a deserted country road to bury her body among a copse of trees not far from Bel Air, Maryland.

Ren's IT team had patched his mobile phone into the feed they were getting from the Farleys' car rental company, which showed him the car's GPS tracker signals all the way from D.C. to New York. Ren smiled as he checked the moving red dot on his phone's screen approaching New York on the I-95. He didn't only have the ability to track the car; he also had the ability to remotely disable the starter and lock or unlock the car's doors and disable the alarm system.

From eavesdropping on the lunchtime conversation of Yasmin and her students the day before, Ren knew the Farley's were going to stay in a hotel in Manhattan, but he didn't know which one. However, Ren's IT team made short work of finding the booking at the One Tree Hill hotel in Manhattan. Getting into the hotel's computer systems was a walk in the park for them. Now they knew the Farleys' room number and had access to the hotel's CCTV.

When the Farleys went out for lunch shortly after they'd checked in, Ren's IT team remotely disabled the CCTV cameras in the basement parking area, disabled the alarm system on the Farleys' car, and unlocked the doors. It took one of the men less than five minutes to enter the parking area and plant the gas canister below the driver's seat, just like they did with Yasmin Burke.

And then they waited and watched the hotel's CCTV feeds.

At 4:05 p.m., when the Farleys left their room, the IT team switched the CCTV cameras for the selected areas off, and within fifteen minutes, they had the unconscious Farleys in the back of a stolen white Ford Transit Courier van with false plates and were on their way to a public parking garage in Jersey City. They had relieved the Farleys of their mobile phones, switched them off, and removed the batteries—preventing anyone from tracking them or activating them remotely.

The IT team disabled the CCTV cameras in the entire public parking garage in Jersey City a few minutes before Ren and his team arrived with their captives. They had about forty minutes before the Farleys would start to regain consciousness. On arrival, Ren scanned the Farleys for bugs and found the personal GPS trackers. He and one of his helpers quickly undressed the Farleys and covered them with white hospital gowns while the third man went out and placed the GPS trackers on a public bus. Less than seven minutes after arrival, the Farleys were in wheelchairs on their way to a safe house downtown three blocks away.

Ren wasn't worried about the CCTV cameras on the streets; his IT team took care of that by switching them off and on as required along the route.

At the safe house, the Farleys were tied up, gagged, hooded, and placed in separate rooms. The safe house was the basement in the residence of a Chinese immigrant family of four, husband and wife in their early thirties and two children, seven and nine. The family was at home. The parents knew that Ren and his men were there with two captives, but the children didn't. It was not the ideal place for an interrogation; an isolated location such as a farm would've been much better; an MSS interrogation room in China would have been ideal. But he had to make do with what he had in the time available.

Ren looked at his watch. "They should start to come around in the next ten to fifteen minutes. And then the waiting will start. It could take anywhere from six to ten hours of no water, no food, no sleep, and sensory deprivation before they'll be ready to talk."

Ren was an experienced and ruthless interrogator. There were very few torture techniques he didn't know about and hadn't used over the years. He had the dubious honor of never losing a prisoner before he got everything he wanted from them. He was raring to inflict pain on the Farleys to revenge the humiliation they had caused the MSS. But he knew the Farleys were trained operators; they would be able to withstand physical torture for much longer than untrained people, much longer than he had time or patience for. The waiting was testing his self-restraint, but he knew his psychological tricks to soften them up would produce results much quicker than applying his usual brutal methods from the outset.

Chapter Twenty-Four

A BRIEFING BY DIGGER

New York, USA

Day 3

The manager of the One Tree Hill Hotel, thanks to Martin Richardson, only asked to see their IDs before handing Rex and Catia a swipe key to the Farleys' room.

As expected, inside the room was the Farleys' luggage, and there were no signs of a struggle. Rex took two pieces of clothing from their luggage, Marissa's blouse and Josh's t-shirt. Rex and Catia were watching Digger closely and could see he knew his pack members had been in the room earlier. It was also evident from Digger's behavior that he had sensed Josh and Marissa were in danger. Rex would never understand how Digger would know, but it didn't matter if he understood it or not; the fact was Digger knew, and that was all that was important.

Rex let Digger sniff the clothing and asked him to find

them. They locked the room and let Digger follow the Farleys scent along the corridor. He stopped at the second elevator door and looked at Rex.

"They went down in this elevator," Rex said.

Rex and Catia were getting a briefing by Digger of what happened from a dog's perspective.

Arriving in the basement, Digger put his nose to the floor and led them straight to the Farleys' car.

At the car, Digger stopped and started growling softly; he must have sensed or smelled something terrible had happened to the members of his pack. With the hair on his neck standing on end and his ears pitched forward, he walked around the car, sniffing and making soft yelping noises. He was in distress.

"He's telling us something bad happened here," Catia said.

"Uh-huh. There're no signs of a struggle. The abductors must have somehow managed to incapacitate them before they could put up a fight," Rex said.

Digger sniffed around the car and made more noises, but Rex and Catia could only guess what he was trying to tell them.

Catia said, "I think forensics experts might find traces of incapacitating agents such as a knockout gas."

Rex nodded. "That's the only way they could've gotten the better of Josh and Marissa without a fight."

Then Digger went to the empty parking space where the white van was parked before. He sniffed around and then sat down where the van's rear end would have been.

"They were loaded into the back of that white van that was parked here," said Rex.

Then Digger headed for the exit. When he got to the street, he stopped and sat down, whining softly and looking at Rex with what Rex thought was a sorrowful expression on his face. He stooped and stroked Digger's head and ears. "Don't worry, buddy, we're going to get them. Okay, let's go over to that parking garage in Jersey City."

So far, Digger's briefing confirmed what they thought had happened based on Greg's analysis of the GPS trackers. Everything now depended on what they'd find in Jersey City.

Jersey City, USA

Day 3

It was 2:50 a.m., almost ten hours since the abduction. The Daltons had less than three hours to find their friends before the FBI and NYPD had to be called in.

The hotel's basement parking smelled of gasoline, oil, and rubber, but this public parking garage was an environmentalist's worst nightmare; it was near suffocation levels. Catia was worried that Digger wouldn't be able to smell anything. But Rex told her that he knew of documented cases where dogs sniffed out methamphetamine hidden in the gas tanks of cars. Digger was not going to have any trouble following the Farley's scent in this place.

And he didn't disappoint. Rex told Digger to find them. Digger led them up the ramps to the third floor and straight to the white van that was still parked there. They expected Digger to lead them to another parking bay where the Farleys would have been transferred to another vehicle, but to their surprise, he didn't. Instead, he led them to the elevator doors and sat down in front of one. They got in and went down to the ground floor.

But if the Farleys were restrained or incapacitated, how did the abductors get them out this way without attracting attention? Wheelchairs? Gurneys? Crates? Guns to their backs? The problem was the CCTV cameras were inoperative at the time. Lots of ifs, but one thing Rex and Catia didn't doubt for a moment was that this was the way the Farleys were taken out of the parking garage. That's what Digger told them, and they knew better than to doubt him.

Digger led them out of the parking area, turned left, and headed downtown.

Chapter Twenty-Five

WE DON'T HAVE TWENTY MINUTES!

Jersey City, USA

Day 3

It was 3:46 a.m. when Digger stopped and sat down on the sidewalk in a poorly lit street opposite a double-story semi-detached red-brick house. The house was dark. No fence or security lights. The neighboring houses were all dark as well. Digger looked at Rex and Catia and back at the house, making a soft whining sound as if to say, "They're in there."

"This could be it," Rex whispered to Catia. "We have to keep moving and find a place to hide from where we can watch the house."

Twenty yards further, they saw a dilapidated convenience store with big For Sale posters on the windows. Rex looked through one of the windows and saw a large space filled with empty shelves. He nodded at Catia and handed her Digger's leash.

She took the leash and turned back to the street to keep watch while Rex picked the lock. The door opened within thirty seconds.

Rex thumbed the switch on the loop around his neck, which had a wireless connection to his Molar Mic, and told Brandt and McArdle in the Ops Center on the Ranch, "We might've found the house where Josh and Marissa are being kept. We can't be sure, though. It's possible that the abductors brought them here but moved them again. But Digger is telling us this is it."

"If Digger says they're there, then they're there," said Brandt without hesitation.

Rex smiled. "Agreed. When in doubt, trust Digger. We're going to deploy the drones to see if we can find out what's going on inside. In the meantime, Greg must get us a floorplan and anything else that might be helpful. Catia will be texting you the address in a moment."

Catia texted the address and then retrieved two mini-drones from her backpack and assembled them.

Mini-drones, known as Personal Reconnaissance Systems (PRS), had been in use by US military forces since 2014. The drones Catia had in her hand looked like mini-helicopters and measured a little over six and a half inches in length and a little more than one inch in width. They weighed less than thirty-three grams, without batteries. The three onboard cameras: one looking forward, one looking straight down, and one pointing downward at forty-five degrees, had night vision and thermal imaging capabilities. They were also equipped with long-wave infrared and day video sensors that transmitted video streams or high-resolution still images to their base station within a range of two and a half miles. The drones could reach speeds of up to twenty-nine miles per hour and stay in the air for half an hour on a single charge.

When the drones were ready, Catia handed both to Rex. He went to the back door, opened it slowly and quietly, looked around, and saw no one. He looked at Digger; he was not indicating any danger. He took a few steps out of the building with a drone in the palm of each hand and nodded for Catia to launch them from the control screen on her Samsung tablet. Less than a minute later, the drones were hovering quietly over the target house.

From CRC's Ops Center, Brandt, McArdle, and Greg were able to see everything on Catia's screen.

She steered the drones in circles around the house at the slowest possible speed, dropping them down in altitude by about thirty feet after completing each orbit.

By the time Greg's team had collected the floorplan from the city council's engineering department database, the team knew from the thermal images provided by the drones that there were four people on the upper floor. They seemed to be asleep, two in one bed and the other two in separate beds in another room. There was no one on the ground floor, but there were five people in the basement. One of them was on a bed in one of the two rooms adjoining a large room and not moving much. Of the four people in the large room, one was in a chair, two were standing on either side of the person in the chair, and the fourth stood in front of the seated person. The figures in the chair and the bed could be Josh and Marissa. The remaining three could be the abductors, and by the looks of it, the interrogation was in progress. But who were the people upstairs?

Greg and his team had done a little digging in the city council's databases and found that the house was registered in the names of Yu Hua and Yu Heng, either husband and wife or brother and sister. If the latter, who were the other two on the upper floor? A few searches in OSINT databases clarified the matter—the remaining occupants on the upper floor were the Yu children, two girls, Lan and Lin, seven and nine years old.

Undoubtedly, the couple upstairs was collaborating with the scumbags downstairs by making their house available as a safe house; the question was, would the couple get involved if someone tried to rescue the prisoners?

Twenty-five minutes after launching the drones, Catia retrieved them, replaced the batteries, and asked Rex to take them outside again for the launch. She had four more backup batteries for each drone if needed.

The drones didn't pick up any signs of an alarm system, and there were no guards outside. The floorplans showed the basement had a narrow window about eight inches off the ground on the side of the house, and apart from the door leading from the kitchen to the basement, there was also a door at the back of the house leading down to the basement. The side window was too small for entry.

"They were abducted more than eleven hours ago," said McArdle. "I assume they've had no food, no water, and no sleep. We've got no idea how long they've been tortured and how much more they can take."

Brandt said, "I think it's time to call in the FBI."

"Agreed," said Rex. "But keep in mind, we don't know who the abductors are. The owners of the property are Chinese, and I suspect so are the shitheads downstairs. The thing is, we don't know how desperate they are. For all we know, they could be suicidal, ready to kill themselves and the Farleys the moment they feel threatened."

"That might be so, but I don't see another option," said

Brandt. "It'll be suicide for you to try and do it on your own."

Rex said, "Okay, make the call. While you do that, we'll see if Digger can get us a view through that side window."

Catia kept the drones going while Rex sat down on the floor next to Digger and rigged him up. Digger's operational harness was equipped with a night vision video camera mounted between his ears. Everything Digger would see would also be visible to Rex. Mini earphones were fitted in Digger's ears, completely invisible, and a mini microphone, not much bigger than a pinhead, was fitted on the harness between his front legs. All of it was wirelessly connected to an iPad mini, which Rex had strapped to his left forearm.

Rex put his face close to Digger's and said, "Okay, buddy, I want you to go and find out if Josh and Marissa are there."

Digger whined softly. He was excited.

Rex opened the flap on his left forearm, revealing the mini iPad screen, and tested the connection with Digger's equipment. Everything was working perfectly. He and Digger went out the back door around the side of the building. Rex pointed to the house across the street and said, "Scout and hide."

Digger reached the side of the house in a flash.

Rex directed him through the earphones to the side where the small window to the basement was. The window was covered with a curtain. Fortunately, the curtain was frayed and a bit too small to cover the entire window. There was a slither of about an inch on either side of the curtain to peek through.

Digger was flat on his belly, crawling forward until he could see through the small opening, which meant Rex and

Catia and everyone in the Ops Room on the Ranch could see what he was looking at.

Digger growled softly, clearly upset by what he was seeing.

A few seconds later, Catia whispered, "Josh... oh my God! They've hurt him—very badly."

Josh was tied to a chair, butt naked, surrounded by three Asian men, covered in white plastic disposable coveralls, disposable shoe covers, black nitrile gloves, and guns in holsters on their hips. Josh's face was one bloody mess, almost unrecognizable. His mouth was covered with duct tape. His body was covered with his own blood. The man standing in front of him, obviously the leader, had a pair of pliers in his hand. His coverall was speckled with blood. The floor was covered with a blue plastic sheet, also covered with blood. The ends of Josh's left index and middle fingers were pulpy messes of blood—the nails were missing.

"Bastards," Brandt hissed through clenched teeth. "Martin said an FBI SWAT team would be on the way within the next half an hour."

Rex murmured, "And probably another half hour before they get here, and only God knows how long to get organized and be ready to move in—"

Just then, the man standing to the left of Josh hit him in the side of the head. Josh's head twisted to the side and then slowly dropped to his chest. The leader grabbed Josh's hair, pulled his head back, looked at his eyes, and let his hair go. Josh's head dropped back to his chest, unconscious.

Rex cursed under his breath. Josh and Marissa were still alive because they hadn't given up any information, or at least not enough to be killed. But for how much longer?

The leader nodded to the man who had thrown the

punch. He turned and walked to the room closest to the back entry, the room where Marissa would be.

Catia retrieved the drones, and by the time she had them in her hands, the man who had gone into the bedroom reappeared, dragging Marissa by her hair. She was completely naked and gagged. He shoved her into a chair next to Josh, who seemed to have regained consciousness, and tied her to the chair with duct tape.

Rex had never heard Catia swear, but now she was firing off a barrage of choice Italian, English, and Hebrew words at the miscreants in that room. Rex felt like joining in, but an overpowering urge to kill the vermin had him clenching his jaws and fists.

The leader pulled his gun out of the holster, fitted a silencer, bent down, and said something into Marissa's ear. Then he walked around to Josh and pushed the gun against his right knee.

Digger was now softly yelping in distress.

"We're out of time, John," said Rex. "He's going to start shooting, and he won't stop until one of them talks. I'm going in."

"Wait. I've got the SWAT team leader patched in; they're about twenty minutes away—"

"We don't have twenty minutes! Josh is going to get his knee blown away in the next minute or two. And not long after, his other knee." Rex was already on his feet.

Catia put her hand on Rex's arm. "I'm going in with you."

Rex nodded. "I'm going through the front door. On my signal, I want you and Digger to create a distraction at the outside door to the basement."

"Okay. Be careful, Rex. Don't forget about the people upstairs."

"If they interfere, they're dead," Rex said. "Pray that the children stay in their beds."

She and Rex checked their P226 Sig Sauers and fitted the silencers. Digger was whining softly in anticipation—he had been very patient thus far. Rex said, "We're on our way, buddy. I want you to go with Catia and make sure she's safe."

Digger yelped softly.

"Okay, John and everyone else tuned in, radio silence, we're going in now."

Chapter Twenty-Six

I TAKE IT YOU'RE REX DALTON?

Jersey City, USA

Day 3

There was no cover for them to cross the street; they just had to do it as quickly as possible.

Rex checked the street; it was clear. He waved at Catia. They crossed the street at a full sprint, splitting up when they reached the other side. Rex reached the front door, tested the handle to see if it wasn't perchance unlocked; no such luck. He already had the lockpick in his hand. Fortunately, it was an old type of lock; it gave way in about fifteen seconds.

He opened the door slowly and quietly, thankful that despite its age, it didn't squeak. He listened for any sounds upstairs; it was quiet.

His Molar Mic vibrated three times; Catia and Digger were in place.

Gun at the ready, he moved slowly to the kitchen, entered, and closed the door. It had no lock. He took a wedge-shaped rubber doorstop out of his pocket and forced it under the door. That would keep the people upstairs from surprising him. He went to the basement door at the back of the kitchen. It was a sliding door with no lock. Great! He opened it very slowly and quietly and heard the voice of the lead thug. "On the count of three, I'm putting a bullet in your husband's knee. Where are Rex Dalton and his wife?"

Closer than you could imagine, asshole.

Rex toggled the on-off switch on the loop around his neck three times, waited for two counts, and toggled it on and off twice more.

The next moment, riotous noise erupted from the back door. Digger was barking; Catia was kicking against the door. This was one of the critical parts of Rex's plan, where the abductors could go for the suicide option and take their hostages with them.

Rex landed on his feet at the bottom of the stairs like a cat. The three kidnappers had their backs turned to him; two had guns pointed at the back door, unaware that the Grim Reaper had arrived behind them. The leader had his gun pointed at Josh's head, finger on the trigger.

The bullet from Rex's gun made a complete mess of his right shoulder, sending his gun flying and throwing him to the floor. He didn't see the heads of his men on either side of him exploding like ripe watermelons in quick succession. He started crawling for the protection of the table a few feet away.

The next moment, with his gun still trained on the crawling man, Rex saw a big black shape coming into his peripheral vision from the right side. Digger landed on the man's back and smashed him face-first into the floor. When

Digger's teeth sunk into the back of the man's neck, he stopped moving.

"Keep him down!" Rex shouted.

Catia was at the bottom of the stairs, gun at the ready. She lowered her gun slowly and said, "I'll get something to cover Josh and Marissa." She ran to the closest room and returned with two sheets, which she quickly draped over their friends before retrieving her combat knife and cutting their ties.

Rex thumbed the neck loop and said, "We got them. They're alive, no gun wounds. Three tangos down, two dead, the leader took a few bullets, but he's alive. Digger has him in custody."

Catia frowned, turned, and looked at the man on the floor, looking for the other bullet wounds Rex was talking about. Seeing none, she looked at Rex askance, holding up one finger. But he had the index finger of his left hand on his lips; she got the message.

"Thank God," Brandt said. "The SWAT team is about fifteen minutes out."

"Call them off," said Rex. "I need time to chat with the surviving scumbag."

"Understood. Let me see if I can—"

"No can do, Rex," it was Richardson. Greg must have patched him in on the comms. "You're in the FBI's jurisdiction. I know you'd like to kill that son of a bitch Rex, believe me, I'd very much like you to, but please don't."

After a long silence, Rex replied, "O-k-a-y," dragging the word out, "you're asking so nicely."

Brandt grinned. *The next ten minutes until the SWAT team arrives is going to be the worst ten minutes of that slimeball's life.*

The Yu family must have been deep sleepers or very scared. Too scared to investigate the tumult that had erupted in their house. Whatever, Rex and Catia were glad they'd stayed put upstairs so far.

Catia had pulled a first aid kit out of her backpack and started tending to Josh and Marissa. Physically, Marissa was unhurt. Mentally, she was shaken and disorientated. Josh had been the punching bag, and although his endurance had kept both of them alive, he was in a world of pain.

In the movies, this was the part when the captives would say, "What the hell took you so long?" But Josh and Marissa didn't say it; she was crying, and Josh could only make groaning sounds.

Rex told Digger to stand down. Digger wasn't happy to let go of the man's neck, but he obeyed, took a half step back, and sat down. All Rex had to do was nod once, and Digger would rip the thug to pieces. Instead, Rex rolled the man over on his back with his left foot and put his right foot on the wounded shoulder.

The man screamed in pain. "I've got diplomatic immunity! You can't do this." He spoke Mandarin.

Since the Shanghai operation eight months ago, Rex and Catia had been learning Mandarin, neither of them was fluent yet, but they had a fairly good command of the language and definitely understood a lot more than they could speak. Nevertheless, Rex knew the man spoke English; he heard him minutes before when he spoke to Marissa in English.

Rex replied in English. "I can't recall establishing diplomatic relations with you. But I'll let your embassy know to put your body in a diplomatic bag when they send it back to China."

The man switched to English and said, "I'm not answering your questions."

"I thought I heard you asking for my wife and me just a

minute ago. I'm Rex Dalton, and that's my wife. Oh, and the guy next to you goes by the name of Digger. He's got a very bad temper. Right now, he's seriously pissed off at you for hurting his friends."

On cue, Digger took a step toward the man and snarled.

The man's eyes bulged, but he made no reply.

"No questions for us?"

The man said nothing.

"Great. We don't have questions for you either. I would've liked to know your name before I shoot you, but it's not that important." Rex pointed the gun at the man's face.

"Ren Shi!"

"Oh, you *have* a name. Care to tell me who you work for? Not that I really care, just as a matter of interest."

"The MSS, China's Minister of State Security. If you kill me, they'll come after you to revenge my death."

"MSS? Never heard of them. But seeing that you've changed your mind about talking to me, who told you where to get hold of my friends here?"

"Facebook."

"Ah, a sense of humor," Rex shot him in the left knee.

Ren screamed and whined. When he finally got his voice back a few minutes later, Rex pointed the gun at Ren's other knee.

"Yasmin Burke!"

Josh mumbled something inaudible. Marissa drew a sharp breath. "We've been on her training course the last few days." She walked over to Rex and held her hand out for his gun without saying a word.

Rex handed the gun to Marissa, hoping she wouldn't kill Ren but not really caring if she did.

Marissa said, "You killed her, didn't you?"

Ren only stared at her.

"Bastard!" She yelled at the top of her lungs and pulled the trigger. If Ren would ever walk again, it would be with artificial kneejoints. Then, with Ren screaming, cursing, and writhing on the floor, very calmly, as if handing Rex a cup of tea, she placed the gun back in his open hand and went back to help Catia dress Josh's wounds.

Rex wasn't entirely surprised by Marissa's actions; she and Josh had gone through an indescribable ordeal at the hands of the man on the floor. He was lucky she didn't kill him. He looked at Ren and said, "Anyone else you came over here to kill?"

Ren hesitated.

Rex pointed the gun at Ren's face.

"General Yuan Lee!"

"Ah, I see. So, it's all about the Shanghai virus your former president wanted to release but failed. Who do you report to?"

"Minister Xuan Bai, head of the MSS."

Rex was about to ask another question when he heard the clamor of police and ambulance sirens. A few seconds later, two men in FBI SWAT gear came in through the back door.

When Ren saw the FBI men, he tried to sit up; he got halfway up, sighed loudly, and toppled over, unconscious.

Rex holstered his gun and waited for the FBI agents to speak.

The older one of them said, "I'm Special Agent West of the FBI. I take it you're Rex Dalton?"

"Yes, I am. This is my wife, Catia. The man in the chair is Josh Farley and his wife, Marissa, next to him. They're our best friends. The asshole on the floor told me his name is Ren Shi, an MSS agent. I didn't get around to asking him the names and occupations of his dead associates."

West's eyes slowly took in everything in the room. He shook his head and spoke into his throat mic. "Everything under control here. Send in the paramedics. We have two dead and three that need medical attention." He looked at Rex and Catia and said, "The two of you'll have to come with us to give statements."

Catia said, "Not before we know our friends are taken care of."

West nodded. "Of course."

Chapter Twenty-Seven

A STAR ON THE WALL

Langley, Virginia, USA

Day 3

Five minutes after the arrival of the SWAT team, Josh and Marissa were in the back of an ambulance on their way to the hospital. Ren Shi was strapped to a gurney, loaded into the back of another ambulance with two FBI agents as escorts, and transported to another hospital where he would be kept in isolation and under guard.

West instructed his team to take the Yu family upstairs into custody but cautioned them to make sure they didn't upset the children and not separate them from their parents at any time.

Martin Richardson had contacted the D.C. Police chief when he heard Ren's unspoken confession about killing Yasmin Burke. The chief told him that Yasmin's family had filed a missing person report that Friday afternoon, about eighteen hours ago. His officers had already been to her house; there was no sign of a struggle, and her car was in the garage. A team of forensics experts was fine-combing the house for leads.

To Richardson, this was part confirmation that she had indeed been killed.

The chief told Richardson that his officers had launched a search and rescue operation but found nothing so far; in fact, they had only one lead to go on, that was footage from the street surveillance cameras showing a white Ford Transit Courier van with false plates in the vicinity of her house. They had expanded their search to all security cameras in D.C. and surrounding areas, but it was going to take time to work through it.

The mention of the white Ford Transit Courier van with the false plates, which were still attached to it where it was parked in the public parking garage in Jersey City, was confirmation that Yasmin gave Ren the information about the Farleys' whereabouts. Richardson was tempted to tell the chief where he'd find the white van, but then he'd need to explain how he knew.

By now, Richardson had little doubt that Yasmin had been killed and that the killer was Ren Shi, but until they could find the body, there would always be some doubt. *I can only hope Ren will talk soon. And if he doesn't, I'll see if I can arrange for Rex and Digger to have an hour with that son of a bitch.*

Within the hour, the president and the DCI, Howard Lawrence, had been briefed by Richardson. The president was livid, ready to get on a personal call with President Liao and give him a piece of his mind, but he knew he had to wait until he got more information from the FBI after Ren's interrogation.

Though they didn't have all the information yet, it was

enough to prove that the MSS had conducted a covert operation on American soil in revenge for the virus debacle eight months before. Was it not for CRC's operatives, Rex Dalton, his wife, Catia, and their dog, Digger, two more American heroes would've been dead.

Richardson couldn't help but think of the stars on the Memorial Wall in the lobby of the Original Headquarters Building. Each of the stars carved into the white Alabama marble wall represented a CIA employee who had died in the line of service. Beneath the stars, framed in stainless steel and topped by an inch-thick plate of glass, was a black Moroccan goatskin-bound book, the Book of Honor. It showed the stars, arranged by year of death. Some stars had names next to them, some not—identities of the unnamed stars remained secret, even in death. He sighed. Another star would soon be added to the Memorial Wall and the Book of Honor.

Chapter Twenty-Eight

HIS PACK WAS SAFE

New York, USA

Day 3

Rex, Catia, and Digger spent two hours in the tallest federal building in the United States, the FBI's field office in the Jacob K. Javits Federal Office Building at 26 Federal Plaza on Foley Square in Manhattan, to give their statements.

When they left the building to hail a taxi to the hospital where Josh and Marissa were being treated, Catia said, "I find it strange that they didn't ask many questions about Ren's bullet wounds."

Rex shrugged. "Just as well. I would've hated to lie to them. It's a federal offense to lie to the FBI, but I was not prepared to drag Marissa into it after what she and Josh had gone through. If she didn't blow that scumbag's other knee away, I would've done it."

Catia smiled. "I agree; Marissa doesn't need more stress

right now. I'm wondering if Martin smoothed things over with the FBI not to ask too many questions about the shooting?"

Rex nodded. "You might be right. I'd have to thank him if he did."

Forty-five minutes later, the three of them arrived at the hospital. They first spoke to the doctor who treated their friends. She told them that Marissa had no physical injuries and would take a little while to get over the emotional shock. "But she's a strong woman; she'll get over it," the doctor said.

They were relieved to hear that Marissa had not been sexually assaulted.

"Josh has multiple external and internal injuries; fortunately, none of them life-threatening. That man is tough as nails. He should be ready to go home in two to three days. However, he'll need a few more days of bed rest and has to take it easy for a week or so."

They thanked the doctor and went to the Farleys' room. Marissa was sitting in a chair next to Josh, holding his hand. Both of them were clothed in clean, blue hospital gowns, and they looked much, much better than when the Daltons last saw them.

Josh had a drip in his arm and looked a bit drugged, probably the effect of the pain medication. He had been cleaned up, but much of his face and arms and legs were covered in stitches and bandages. His face was bruised, his eyes swollen shut, and his lips cut in many places. Yet, he tried to smile when he heard his friends.

Marissa hugged Catia, Rex, and Digger in turn. "Thank you for saving us, we—"

Josh mumbled something which sounded like, "Thank you."

"No problem," Rex said. "We were in the neighborhood and thought you wouldn't mind us dropping in unannounced."

Marissa smiled. "We don't mind at all. You're always welcome to drop in unannounced like that."

Rex said, "Oh, by the way, I spoke to your doctor. She begged me to help her get you out of here ASAP. She needs these beds for sick people."

Catia punched him in the shoulder.

Josh raised the middle finger of his right hand.

Rex laughed. "That's the spirit, buddy. The CRC jet is on standby to take you back to the Ranch. Unless, of course, you and Marissa want to complete your pilgrimage to Martha's Vineyard."

Josh shook his head slightly.

"Another time," said Marissa. "Now tell us, how did you know where to find us?"

Rex and Catia told them. And then Marissa filled in the parts that they didn't know. When they came to the end of their narratives, they found themselves staring at Digger. He was fast asleep on a sunny spot in front of the window, obviously content that his pack was safe, but totally unaware of his hero status.

Chapter Twenty-Nine

I WANT TO MAKE A DEAL

Beijing, China

Day 3

By 8:00 p.m. Beijing time, 8:00 a.m. in New York, Xuan Bai of China's Ministry of State Security was a worried man. He had been expecting a call from Ren Shi for hours. He called and texted but got no reply. The last message he received from Ren was shortly after 5:00 a.m. Beijing time. That was to let him know that the Farleys had been captured and were held in a safe house in Jersey City where they would be interrogated and terminated.

Xuan had been in the intelligence business all of his adult life and had developed a sense of knowing when a mission had gone south. Fifteen hours without news from the mission team had only one explanation—trouble. Missions often got into trouble; that was part of life. But trouble came in different shapes and sizes. If Ren and his team were dead, no problem, just like Stalin said, "Death solves all problems - no man, no problem." But if they'd been captured alive, it would be the worst scenario imaginable, especially if Ren was alive.

Although the president personally ordered this mission, Xuan knew he was the one who would bear the brunt. This was the problem with these kinds of missions where the agents had no backup in the theater of operation. But the President would probably not be interested in that.

Ren was a senior agent, one of their best. He had been on many missions, and he carried a lot of very damaging information between his ears. Xuan was starting to wonder if it was time to activate the damage control protocol—warning MSS's American spies and moles to get out of the country.

Another hour had passed when Xuan was at the point where he had to decide: Tell the president the bad news or wait a few more hours. If the latter, he was running the risk that the president might hear about it on the American news. He decided it would be better for his career and longevity to rather prepare the president to expect bad news than let him hear it from the Americans.

He picked up the phone.

Unknown location, New York, USA

Day 3

Ren had regained consciousness in the back of the ambulance on the way to an unknown location. He didn't expect to be treated like a royal on arrival. Although he wasn't mistreated or tortured, he wasn't treated with much compassion either. They took him to a single room where he was placed in restraints on a hospital bed. A dispassionate doctor examined him and instructed the equally impassive nurse to clean up and dress his wounds, administer antibiotics and mild painkillers, as well as a blood transfusion. Throughout it all, two stern-faced FBI agents with guns were in the room and two more outside.

As soon as the doctor's orders were executed, the nurses left, and Special Agent West, accompanied by a Chinese-speaking FBI colleague, entered.

From the moment of Rex Dalton's appearance in that basement a few hours before, Ren knew his mission was an epic disaster, and life as he knew it had changed irreversibly. He had no means to commit suicide and doubted he would get an opportunity to do so—at least not until they had sucked every bit of information out of him.

However, he still preferred life over death. Better to be a live traitor than a dead patriot. But then, whichever way he looked at his situation, death was staring back at him. If he were extradited to China, he would be taken to a prison and shot in the back of the head shortly after arrival. If he were kept in America, he would be put on trial for the murder of Yasmin Burke and executed. His best-case scenario was life in a maximum-security prison. Sometimes they kept people like him in prison, just in case he could be part of a prisoner exchange in the future. He couldn't help but think his dead assistants were the lucky ones.

He had one ray of hope, though, the information in his head. Not only about the current mission but everything he had come to know about the MSS over a period of twenty-five years of service.

West took a recorder out of his jacket pocket, switched it on, and started by asking him through the interpreter if he wanted to be addressed in Mandarin or English. He told West that he was fluent in English. He didn't lie; his English was perfect, albeit accented. West read him his Miranda Rights and placed him formally under arrest for murder and attempted murder, and explained more charges would be forthcoming. Ren confirmed that he understood the charges and his rights and waived the right to an attorney.

West turned to leave the room, but Ren said, "I will give my full cooperation. I'll neither lie to you nor try to mislead you."

West grinned. "Wise decision, though I get the impression there's a condition attached to your willingness to cooperate?"

"Yes, only two conditions: One, no extradition to China, ever. Two, I tell you everything I know in exchange for a place in your witness protection program."

West shook his head. "Not within my power to make deals. But if you put on record what you're offering, I'll present it to my superiors. That's as far as my authority goes."

"I'll start with the current mission and tell you who authorized it and what my orders were. I'll give you the names of past and present Chinese spies and moles active in your country and elsewhere, and I'll tell you about all MSS operations I've been part of and know of."

West turned back and approached the bed. "As I said, I'm not authorized to make a deal, but I can imagine that it might count in your favor with those considering your request if you were to tell me everything about the current mission—a goodwill gesture from your side."

Ren nodded slowly, contemplatively. "Okay, I'll tell you. Is the recorder on?"

"Yes."

Ren started with the role he had played in the investigation of General Yuan's defection and his appointment as the lead investigator by the Minister of the MSS, Xuan Bai. Also, how they'd tracked down Yasmin Burke, her surveillance, interrogation, and killing, including the exact location where they'd buried her body. He told West how they'd tracked down the Farleys, their kidnapping, and torture.

Two hours later, Ren received a dose of painkillers that knocked him out, and Special Agent West hurried across town to the FBI offices with the recording.

Ren Shi's full debriefing was going to take many months, and the information he would provide was going to throw some of the MSS's spy operations in the USA into turmoil.

New York, USA

Day 3

The FBI investigators interviewed Yu Hua and Yu Heng separately. Initially, they tried to convince the interviewers that they had no idea who Ren Shi was, that they'd never met him or his men, that Ren and his men had broken into their house and locked them up in their rooms and told them to remain there until told they could come out.

The Yus story quickly fell apart when the interviewers

pointed out that their bedroom doors were not locked, they were not tied up, and they had their cellphones with them. Besides, by the time they were interviewed, Ren had already sunk their ship when he told Special Agent West that the Yus were MSS agents and that their basement had been used as a safe house for other missions in the past.

It didn't take long for the Yus to confess.

They were naturalized citizens of the USA; therefore, they would be charged with treason. The law stated: *Whoever, owing allegiance to the United States, levies war against them or adheres to their enemies, giving them aid and comfort within the United States or elsewhere, is guilty of treason and shall suffer death, or shall be imprisoned not less than five years and fined under this title but not less than $10,000, and shall be incapable of holding any office under the United States.*

Over the course of the next few days, the Yus' lawyer negotiated that the children would, instead of being placed in the care of social service agencies, go to China to live with their maternal grandparents. Eventually, the Yus would serve five years of a ten-year sentence, be stripped of their citizenship, and be deported back to China.

Chapter Thirty

A PRESS RELEASE

Situation Room, White House, Washington, D.C., USA

Day 3

It was late afternoon on Saturday when DNI Tia Chapman, DCI Howard Lawrence, SECSTATE, Lauren Woods, Director-General Department of Justice and Attorney-General (DJAG), Ben Lloyd, and the White House Chief of Staff, Hayden Price, were in the Situation Room where Douglas Cole, the Director of the FBI briefed the president about the events of the past few days.

Cole started with a condensed version covering the essential aspects of the full brief, sometimes referred to as an elevator pitch—from the idea of having to impress a senior executive during a brief ride in an elevator—that's how the president liked it.

"I remember those names," the president said when Cole finished the summary. "They were the team who got

General Yuan Lee out of China and saved the world from that nasty virus, right?"

"Yes, Mr. President, it's them," said Chapman.

"So, this MSS operation was meant to be retaliation for us throwing a wrench into their virus works?"

"Yes, Mr. President, Ren Shi admitted as much," Cole replied.

"Has Ms. Burke's family been notified?"

"Not yet, sir," said Lawrence.

"Will you please get me their contact details? I'll call them as soon as this meeting is over. I take it she's going to get a star on the wall at Langley?"

"Absolutely, sir," Lawrence said.

The president returned his gaze to the FBI director and said, "Apologies for interrupting, Douglas, please continue."

The briefing ended half an hour later.

The president said, "So, that son of a bitch wants to make a deal?"

"Yes, sir."

"Do we want to make a deal? We have a policy of not negotiating with terrorists. But all rules have exceptions. Is there anything this guy can offer us that we won't get out of him over time?"

"Sir, this might be one of those occasions where we'd have to make an exception," said Cole. "We need to get the information about their moles and spies in our midst as quickly as humanly possible. The moment the Chinese hear about it, they'll warn their assets. As much as I hate to do it, I recommend we make a deal. We've got him in a secured location, and everyone who knows about it has been warned to keep it a secret."

"I agree with Douglas," said Lawrence. "We might not want to arrest all the spies; some we might want to leave in position so we can keep an eye on them and see who they interact with.

"Mr. President, I'd suggest we issue a statement saying three Chinese spies were killed in a shootout during a raid. We tell them nothing else. Let them speculate. Let them worry. Let them come to us if they have questions.

"If we can make them believe that their agents were killed without giving us any information, they'll keep their network in place, and we can watch them and use them to feed false information to pass on to their masters."

The president smiled. "In other words, treat them like mushrooms?

"Sir?"

"Keep them in the dark and feed them manure."

"Exactly, sir," Lawrence said through the chuckles.

"Everyone agrees?"

A chorus of yeses followed.

"Then that's what we'll do. Ben, work with Douglas and the others and make the deal. But make sure that scumbag understands that the deal is off if he utters so much as one word of dishonesty. And the same goes if he doesn't supply us with a full list of MSS assets in the US within the next two hours."

"Will do, Mr. President."

Chapter Thirty-One

YOU FAILED

Zhongnanhai, Beijing, China

Day 4

Despite Xuan Bai's insistence that he had to meet with the president about an extremely important matter, he was only given a fifteen-minute slot the next afternoon at two o'clock. He didn't sleep that night. He kept on checking his phone every few minutes, hoping against hope for a message from Ren. The message never came, and the more he checked, the more anxious he became. In China, senior officials understood two unwritten rules very well; never disobey an order from the president and never make him look bad.

With his nerves in tatters, nauseated from stress and lack of food, he arrived an hour early for his appointment and missed the breaking news out of America. When he stepped into the president's office, the president didn't get up to welcome him. In fact, the president didn't even look at him;

he only pushed the button on the remote on his desk to increase the volume on the TV showing CNN news.

On the screen, the red breaking news banner was flashing.

FBI AGENTS KILL THREE CHINESE SPIES IN EARLY-MORNING RAID

"You failed."

Xuan was ashen-faced. His knees were shaking. He stuttered, "Sir, I... have been trying... to uh... get a meeting—"

"Cut the excuses, Xuan. How bad is it?"

"I don't know, sir. I lost contact with Ren Shi, the lead agent on the mission, about thirty-six hours ago. I don't know more."

Thus far, Xuan had avoided looking the president straight in the eyes, and when he did so now, he stopped mid-sentence. That's how the CCP conducted their affairs —failure of this magnitude always ended in death or lifelong imprisonment for those who oversaw the disaster. His hour had arrived.

Over the course of the next twenty minutes, he imparted everything he knew about Ren Shi and the knowledge Ren had of MSS operations and assets across the globe. When he finished, the president told him to wait in the anteroom outside the office. Ten minutes later, two security officers arrived and escorted him off the premises to a waiting vehicle.

Within the hour, Xuan's second in command, Shen Delan, was promoted to minister in charge of the MSS.

An official statement was issued twelve hours later. Minister Xuan Bai had been replaced. No explanation was given. Xuan could not be reached to comment; his whereabouts were unknown. He could've been in prison or a labor camp, or he could've been dead.

Chapter Thirty-Two

CANDY FROM GRANDMA

Beijing, China

Day 4

Although the government wanted everyone to believe there were no bad neighborhoods in China's cities, there was a saying among the citizenry; wealthy east, noble west, poor north, and humble south. Sun Jia lived in a small three-room dwelling in a very poor area on the north-side of Beijing in what was known as a *hutong*, a narrow alleyway formed by traditional courtyard houses. The subway station in this area was a two-mile walk from her house. Her immediate neighbors were nice people, old and dirt-poor like her. However, there were also a lot of bad and unruly characters in the area, drunk and noisy most of the time.

By 7:00 a.m. on Sunday morning, Jia locked the bright-red front door of her ramshackle abode and walked the two miles to the subway station where she would catch the train for the one-hour ride to the humble south-side neighbor-hood where her son, Sun Yan, lived with his wife and their four-year-old daughter. Her handbag was a plastic shopping bag containing her ID card, party membership card, fifty yuan (the equivalent of about seven US dollars), a scarf that her son gave her for her birthday, and a small plastic bag of candy for her beloved granddaughter, Sun Lei. Her name meant flower bud, and to Jia, Lei was the prettiest little flower on earth. Lei loved her *năi nai* (grandma) to bits. She always nagged her parents about when *năi nai* would come to visit again. Lei loved nothing better than to sit on her *năi nai's* lap and listen to her stories, playing with her gray hair, nuzzling her little nose in her neck to smell her, and, of course, enjoy the candy she always brought with her. She always squealed with laughter when *năi nai* tickled her.

Jia and her daughter-in-law, Ming, got along very well. Ming was a qualified nurse and used to work at a nearby hospital in the city before Lei's birth. She was planning to return to the workforce when Lei turned six, the age when Chinese children had to start attending school.

Jia only knew that her son worked for the government. A software engineer is what Yan told her. She had no idea what that meant, but she was very proud of him. While he was studying to earn his degree in computer science, he held two jobs, one as a meat-packer and another as a cleaner, to pay for everything and help support her. It was hard, but he persisted and succeeded.

The Sun family were all card-carrying members of the party; it was the first thing a hiring manager looked for on the résumé of any prospective employee, even that of a lowly office-cleaner like Sun Jia.

Besides ticking the right boxes with his qualifications and party membership, Yan was a conscientious and intelligent worker, which was why he was making steady progress up the promotion ladder and already held a middle-management position with a team of fifty IT experts reporting to him. What Jia didn't know, and even if she did, wouldn't have any idea what it meant, was that her son worked for Unit 61398.

Ming knew Yan had become deeply disenchanted with the CCP over the years, just like she had. Not that they didn't love their country and its people; they were patriots. What they loathed was the Communist Party.

After the 2008 global financial crisis, China had become the key engine of world economic growth. Yan and many others like him were excited about the prospect that China would finally move away from the oppressive communist system to embrace capitalism and basic human rights. Alas, soon, their excitement turned into discontent as they realized the CCP had no intentions to do any of that. The fiscal windfall from the economic growth was instead used by the CCP to expand their hold on the citizens of the country, to increase surveillance on and control over them, to expand the military, and extend their influence across the globe, to threaten neighboring countries, and to interfere in the governing of Macau, Hong Kong, and bully Taiwan into submission.

In 2019, more than a hundred million Chinese featured among the top ten percent of the world's richest people, while, at the same time, there were ninety-nine million from America on that list. But one had to understand that the American economy was almost forty-five percent bigger than China's. A simple comparison of the personal and economic freedoms enjoyed by US citizens to those of the PRC showed the citizens of China were getting the short end of the stick from their government.

For the ordinary citizens of China, nothing had changed while a privileged few prospered. But the citizens were not stupid; it was no surprise that the vast majority of the Chinese people, including the ninety million members of the CCP, among them Sun Yan, wanted to see the disappearance of the Communist Party, who, in reality, existed only to serve a few hundred or so self-appointed elitists.

Yan had never signed on with Tuidang; doing so would have brought his career to an abrupt end and made him unemployable. If not for that, he and Ming would've joined the movement. He never discussed his political opinions with anyone except Ming, not even with his mother. At work, he and his colleagues were constantly bombarded with the message that his country was at war. He and his comrades were fighting on the front lines. As a patriot, even if he disagreed strongly with his government's policies, he was a soldier serving his country and its people, and soldiers didn't question their orders.

He was happy to see his mother, and so was his wife. Lei was over the moon. It never ceased to amaze Yan and Ming what a good story-teller Jia was, especially in light of the fact that she was near-illiterate.

She seemed to never run out of stories to tell her granddaughter. Among them was always at least one story from the Bible, even though she didn't own a Bible because she wouldn't be able to read it. But clearly, there was nothing wrong with her memory. Today's Bible story was about David and Goliath. Yan and Ming enjoyed the story almost as much as Lei did, but they would've been horrified to know how soon they would be facing their own giant.

The time flew that Sunday, as it always did when she came to visit. Lei was crying when the time came to say goodbye to *năi nai*. Jia put the little one on her lap, gave her the bag of candy, and told her if she ate one a day, by the time the bag was empty, she would come back with another, and more stories, of course. That was enough to appease the little girl and put a smile on her face as she opened the bag and looked at the sweet temptations.

"You know the rules, Lei," said Jia with feigned strictness. "One candy per day, after lunch, starting tomorrow. Otherwise, you're going to run out before I come again."

"I know *nǎi nai.*" Lei sighed, clearly not happy about the draconian rules imposed on her.

Yan and Ming had never asked Jia where she got the assortment of candies every month; they assumed she was saving some of the little money she had to buy the candy for her only grandchild. After all, what kind of grandma would not want to spoil her granddaughter if she could? Lei, of course, didn't care at all, as long as *nǎi nai's* supply didn't dry up.

Chapter Thirty-Three

QUESTION HER, YOU IDIOT!

Beijing, China

Day 5

The failure of the first covert mission ordered by Liao as president was an unmitigated disaster, to be sure. It had the potential to blow his cover as the political dove, the peace-loving economic liberal who would lead China to democracy. Any trust, as misguided as it was, that the international community would've had in him as the great reformer of communist China was going to suffer a severe blow.

The Trustees and General Tao, however, had a different view. They were hawks, fixated on world control. This was only one battle in the war, they argued. A setback, no doubt, but by no means a reason to abandon their plans or change them. If anything, it was necessary to step up their preparations.

Generals Dai Min and Wan Huang, always more than a

little nervous that their cooperation with the CIA to help General Yuan Lee defect eight months before might come to light, were secretly relieved to hear the news of Ren's demise. If his mission were successful, Ren was bound to eventually unearth the details, which would've put the two generals in an untenable position.

General Lang arrived in his office earlier than usual on Monday morning, highly motivated to complete his reading and comment on the Operation MK plan provided by Zhì Zhě. He was not surprised to find his secretary at her desk —he had never been able to beat her to the office in the morning. Maybe his driver alerted her when he was about to head to the office. He had never asked her how she managed to do it nor thanked her for being so conscientious.

She greeted him, followed him into his office, placed a cup of tea on his desk, and left as he headed for the wall safe.

Lang opened the safe to get the USB drive. It wasn't there.

I put it here on Friday night... Or... hmm... in my tunic pocket...

Ten minutes later, his wife had checked every pocket of the uniform he wore on Friday but couldn't find the red thumb drive. He called his driver to bring his car around. He searched the car personally, twice—no red thumb drive.

Half an hour later, he was a worried man. He was in his chair behind his desk. His head in his hands, his eyes closed as he tried to reconstruct his every move of Friday night. He gave up a few minutes later; he simply couldn't remember. He had to admit, it was true—excessive alcohol abuse over a long period had an amnesiac effect.

Amnesiac or not, I'm in serious trouble. If anyone gets hold of that drive, I'm as good as dead.

He couldn't help but think of Xuan Bai's fate.

Wait, the document is password protected; no one can access it without the password.

Lang picked up the phone and dialed General Dai Min.

"Min, good morning. I trust you had a good weekend?"

"I did, Jianhong. How was yours?"

Lang laughed. "On the insistence of the missus, quiet and relaxed."

Dai chuckled. "Good, the wives know when we need to relax. But I'm sure you didn't call me only to find out about my weekend."

"Ah... well... I'm a bit embarrassed. You see, the thing is, I had a little accident. I destroyed my red thumb drive last night."

"How did you manage to do that?"

"An accident, Min. A stupid accident. I had a few too many whiskeys while working on the document. When I finished, in my clumsiness when I took it out of my laptop, I dropped it on the floor, and when I pushed my chair back to look for it, one of the wheels crushed it to pieces. For obvious reasons, it's not something I could ask a technician to try and repair. So, I destroyed it completely and burned what was left of it."

Dai laughed. "Jianhong, there's a reason why the Americans call it firewater. You have to go easy on the stuff. Especially when you work on beyond top-secret documents." *But you're an alcoholic. You just haven't come around to admitting it.*

Lang chuckled. "Yeah, yeah, I know. I'll go on the wagon, as the Americans say. Can I come over and get a copy from you?"

"No problem. I'll be in my office for another hour."

"Thanks, see you soon."

Lang sighed, partly in relief, partly in distress. That

solved only half of his problems. He had literally dodged a bullet. But only for now. As long as that little red thumb drive is missing and not found and delivered to him, he wouldn't be able to sleep peacefully. A cold shiver ravaged his body as he had a vision of himself with a gaping bullet hole in the back of his head.

He called in his aide and ordered him, without telling him what was on the drive, to drop everything he was doing and find out how it was possible that the red USB drive had grown feet.

Three hours later, the aide was back with a full report. While the general was out to see General Dai Min, the aide and the secretary had searched the office from corner to corner. The aide and two guards then checked the rubbish bins in the basement. Fortunately, the garbage truck had not turned up to remove the rubbish yet. Nevertheless, there was no red USB flash drive among the rubbish. The aide then turned to the guards who were on duty on Friday and over the weekend, questioned them at length, and inspected their logs. None of them had been in the general's office during that time. The only person who had entered the office was the cleaner, Sun Jia, at 10:03 p.m. on Friday night. The guard who let her into the building was also the one who unlocked the doors of the offices, which she had to clean. He was also the one who locked the doors when she was done.

When the aide finished his report, he asked, "What do you want me to do?"

Lang roared, "Get hold of the cleaner and question her, you idiot!"

Chapter Thirty-Four

PLASTIC CANDY

Beijing, China

Day 5

Yan worked 12-hour shifts, five days on four days off. Every 28th day he would switch from day-shifts to night-shifts. His last five-day shift ended the previous Friday. He cherished the time off to rest and be with his family.

After lunch on Monday, Lei reminded her mother that it was time for one of *nǎi nai's* daily treats. Ming laughed. "You forget many things that I ask you to remember but never *nǎi nai's* candy. I wonder why that is?"

Lei only giggled in reply.

Ming retrieved the little plastic bag from the kitchen cupboard, opened it, took out one candy, and stared at it.

Yan, who had been following the conversation, blinked twice and asked, "Is that a USB drive?"

Ming turned it around a few times as if to make sure it

was what her eyes told her it was. She nodded. "Y-e-s. B-u-t... why... I mean... how... where..."

Yan held his hand out. She gave it to him and took a real candy from the bag, which she gave to Lei.

Yan studied the red, rectangular device, about half an inch wide by two inches long and a quarter of an inch thick. A USB thumb drive, no doubt. He couldn't help himself; he had to know what was on it. He went to his study nook and plugged it into his laptop after disconnecting it from the internet. That was the second-best way to keep a computer from being hacked; the best way was to switch it off and unplug it.

He was a little bemused at the password challenge when he tried to access the folder. But the author probably never thought that one of the top hackers in the world would have reason to access the folder's content. Yan had a little smile playing on his face as he hummed a tune of one of his favorite pop bands while he cracked the password within the next two minutes. And then it disappeared, the smile that is, as he read the first paragraph of the first page of the executive summary.

Ten minutes later, as he got to the end of the executive summary, he was about to throw up. *My mother is in mortal danger. And my family. I have to get to her and find out where she got this drive. Maybe she can take it back.*

He grabbed his small canvas handbag, put his cellphone and wallet into it, and stood to leave.

Just then, Ming came in. "Yan, what's wrong? You look like death."

"It's my mother. She's in big trouble. And she doesn't know it. I'm going to her to see if I can help."

"What's wrong, Yan? You're shaking. How do you—"

Ming was still talking when Yan planted a kiss on her

mouth, hugged Lei, grabbed the car keys, and headed to the front door, saying, "There's no time, Ming. I'll explain when I get back. Keep your cellphone on in case I need to get hold of you."

A few minutes later, he was on the highway, northbound toward his mother's house. He looked at his watch. It was going to be a very long hour. His mind was awash with questions and more questions and no answers, but most of all, his mind was besieged by fear—raw nauseating fear—for his mother, himself, and his family. Every slowdown in the traffic made him hit the steering wheel in frustration. It felt like an eternity.

Beijing, China

Day 5

It was 1:15 p.m. when the official vehicle pulled up in front of Jia's little home and blocked the entire alleyway. Two men in black suits and dark sunglasses got out and knocked on the front door.

Jia answered the door, saw the men, smiled, and invited them in.

There was no one in the street. The people in this area often got visits from men in official vehicles and knew better than to be inquisitive. It didn't stop them from peeping through their front doors or windows, though. Or wonder what this was about. Sometimes one or more of the occupants of the house that gets such a visit would leave with the visitors—in the back of their vehicle, handcuffed—troublemakers. Of those who left in that fashion, some returned after a while and became model citizens, and some would never be seen or heard of again. The message was unambiguous, don't be a troublemaker.

But Sun Jia was no troublemaker unless it was an offense to be a friendly, poor, and uneducated old woman. Then again, one would never know what people do in the privacy of their own homes. For all they knew, she could have been a drug smuggler; hence the secret train trips to an unknown location once a month. Maybe she was involved in some kind of conspiracy against the government. Whatever Sun Jia did or didn't do, the fact was, official vehicles didn't come to your home unless you'd done something wrong.

Had the residents in the area been given the opportunity to sit in on the questioning of Sun Jia, they would've been shocked to the core, not about the questions the men asked her and the confessions she made but the way they treated her when they thought she was lying. As it were, they were not privy to the conversation. They only heard her blood-curdling screams. She must have done something very bad.

Jia was honest. She didn't lie at all. She immediately confessed to stealing two candies from the general's candy bowl five nights a week for the past seven months. She regretted what she did and promised to pay the general for every candy she had stolen. They never asked her why she did it. But she told them she ate one every night and saved one for her granddaughter. But the officials were not interested in recompense. They didn't believe her when she told them she had no idea what the words USB or thumb drive meant. She had no idea what any of those looked like. Her interrogators showed her a photo of such a device. A black one. Of course, she'd never seen one of those. The one she saw was red, but they didn't ask her that.

By the time they had broken many of her ribs and fingers and hit her in the head so many times she was barely able to speak, one of them had the sense to mention that the device they were looking for looked exactly the same as the black one in the photo except it was red.

She still had enough life left in her battered body to tell them she had seen one of those. It was in the little plastic bag with the other stolen candy she had given to her granddaughter the day before. Then she lost consciousness.

No amount of hitting, or slapping, or kicking, or yelling, or cold water revived her. Therefore they couldn't get her son's address. But that was more of a nuisance than a problem. The government kept very comprehensive records of its citizens. Getting the address of a government employee, even if they didn't know which department her software engineer son worked for, was easy. By 3:00 p.m., the two men left Sun Jia still in a state of unconsciousness in her house, got into their official vehicle, and raced across the city to the south where Sun Yan, his wife, and daughter lived.

None of the neighbors or anyone in the area dared go into Jia's house to check on her. Interfering in official government business was a serious offense.

Chapter Thirty-Five

GET HIS FAMILY TO SAFETY

Beijing, China

Day 5

Yan parked his car in front of his mother's house in the same spot the official vehicle had vacated ten minutes before. He knocked on the door, no answer. He turned the handle. The door was unlocked. Strange. This was not a safe neighborhood. His mother promised him she'd always keep the door locked, and she did. He took one step into the house and knew he was too late. Jia lay on the threadbare carpet in a pool of blood.

"Mom!"

He rushed to her, sat down on the carpet, and lifted her upper body onto his lap. Her head tilted backward. He put his hand under her head and raised it. Her eyes opened slowly, painfully.

"Mom, what happened? Who did this to you?"

"Ge... genera... La...ng. Men... came... I... too...k... can...dy. Red... plas...tic... can...dy. I...in bo... bowl. On... de...desk."

Yan's blood was running cold. *That's where she got the candy from. General Lang's office. She had no idea the USB drive was not candy. But what was the device containing the most secret, most evil document in the history of the CCP doing in a candy bowl on the general's desk?*

Jia's breathing became labored. She coughed once, weakly. Blood started running out of the corners of her mouth.

"Run, Yan," she mumbled almost inaudibly. "Ta...ke... Mi...ng...Lei... go away... th...ey... kill...you... ah... sorry."

She took one more breath. Her eyes turned in their sockets as she died in her son's arms.

Yan felt the world tumbling down on him. He had no first aid training. He was helpless. He yelled for help, and he cried as he rocked back and forth with his mother's broken body on his lap. No one came to help.

Later, he had no idea how long it was; a thought exploded in his mind. Ming and Lei. They had to get out of the house and find a place to hide. He had read enough of the Operation MK plan to know that by doing so, he had signed his own warrant of execution, probably also those of his wife and daughter. The people who did this to his mother, a poor, lonely, uneducated woman, would have no compunction to kill him and his family. It wouldn't matter if he gave the USB drive back to them in person. They would kill him after they'd tortured him to find out if he'd read the document, made any copies, or if he'd given copies to anyone else. Even if he didn't read the document or hadn't made a copy of it, they would rather err on the side of caution and kill him and his wife just in case. The fact was, even if it was only the summary he read, he knew too much of their evil plan. And he knew the names of the thirteen men who created the plan.

He took his cellphone out of his bag and phoned Ming. When she answered, he said, "Ming, listen carefully. Don't interrupt me. Mom is dead, killed. I'm sure the people who killed her are on their way to our house as we speak. They could be there any moment. Grab a change of clothes and toiletries for you and Lei, put it in a backpack with my laptop, and leave the house immediately. Go to the subway station, take the train to the place where I proposed to you. Put scarfs around your heads and put on facemasks. I will meet you there in the next two hours."

He didn't tell her what to do if he didn't turn up at the rendezvous point. There was no point in scaring his wife any more than she already was.

"What—"

"Ming, there's no time to answer questions. Just do it right now. They're going to kill all of us if you don't. Switch your phone off and take the battery out the moment you leave the house. I'll see you in two hours. Don't forget the laptop. We'll need it if we want to stay alive."

Yan ended the call, laid his mother's body gently on the floor. Then he got a blanket off her bed and covered her body from head to toe. He went to the kitchen and washed his mother's blood off his hands and clothes as best he could, and left the house without closing the front door, hoping that at some stage, curiosity would get the better of the neighbors, and they would find her body and phone the police. He switched his phone off, removed the battery, and put it back in the canvas bag before he started the car engine.

He drove to the subway station, pulled the hood of his

jacket over his head, and donned a facemask. It was cold. Many people were covering their heads. In Beijing and most of China's cities, because of air pollution, people wearing facemasks were a common sight. He found an ATM machine and emptied their savings account, 15,000 Yuan, about 2,200 USD. He got another 1,317 Yuan, about 200 USD, from their current account. That was the last time he'd access their accounts. He looked at the money in his hands—it was all the money they had. With that, they had to run, hide, feed themselves, and get out of China. Where they were going to run to or hide without passports, he had no idea. But he knew if they didn't, they were going to die.

He felt as if his heart had been torn to pieces as he turned onto the highway and sped away to Beihai Park, also known as the Winter Palace. The former imperial garden built in the 11th century was located in the northwestern part of the Imperial City. It was the place where he had asked Ming to marry him six years ago. He had to fight the emotions threatening to overwhelm him about his mother. He didn't even get a chance to tell her how much he loved her. He wouldn't be able to be at her funeral. The thought that no matter what he did, she was gone, never to return, never, was driving him to the edge of insanity. At times he felt like pulling off the road to just sit there and cry. But he knew he couldn't; he had to get his family to safety.

Beijing, China

Day 5

General Lang's aide and his assistant were terrified. They had arrived at Yan's home half an hour after Ming and Lei had left. It took the two hapless men the best part of an hour to question the neighbors to establish that and assure themselves that none of them were hiding the woman and her child. What they needed urgently was a lot of police to help them, but they had their orders—no police.

The aide called the general. He was livid when he heard the report. With a tsunami of choice words, he ordered his incompetent minions to return to the cleaner's house, pick her up, and bring her in for more questioning—this time to find out where her son was hiding. And if she didn't know, to keep her in custody to use as leverage against her wayward son.

It took the men another hour to return to Sun Jia's house only to find that she was dead. The open front door and a blanket covering her body told them someone else had been there since their first visit.

The aide made another call to the general. After listening to the report, the general ordered them to cover the body with the blanket as they found it and return to the office. The neighbors will succumb to their nosiness sooner or later, find the body, and call the police.

While waiting for his men to return, Lang had time to consider his situation. The problem he had was that Sun Yan had the time and opportunity to read what was on the device, even make a copy of it. The only way to know was to apprehend and question him.

He would let it be known that somehow the cleaner had managed to get the combination to his wall safe and remove top-secret documents. She then handed them over to her son, who was now suspected of being a threat to national security—a spy—and on the run. He desperately wanted to believe that Sun Jia's son was not able to break the password, but the fact that Sun Yan worked for China's foremost hacking outfit, Unit 61398, dashed the hope.

"The old woman told you she accessed my wall safe. Right." It was not a question.

The aide immediately caught on to it. "Yes, General, that's precisely what she told us." He ignored his assistant's frown.

"She refused to tell you where and how she got the combination of the lock to the safe. Right."

"Yes, General, she refused. We left it at that because we had no time to waste; we wanted to get to her son's house as quickly as possible to retrieve those top-secret documents before he passed them on to someone else."

"Did you hurt her in any way, shape, or form during the interview?"

"No, General. Not at all. She was very scared. She voluntarily admitted to wrongdoing. There was no reason to intimidate or hurt her at all."

"Who do you think would've killed her?"

The aide shrugged. "Difficult to say, General. It's a dangerous neighborhood. There are lots of unsavory characters wandering the streets looking for easy prey. She could've been involved in some kind of criminal activity, and it's entirely possible that she had hacked off some of her enemies. But, when we went back to her house, the neighbors told us that a young man in a blue car arrived about ten minutes after we'd left the first time. He was inside the house for about twenty minutes, came out in a hurry, jumped in the car, and left without even closing the front door. He's probably the killer."

Lang shook his head. Not the answer he was looking for. "So in your considered opinion, given the fact that she stole top-secret documents from my office, is it not possible that this woman could've been part of a spy ring, and they got rid of her after taking delivery of the documents so as to leave no loose ends?"

"Come to think of it, General, in my considered opinion, I'd say that's the only explanation that makes sense."

Lang nodded. "Well then, let's go to work. We've got ourselves a spy ring to break up. And it can't be done soon enough."

Chapter Thirty-Six

TIME TO GET AWAY

Beijing, China

Day 5

Yan got to Beihai Park much earlier than he thought he would. Ming and Lei weren't there. It didn't worry him. The train trip from where they lived to the park was more than an hour. They probably had to wait to catch the right train. He would start to worry if they didn't arrive within the next hour.

He had time. He did his best to push his emotions aside and think about their situation and what to do. The one thing he was sure of was that he was done with the Chinese Communist Party, not with the Chinese people, the party. All his life, he had seen how they treated people, their corruption, their favoritism, their elitism, their brutalities, and their merciless suppression of the people. For years those things had been troubling him, but as long as it was happening to someone else and not to him or his loved ones, there was always a false sense of security. The barbaric killing of his mother epitomized everything that was wrong with China's communist system—infested by animals who entitled themselves, by virtue of their position, to kill a defenseless, innocent, old woman who wouldn't harm a fly.

In those few moments of reflection, Sun Yan's sorrow was transcended by rage. He made a silent oath; he was going to fight this regime until he had no life left in him.

He never held a gun in his hand, had never been in a uniform. Yet, he was a soldier in the trenches on the front-line; that's what his superiors told him every day. He agreed. He *was* a soldier, a Special Forces operator, not the door-kicker and snake-eater kind; no, he was a Special Forces soldier on the battlefield of technology. And he was one of the best in the world.

His and his family's photos would soon be in the hands of all law enforcement agencies across the country and would also be fed to the facial recognition software moni-toring the 170 million CCTV cameras, one for every twelve people in China, to find matches and track their every move wherever they go. And so would be the license plate number of their 2012 blue Nissan Sylphy.

For any ordinary citizen without an in-depth under-standing of how the state's oppressive surveillance apparatus worked, it would have been all but impossible to avoid capture for much more than a day, two at best. But Yan had an intimate understanding of their systems, for he had been involved in the development of some of them. He didn't only know how to hack them; he also knew how to circum-vent them.

Notwithstanding, he knew at Unit 61398 they would soon, if not already, disable his account and block his access to all systems. But as long as they didn't force a password change for everyone in the unit, a standard operating procedure in the event of a security breach, such as an employee who had disappeared or had walked off the reservation, like he did, he would still have access.

All he required was forty-five minutes of uninterrupted access. The moment Ming and Lei had arrived, he would do it and get out of Beijing.

The closest safe haven would be South Korea or Japan, but that would mean air or boat travel for which he didn't have enough money, to begin with, on top of the fact that ports of exit would be swarming with security staff, CCTV, and a legion of officials on the lookout for them. Besides, that's probably exactly what their pursuers would expect them to do. But there were many other options; China was not only the most populous country in the world, but it also had the largest number of neighbors, 14 in total, sharing its 13,670 miles (22,000 kilometers) of land borders.

Yan and the other managers at Unit 61398 all had VPN, virtual private network, access configured on their cellphones and laptops to access the work servers whenever they were not on site. With the VPN using proxy servers that would hide the location of his real IP address, he would be able to access the servers without letting them know where he was. But he knew better than most that even a VPN, which most people wrongly believed was totally secure, could be hacked by someone with the expertise and a bit of time.

Unit 61398 and their colleagues in the Social Media division didn't only focus on external enemies; they had sections dedicated to the internal enemies of the state, spying on them and censoring their communications, often blocking them completely. Unit 61398 was responsible for hacking into the computers of said enemies of the state to enable the spies and censors to do their job. That was another reason Yan needed access to the Unit's servers— sometimes, when in trouble, it was helpful to not only know people in high places but also in low places. In this case, not so much knowing them but rather knowing all about them, and that information was on the Unit 61398 servers.

Just then, he spotted Ming and Lei among a group of tourists heading in his direction. He got up from the bench and went to meet them. A few minutes later, he was seated on a bench under a tree. He had his laptop up and running and activated the VPN while Ming and Lei played hide and seek. Ming was keeping an eye out for police or anyone that looked suspicious. Not that she or Yan had the countersurveillance skills to spot suspicious-looking people of the kind that would pose a threat to them. At least the thought that she was keeping a watch provided a sense of safety.

Jia was a Christian. She didn't understand dogma and theology. To her, it was simple, God and His son Jesus were real, and the latter died for our sins. When you die, you can go to heaven where you will be with God or hell where you will be with Satan. If you believed in God and His Son Jesus, you go to heaven, and she believed that without questioning or hesitation, like a child. Yan smiled sadly as he recalled when Lei once had a high fever when his mother came to visit, and she told him that she'd pray to the devil. When he said, "Mother, surely, you mean pray to God?" she'd shaken her head and said, "No, the devil. God already loves her. It's the devil that needs to be told to leave the child alone."

If indeed there was a heaven as she believed, that's where she would be—despite stealing General Lang's candy, which she had confessed. Somehow, those thoughts brought Yan a small measure of solace.

He and Ming were neither atheists nor agnostics. They both believed there was a deity out there, but which one, if any, of the many gods of the many religions of the world that deity was, they'd never thought about. Even so, Yan knew whoever that deity was; he was in desperate need of divine intervention to get him and his family to safety.

Before entering his manager's credentials to access the Unit's servers, he whispered a simple prayer. "God of my mother, please let this work, and help us escape from our persecutors." No foxhole promises of if you help me, I will become a Christian, go to church every Sunday, say my prayers every day, love my neighbors, and live a good life. There was no time for it in any event.

Yan's manager was a complete jerk who terrorized his subjects; Hǎi'ōu, Seagull, they called him behind his back. It was for two reasons: the ringtone on his phone, that of a screaming seagull, and his management style reminded them of a seagull—fly in, make a big noise, shit all over the place, and leave with a big noise. He was a rude, self-aggrandizing twit, who, among other stupid things, also believed security measures such as not writing your password down was below a man of his stature, too busy to bother with remembering passwords. He kept his password on a sticky note on the side of his screen. That kind of arrogance was one of the many traits that Yan always hated about the dimwit, but now he felt like sending him a thank-you note for it as he downloaded all the information he wanted from the Unit's servers.

Forty-five minutes after he started, to his mother's God, he whispered, "Thank you," disconnected the VPN link and shut down his laptop and cellphone. He didn't have to wipe out his tracks on the servers. He was never there; the logs would show that Seagull had accessed them. And unless they conducted a very meticulous audit, which they'd never done before, they would never know Seagull's account had been hijacked, and neither would Seagull. But if they did, Seagull would get the ass-chewing, which, of course, would please Yan and his former colleagues to no end.

He signaled to Ming that he was done and that it was time to get away.

Chapter Thirty-Seven

WE HAVE A DEAL

Beijing, China

Day 5

All the excitement had left Lei tired—she fell asleep in her safety seat in the backseat minutes after the car had pulled out of the parking lot at Beihai Park. That gave Yan the chance to tell Ming what had happened. She was crying as she listened to him. But she agreed they had no choice. It was either handing themselves over to the authorities, which was the same as reporting for their own execution, or flee the country. She'd lost both her parents at the age of ten and grew up in a foster home. There was no family that could be intimidated or used as leverage against them.

Yan explained to her how the CCTV and facial recognition systems worked. Wearing the right disguises, they would be able to evade detection. But they needed something much more sophisticated than headgear and facemasks.

However, for now, until they reached their first destination, ballcaps, facemasks, and sunglasses were all they had.

The second problem was the car. Every car in China was registered in a database. All the police had to do when they got the call to find it was to feed the details to the CCTV systems, and they'd track it down in minutes. Ming suggested they steal the plates of another car, but Yan explained that the system was programmed to look for cars whose make, model, color, etcetera didn't match the number plates. "So, swapping plates with another car will be the same as walking into the police station and asking them to please arrest us."

"In other words," Ming said, "all we can hope for is that we can get to the panelbeater (auto body mechanic) without detection?"

"Yep. But once the police get the alert, they'll feed the car's details to the system, and from the historical data, they'll be able to track the car down very quickly. We need to dump the car somewhere and use alternative transport to get to the panel beater."

Yan needed another favor from the God of his mother. If He would be so kind as to make sure the news of their escape wouldn't reach the ears of the police before they had reached their destination, he would be very appreciative.

Uber sold its China operations in 2016. In its place came Didi Chuxing, Didi for short; they were now the world's largest ride-hailing service. All one had to do was install the Didi app, load some credit, and you were ready to book a ride. The problem was if Yan did that, there would be a record of the trip, complete with his name, address, and photos of him and his family from the cameras the Didi drivers had to install in their cars.

Fortunately, there was a way around it; find a Didi

driver who was waiting for a call and offer him or her cash, provided the trip was off the books, and there were no cameras on. There was a thriving black market for that among Didi operators. They took cash, didn't declare the income, and didn't share the fare with Didi.

Yan drove into an underground parking garage beneath a shopping mall. There were CCTV cameras everywhere, but it couldn't be helped; he knew of some unmonitored side alleys close by where Didi operators parked while they waited for calls to pick up customers, usually shoppers from the mall.

They disguised themselves as best they could with what they had and went out to find a Didi driver. Within minutes the deal was made, and cash had changed hands. Twenty minutes later, they were dropped off at another mall, and Yan made another deal with a different Didi driver. They went through the same routine twice more before they were dropped off at another mall about two miles from the panel beater's house shortly before seven that night.

Beijing, China

Day 5

Gao Rong was the panel beater's name. Fifty-one, married, a son of 30, member of Tuidang, and leader of a well-organized syndicate of car thieves.

The average family sedan car was made up of about 2,400 pounds of steel plus copper wire, plastic, rare earth metals, platinum, lead, aluminum, electronics, and other recyclable materials. The average price paid to the owner of a family sedan that had reached the end of the road, so to speak, was about 2,300 Yuan, 350 USD. However, if the owner stripped the car down to its component parts, it would save the recycling company the cost of doing so, and the owner would receive three to four times more. But very few vehicle owners had the know-how or the tools to accomplish the task.

And that's where Gao saw the opportunity. One man's junk was another man's treasure. The income from his panel beater business was enough to put food on the table for him and his family, but he was not going to get rich from it, and Gao had an entrepreneurial spirit, it was part of the reason he joined Tuidang; he didn't like the government telling him how to run his business. He decided to branch out into recycling. A few years later, his chain of panel beater shops had spread across China. They were equipped with the tools and facilities to reduce a car to its recyclable parts in less than an hour. They had trucks roaming the country picking up end-of-life vehicles directly from vehicle owners, many of whom were happy to give it away for free just to save themselves the schlepp of the paperwork and cost of having it towed away.

In the beginning, Gao's business expanded rapidly but so did the competition, and his business began to stagnate as the supply dwindled. The answer was to expand his supplier base to the 260 million private vehicle owners of China. His supply chain issues were solved.

Yan knew all of this because he had hacked into the network of a company in Shanghai at the behest of the MSS, who suspected there could be more to the company than only recycling. Seagull gave the job to Yan three weeks ago, which he, at the time, wanted to give to one of his team but was told to do it himself—Seagull's way of making sure Yan still knew who the boss was.

Seagull told him it was not his highest priority but that he still expected a full report in four weeks. He might as well have added, "I expect you to do it in your spare time—after hours."

Yan went to work on it that same night when he got home. It didn't take him long to figure out that the Shanghai company was above board, but one of their biggest sources of recyclable materials was not. Gao's panel beater business.

He was wondering how to approach Gao. He could make a computer do whatever he wanted, humans not so much. Discussing his dilemma with Ming, she suggested, "In the hospital, we learned that it's always better when patients know what's wrong with them rather than hiding it from them. I'm not saying you should give him the keys to the vault, but tell him what you know, how you came to know it, and what you can do to help him."

Yan left Ming and Lei at a McDonalds restaurant with a nice big playground for children, shouldered his laptop bag, and walked the two miles to Gao's house.

He knocked on Gao's front door and, when his wife opened the door, introduced himself as Tang Ru, the owner of a scrapyard who wanted to talk business with Mr. Gao. She let him in and showed him to the family room where her husband was watching TV and smoking a big fat Cuban cigar while working his way through a bottle of baijiu, a beverage that was pungent, distinctive, and clear as mineral water—an acquired taste—but it was the national drink of China, often cited as the most consumed liquor in the world, 2,6 billion gallons (10 billion liters) per year.

As can be expected, Gao was not impressed by Mr.

Tang's audacity to turn up at his house uninvited, let alone disturbing him while he was relaxing after a hard day's work. But Yan was not going to let him make too much of a scene; he got to the point quickly. "I'm not the owner of a scrapyard. I work for the government." That was a half-truth. Although he had abandoned his position, he would still be on the books as a government employee.

Gao stubbed the cigar out in the ashtray next to him, downed the last bit of baijiu, and said, "Then state your business."

Over the course of the next half hour, Gao went from red-faced anger to ashen-faced trepidation as Mr. Tang told him more about his own business than he himself knew. He was too terrified to ask how Mr. Tang had managed to come by all this condemning knowledge. But he must have realized that if Mr. Tang were there to arrest him, he would have done so shortly after entering the house. "I take it you came here to blackmail me. So, get to the point and tell me what you want."

"No, sir, no blackmail. I'm not going to let the authorities know about your illicit business dealings. My problem is I don't have money to pay you for what I need from you. However, I can delete all that information, which would assure that the authorities won't ever know about the unlawful side of your business. In other words, the bartering of services is what I propose. If it's unacceptable to you, I'll leave, and you won't hear from me ever again."

"But the police might come knocking on my door, right?"

"Yes, sooner or later, they will find the information without me telling them."

"How will they know if you don't tell them?"

"I've collected all the information about your business,

and it's currently residing on a certain computer that only I have access to, for now." That was not entirely true either, but necessary for the sake of keeping things simple for Gao. Seagull had access to the folder but hadn't looked at it as yet. Yan had confirmed that while he accessed Unit 61398's servers earlier. "Once my employer knows I'm not coming back to the office, that might change."

"How much time do we have?"

"I'd say another hour or so. Could be more, but if I were you, I wouldn't take any chances."

"So, when you've deleted that information, what makes you think I'll still be motivated to help you get out of the country?"

Yan grinned. "I have to trust *someone*, sir."

"And I'm to trust that you haven't made a copy of it?"

"I already have a copy."

Yan's honesty must've convinced Goa. He relaxed visibly. "We have a deal."

Three-quarters of an hour later, they'd agreed the terms of the deal. Goa, with Yan in the passenger seat, pulled up in the parking lot of the McDonalds in his white Volkswagen Lavida, the second most popular car in China. Yan got out and went to collect his wife and daughter.

A few minutes later, the rest of the Sun family were introduced to Gao's family, his wife, Qiu, his son, Yong, and his wife, Bo. Gao's property was a duplex, two two-bedroom homes sharing a common central wall with an interleading door. The Sun family was going to stay with Yong and his wife for the next week or so, maybe longer, depending on the plan of escape they'd come up with over the next few days.

Bo led Ming and Lei to their house, and the men went to Goa's home office. Yan started his laptop and again used

Seagull's credentials to access the Unit 61398 servers and deleted Gao's file completely. While he was at it, he made a few minor and undetectable changes to the Unit's firewall for future use if necessary. He terminated the connection and hacked into the Shanghai recycling company's network, and deleted all the evidence in their files, which had led Yan to Gao in the first place. Then he hardened Gao's firewall so that no one else could access his network like Yan did. Finally, he moved all the damning evidence off Gao's computers onto an external hard drive and schooled Gao and Yong about online security and how to make sure that their sensitive information would never be accessible via the internet ever again.

Yan concluded, "Mr. Gao, that's my end of the deal. My family and I are now at the mercy of you and yours."

"First of all, you may call me Rong. Second, I've had enough time to observe you, and I've decided that you're a trustworthy man. You and your family have nothing to fear. I will fulfill my part of our agreement. And, of course, you're welcome to remind me if I forget that you still have a copy of the incriminating evidence. We've got a lot to talk about, but you and your family have had a long and stressful day. I suggest we all get some sleep and start planning your escape in the morning."

By 11:30 p.m., they were all in bed. Lei had fallen asleep within minutes after Ming had put her to bed soon after their arrival. Yan and Ming were whispering quietly. It was the scariest situation they'd ever found themselves in. Having a copy of the condemning business data was not as much of an insurance policy as Gao thought, and he'd figure that out sooner or later and possibly change his mind. But there was no alternative; they had to trust their hosts. All they could hope for was that Gao, as a member of

Tuidang, would not be inclined to betray them. They both would've had a less fitful night if they knew what Gao was going to tell them in the morning.

It was almost two in the morning when Yan heard Ming's breathing becoming regular as she fell asleep. He closed his eyes, took a slow, long, silent breath, and exhaled softly. Within minutes he also drifted off.

Beijing, China

Day 6

Less than thirty miles from where Yan and his wife were sleeping, Seagull was in the embrace of his mistress, also fast asleep, but only until the sound of seagulls roused him. He leaned over and grabbed his mobile phone.

Less than an hour later, he was in the director's office answering his and General Jin Ping's questions. No, there were no prior warning signs that Sun Yan could be a traitor. No, there was nothing that he could think of that would've aggrieved Sun so much that he would turn traitor. No, the monthly security checks, which included a personal interview, financial checks, checks on friends and family, internet and telephone use, didn't flag anything, and it was the same for all months prior. His background check when he was recruited for the unit was above reproach. No, none of his subordinates ever filed a negative report about him.

"So, in your opinion, Sun was a model employee, patriotic, intelligent, hardworking, and respectful?" said Ping.

"Yes, General."

"Yet, he and his mother collaborated to steal top-secret documents from General Lang's safe. And most bizarre of all, it seems he killed his own mother after she delivered the documents to him. Any sociopathic tendencies that you've noted during the time he worked for you?"

"No, General, none whatsoever. His last psychological evaluation, about six months ago, raised no suspicions either."

"Well, something has gone wrong with him, and you missed it."

The blood started draining from Seagull's face. He swallowed hard. This was a big mess. He was in charge of the man who caused it. Managers could delegate work, never responsibility. "I must've, General—"

"Presumably, you have a list of projects he and his team have been working on now and in the past. Let's look at it. I want to know how much damage this man can cause us."

For the next two hours, Seagull took them through the projects. If he got the call a few hours earlier, there would've been one more project to look at. But, as it were, now it didn't exist, and Seagull either forgot about it or didn't want to exacerbate his already precarious situation.

Sun Yan's network account had been disabled hours before when the director got the call from General Ping. His computer was already with the forensic analysts, who would be scouring it for any malicious applications and code. His activity-log would be scrutinized to see when did he access what. They would find nothing.

Shortly after Seagull produced the list of projects, everyone in Yan's team was on site. Their accounts had been disabled at the same time as Yan's and would only be reactivated once they'd been interviewed by experienced interrogators, one by one, and they'd passed a thorough security check. In China, law enforcement agencies didn't trust lie detectors nearly as much as their skilled interrogators to get to the truth. Fifty hackers of Unit 61398 would be scared out of their minds and totally unproductive for the next four days.

Seagull eventually got away with only the ass-chewing Yan wished upon him. No demotion. They didn't even change his password, which would expire in thirty-five days' time.

Chapter Thirty-Eight

WEDDING PLANNING

The Ranch, Arizona, USA

Days 6 to 10

Three days after their rescue, the Farleys and Daltons arrived back on the Ranch on CRC's Dassault Falcon 2000 DX private jet to a heroes' welcome.

The Old Man, clearly very happy to see Josh alive, shook his hand and said, "You should thank the guy who did your facelift. He did something I would've thought impossible; he improved your looks."

Christelle was visibly disturbed when she saw Josh's condition. He noticed it. "Don't worry, Christelle, come Saturday, you'll have the honor of watching me on TV taking my place at the starting line for the Iron Man competition."

Rex grinned. It was good to see his best friend was rapidly recovering his health and sense of humor.

For the next few days, Digger got much more than his usual number of jerky treats from the Old Man, Marissa, and Josh. Rex and Catia quickly became aware of the conspiracy when they noticed Digger was almost constantly busy sniffing out one of three jerky-carriers and, when he found them, made it look as if he was just checking in to see if they were still okay. Strange, Cupcake seemed to have never gotten an invitation to join Digger on those missions of compassion.

With the wedding two weeks away, the occupants of the Ranch were besieged by wedding planning and preparations.

Rex and Josh had the most recent experience in matters related to getting married. Specifically, a man's role in the planning thereof, which is the reason they did everything within their means to stay out of it. If somehow they got dragged into it, they were very diplomatic, which meant not to give an opinion unless asked for and then to restrict it to one of two responses only: I like it or, I think it's a brilliant idea.

But the Old Man had forgotten all about the intricacies of wedding planning. The last time he got married was almost forty years ago. Rex and Josh felt for him, and more than once stepped in to rescue him from ruining his marriage before he could put the ring on Christelle's finger.

The wedding location was Hạ Long Bay in northeast Vietnam, an idyllic location known for its emerald waters and thousands of towering limestone islands covered by lush-green rainforests. The region was popular for scuba diving, rock climbing, and hiking, particularly in the mountainous Cát Bà National Park. The wedding venue was the *TOMATS*. Declan Spencer was going to be the officiant and Rex, the best man. Margot Lemaire, a deputy minister in the French government, was going to be Christelle's maid of honor.

Rex and Digger had rescued Margot Lemaire a few years ago from the claws of Russian mobsters, acting on behalf of the President of Russia who wanted to use her as leverage against the French president to get him to sign an agreement which would've tied France to a Russian gas pipeline in perpetuity. Margot's four-year-old daughter, Rowena, was named after Rex before Margot was let in on the secret that the real name of the man who rescued her and saved France from an enormous international embarrassment, whom she knew as Rowan Donnelly, was actually Rex Dalton. Rex was Rowena's godfather, and she was going to be the flower girl.

Spencer with his wife, Simona, and the crew had been sailing in the direction of Vietnam crossing the Mediterranean Sea, Red Sea, Gulf of Aden, Arabian Sea, around the tip of India, through the Straits of Malacca, past Singapore into the South China Sea to Hạ Long Bay. They made a quick stop in Mumbai, where Rehka Gyan joined them.

Rehka was the daughter of Rex's friend from Bilaspur, India. Rex and Rehka had met when he and Digger liberated her and six other women from a Saudi Arabian prince (Mutaib bin Faisal bin Saud), an international black-market arms dealer and human trafficker.

Rehka was Rex's technology expert, virtual assistant, researcher, and friend. With a master's degree in computer sciences, she had exceptional skills in programming and online research. If anyone anywhere left a digital footprint, be it on social media, email, or online searches, she could track that person down. She had enough black hat and gray hat skills to operate anonymously on the Darknet and get unfettered access to some of the most secure private, government, and law enforcement databases across the globe without leaving so much as a hint that she had been there. And since she had met CRC's IT guru, Greg Wade, and worked with him on a number of missions, her knowledge and skills had gone from strength to strength. And they were in love.

Chapter Thirty-Nine

ALL WAR IS BASED ON DECEPTION

Undisclosed location, New York, USA

Days 6 to 10

Ren Shi had not received knee-replacement surgery yet. That would come later. In the meantime, he was kept reasonably comfortable, fed properly, supplied with anti-inflammatory medication, and kept in a near-constant state of euphoria with painkillers, which had the side-effect of making him very loquacious.

Within two hours after his offer had been accepted, Ren had spilled the names of the four spy-handlers reporting to him, including the details of the traitors controlled by them: A Rear Admiral with a sexual preference for underaged boys; a communications officer on a Los Angeles-class attack submarine in desperate need of money after losing everything he had on the Forex markets; a senior analyst in the CIA's Office of South Asia Analysis with a nymphomaniacal Chinese mistress; a senior staff member with a gambling problem in the office of the Secretary of Defense; a congressman who wanted to retire early and rich; two network specialists in General Caiden McKnight's Cyber Command, one with a drug problem and the other who secretly believed the Chinese blend of communism would cure the world of its ailments; and two middle-managers who felt victimized for being passed over for promotion too many times, one in the office of the Secretary of State, the other in the office of the Department of Homeland Security.

One senior MSS agent managed four spy-handlers who controlled nine traitors and a network of almost fifty informants in-country. How many more senior MSS agents such as himself were there running? How many handlers, spies, and agents in the USA? Ren didn't know but guessed the number of MSS agents like him to be a hundred or more. The total network of spy-handlers, agents, and traitors would probably be running into the thousands. It was at once sobering and gut-wrenching for the FBI's counterintelligence officers listening to Ren. It was their job to sniff out spies and traitors. They knew the PRC had vast espionage networks in the USA, and Ren Shi's information served to confirm just how pervasive the infiltration was.

Naturally, the first instinct would be to shoot the traitors, arrest their handlers and all agents, and hold their feet very close to a nice big fire until they'd given up everything they knew. But it's quite possible that the FBI and CIA read the Bible: "For by wise counsel thou shalt wage thy war." Proverbs 24:6. Or studied Sun Tzu: "All war is based on deception." Or remembered the motto of one of the best intelligence agencies in the world, the Israeli Mossad: "By Way Of Deception, Thou Shalt Do War." Notwithstanding what they've read, through hard-gained experience, they knew that spying was all about deception. The capturing of Ren Shi gave them a much-awaited opportunity to return a few long-overdue favors to the PRC's intelligence agencies.

They issued a statement to the media that three Chinese spies had been killed in a raid. To this fiction was added a bit more of the insider details, all of it false, of course, and repeated in a few secured meetings where some of the traitors happened to be present. Two of the spies were killed right away in the firefight. The third was alive but unconscious after the raid but unfortunately succumbed to his wounds without uttering a single word to the FBI. Through the traitors, that information would soon reach the ears of the MSS, giving them the much-needed reassurance that their network had not been compromised. What a relief.

Ren's network was placed under surveillance, electronic and physical. The traitors were going to be fed the information that the CIA wanted the MSS to hear.

It took days to get all the details of what Ren had direct knowledge of before they got to the information that he had come by from overhearing conversations, glancing at emails and documents not meant for him, adding two and two together, etcetera. And rumors, such as an operation against two IT companies based in Silicon Valley contracted to do work on some top-secret government IT systems. Another rumor was about a senior senator who they'd been studying for possible recruitment. If they were successful with the senator, it could turn out to be one of the biggest intelligence feats in the PRC's history. Ren had a lot more unsubstantiated information. Some of it contained names or positions or both and was actionable. But much of it was just that, too vague to action, but not ignored. Those were pieces of a puzzle. As more pieces became available, the full picture would reveal itself.

The USA and China were already at war with each other. The trade war, the cyberwar, and the war of words. The Ren Shi incident added another dimension to the war, the start of the Second Cold War. And by all indications, it was going to be every bit as brutal, if not much worse than the first.

Beijing, China

Day 6

General Lang was making his own plans of deception. After learning that Sun Yan worked for Unit 61398, under the command of General Jin Ping, he phoned the general and told him that one of his men was a spy and traitor who used his mother, the cleaner, to steal top-secret documents from his office, then killed his own mother after receiving the documents, and was now on the run, probably trying to get out of the country.

Then Lang poured himself a stiff shot of whiskey and sat down in his chair with his feet on his desk to take stock of his situation. He was walking a very tight rope. Thus far, no one had asked what was in those top-secret documents. He could get away with telling anyone who wanted to know that there was a reason it was classified as top secret; only those who had a need to know could be told. Besides, how would knowing what was in the document help them find the traitor who stole it? He nodded to himself; *that ought to do it.*

But how did it come to this in the first place? He couldn't bring himself to confess that the causal connection was the liquor in the glass in his hand—too much of it too often.

By the time he poured the second whiskey, he had turned his thoughts to those *he* believed should be blamed for the mess; the bungling aide and his idiotic assistant. They didn't have to kill the woman. That's why Sun Yan had chosen to run instead of doing the logical thing and return the USB drive his mother had stolen. He picked up the phone to arrange for them to be taken into custody for murder but then hesitated and put it down. He was still sober enough to realize that those two were the only ones besides himself and Sun Yan who knew the truth. Sun, he expected to be dead very soon. Still, the aide and his helper were the last two men on the planet he wanted to upset right now. Unless, of course, he arranged for them to be silenced, permanently. But maybe he should wait and see if they were able to get hold of Sun. This time his instructions were clear: "He must be taken alive."

Chapter Forty

ETHICAL THIEVES?

Beijing, China

Day 6

Yan couldn't help but think about his prayers to the God of his mother the day before. That God must have taken a liking to him and his family. How else could it be explained? Coincidence? Good luck? Highly unlikely. No one could have that many coincidental strokes of good luck all in one day and then have it continue the next day.

Listening to Gao early that morning, all doubts Yan had the night before about the wisdom of entrusting his family's lives to a professional car thief were dispelled.

Gao and his son, Yong, were both Tuidang but also part of a secret resistance network. An organization with no name. Gao was in command. They had twenty branches across the country, all fronted by a real panel beater shop. Tuidang members found it near-impossible to get jobs in the government or government-controlled enterprises. They had to make their own living. Yes, they were car thieves, but in Robin-Hood-style, they stole cars only from rich communist party members, and the bulk of the proceeds went to growing the resistance and caring for Tuidang members in need.

Yan struggled to keep his jaw from dropping. Ethical thieves? None of that was evident from the information he'd collected from Gao's computer when he hacked into it. Which explained why Gao was so agreeable to his suggestions the night before. Getting caught for car theft would end in a lengthy stint in jail for him and his son. Getting caught for organizing a resistance movement against the PRC government would've ended with a bullet in the back of the head of everyone involved, without exception. More than enough to trigger anyone's nerves.

Gao told him that they had assisted a few people to escape from the country in the past. He would discuss the matter with the second in command in a few days' time when he met with her. "But I need to know what is it that you've done that would be so important to them that they'd kill your mother and want to do the same to you and your family? And, of course, so important to us that we'd want to put ourselves in danger to get you out?"

Yan had a dilemma. Though he'd read only the executive summary, the information was earth-shattering. It had the potential to expose the CCP for who they were, even destroy them. And therein lay the problem. Not only would the authorities kill to get it back, but also anyone who knew what he had could kill him to get their hands on it and use it to enrich or protect themselves. That information would be invaluable to western intelligence agencies. Why would Gao and his outfit need him if they could do it themselves and profit from it? But, then again, anyone who had the opportunity to see that information would be in the same danger as he was.

"Rong, the information I have already caused the death of my mother. I won't tell you what they did to her. It was barbaric, horrific..." He stopped to fight back the tears. "Please let us not put more lives in danger. As it is, my family and I can't get out of it; let's keep it limited to us. But I'll give you a bit of background."

Gao nodded.

Yan continued. "Until yesterday, I worked for a top-secret unit in the cyber warfare division of the PLA's Information Operations and Information Warfare division. Our government denies the existence of the unit. Very few people know about the unit's existence. Our job is to penetrate the computer networks of the enemy, domestic and abroad. I stumbled across the information about your business quite by accident." It was a lie, but it kept things simple and didn't involve his mother. "I'd appreciate it if we leave it at that and ask that you trust me when I say that this information could bring the Communist Party down, something I want, and I'm sure Tuidang wants, too."

Gao nodded pensively and looked at his son. Yong also nodded.

"I'll talk to my second in command. We strongly believe that the people of China should resolve the problems of China. But be that as it may, we are not too stubborn to accept help from the outside as long as they don't dictate to us *how* we should reform our country."

"I agree with your approach; that's how it should be."

"Good. We might want to ask you to help secure the organization's computers in the same manner you secured mine."

"It'd be my pleasure."

By 9:00 a.m., the Sun family's pictures were on all TV stations. "Traitors!" The headlines screamed. "If you see them, report them. They're a threat to our country. They must not be allowed to escape. They broke into a general's office and stole top-secret documents. Don't try to apprehend them; they're dangerous. That man killed his own mother when he discovered she'd reported him. Call the police. Here's the number. There will be a big reward for anyone who provides information that leads to their arrest."

From that moment on, at least half a billion people would be on the lookout for the three members of the Sun family.

For the next two weeks, until the plan of escape had been finalized, the Suns would not leave the Goa family's houses while hoping and praying that the neighbors would not become aware of their presence, and the police would operate on the belief that the Suns would not have been so stupid as to hang around Beijing.

Chapter Forty-One

SIX DAYS OF FUN IN THE SUN

Hạ Long Bay, Vietnam

Days 11 to 17

The Daltons, Farleys, and Greg Wade, flew on a Cathay Pacific flight from Los Angeles via Hong Kong to Ho Chi Minh City and on a domestic flight from there to Hạ Long Bay arriving a week before the wedding. Apart from the bandages covering his left index and middle fingers, Josh was in good shape and getting better every day. Marissa was also doing very well. Helping Christelle and Catia with the planning and preparations helped a lot to take her mind off the horrors. But the nightmares wouldn't let themselves be brushed away so easily. It was going to take a long time to subdue them, and even then, they'd probably never go away completely. They'd only visit her less often.

Rex and company arrived at the marina at Tuần Châu Harbor, Hạ Long Bay, Vietnam, where the *TOMATS* was moored six days before the wedding. Apart from Spencer, Simona, and Spencer's first mate, Billy Walton, the crew was made up of three CRC agents, single, three Navy SEALs with their wives or girlfriends, three Delta Force operators with their wives or girlfriends, and a husband-and-wife chef team.

Although Rex and company were tired from the long flight when they arrived on the *TOMATS* shortly before 10:00 a.m., they decided to stay awake for the rest of the day in order to get their body clocks adjusted to the time difference as quickly as possible.

Naturally, Greg and Rehka, who hadn't seen each other for a few months, couldn't keep their hands off each other. And Digger was almost beside himself with joy to see Rehka, Spencer, and Simona. It was now only Brandt and Christelle that were missing from his pack.

Spencer was like a proud father showing off his first-born as he showed the new arrivals the upgrades that had been made to the *TOMATS*. The latest communications equipment, satellite links, the newest radar, and sonar technology—most of it top-secret.

Spencer saved the best for last. It looked like an over-sized fish oil capsule, thirty-six feet long, with a glass dome on one end and a propeller at the other. It bore no livery or markings.

"A midget-submarine," Rex crooned as he touched the hull.

Spencer was smiling from ear-to-ear. "Yep. DARPA-designed. SEAL teams have been testing it on missions for the past two years. This is the latest model. She carries a pilot and co-pilot/navigator and six fully equipped operators. She can dive up to two hundred feet and stay under for more than twenty-four hours. She cruises at five knots, maximum speed fifteen. She doesn't carry any weapons, but she's stealth."

For decades, the Navy SEALs had been using 'wet' mini delivery vehicles in which the compartment was flooded, and the riders had to wear SCBA masks (self-contained breathing apparatus) to get the operators stealthily to their targets. It was not ideal; therefore, the United States Special Operations Command (USSOCOM), the unified command of the special operations of the Army, Marine Corps, Navy, and Air Force, had been working on a non-attack mini-submarine (midget submarine) DCS (Dry Combat Submersible) for years.

The model that Spencer was showing them now was one of the prototypes, tested in battle conditions and found not to be wanting.

"Hmm, who's going to drive this thing?" Josh wanted to know.

The two SEALs who were part of the group smiled. One of them said, "As Captain Spencer said, we've used the model before this one a few times on some of our missions. This lady here, we took out quite a few times during the trip over here. She's a beauty."

That was all Rex needed to hear. "Well, what are we waiting for? Lower the lady, and let's take her for a spin."

"Not so fast, buddy," said Josh. "I ain't getting onto no ship if it ain't got no name."

"Boat," said Spencer.

"What?"

"It's called a boat, not a ship. And this one you get into not onto."

"Ah, okay. The same rule goes for a boat. I'm not getting *into a boat* with no name."

"O-k-a-y, what shall we name her?" asked Spencer, smiling.

Everyone looked at Josh.

"Not without a bottle of champagne."

A few minutes later, Spencer was back with a small bottle of champagne, which he handed to Josh.

The tradition of christening a ship dates back several millennia. The ancient Greeks had their new vessel blessed by the builder before it was launched. The Vikings brought a human sacrifice to appease the gods of the sea, a bit too barbaric for the modern-day. Instead, an expensive bottle of wine was sacrificed on the ship's bow. It didn't matter what the bottle contained—wine or Champagne, as long as it was a precious beverage—what was more important was that the bottle smashed and spilled its contents over the bow.

Apparently, the first time this method was used, it ended in humiliation for the princess from the House of Hanover when she missed the bow and hit a spectator with the bottle instead. The injured man sued for damages.

In the era before liberation, it was tradition that a woman would do the honors. Not anymore. Josh was going to do it. He took a step forward, smiled, and said, "God bless this shi... ah, *boat* and all who sail *in* her." Then smashed the bottle on the bow.

Everyone cheered.

Marissa laughed. "You forgot the name."

"Nemo, of course. What else could it be?"

Josh was referring to Captain Nemo, the fictional character in the French novelist Jules Verne's science-fiction classics, Twenty Thousand Leagues Under the Seas and The Mysterious Island.

Half an hour later, Nemo was lowered into the special bay which the boat builders had created on the stern side of the lower deck. No one watching the *TOMATS* would've been able to see that it was carrying the mini-sub or when it was being submerged.

Greg and Rehka didn't go on the trip. They didn't like cramped spaces. Rex, Catia, Josh, and Marissa couldn't get in fast enough. As far as Rex knew, Digger had never been in a submarine, but he went where his pack went. *Someone* had to look after them.

An hour later, Nemo was hoisted back into the bay, and her passengers were still babbling about the experience when they sat down for lunch.

Hạ Long Bay, Vietnam

For the next six days, until John and Christelle arrived on CRC's private jet, they spent their days jet skiing, kayaking, snorkeling, hiking, swimming, and taking more underwater excursions in Nemo. Digger had the time of his life as he accompanied his pack on every adventure. At nighttime, they visited the popular tourist waterholes.

On the day before John and Christelle arrived, the six guests were invited by the crew members who were not on duty that night, including Spencer and Simona, to join them for what they promised to be 'the gastronomic experience of a lifetime.'

They should've known better. Special Forces operators were famous for the pranks they played on their friends. Digger tried to warn his pack, but they thought he was just excited about all the people around him. As it were, they walked into it with open eyes.

They were in the center of town, where there were

numerous stalls of street hawkers selling their wares, and ended up at a small restaurant where the owner was very glad to see them again and meet their six new friends. They were seated at a u-shaped table where the chef prepared the food right in front of them. The lead conspirator, Spencer, said something to the chef in broken Vietnamese.

The chef smiled and went to work.

They sipped on their beer and talked until the main dish arrived. It was thinly sliced raw beef dropped into a large bowl of boiling broth containing pork knuckles and unknown herbs. Delicious. Digger agreed; he couldn't get enough of the beef and pork.

When they had their fill, the chef served what Rex thought to be the Vietnamese version of an after-dinner cheese platter, except there were no cheese or crackers. This platter consisted of fishcakes, mini spring rolls, hot peppers, and a bowl of what they were led to believe by their companions was a fish sauce dip.

This was when Digger tried to warn Rex and the others with a yelp but got ignored.

The chef kept a straight face as he demonstrated how to eat this dish. He combined one of the hot peppers with a piece of fishcake, dipped it in the sauce, dropped it into his mouth, chewed, and swallowed. Easy. He smiled and nodded for them to do the same.

That was when Rex and company should've noticed that their companions had not been served with the same fish sauce dip they'd received. They should also have noticed that their companions had all stopped eating and were watching the six of them.

As if on cue, the six did it exactly as the chef had demonstrated. And then pandemonium erupted. Rex was screaming, "Water! Water!" at the top of his lungs. Catia's face was wet with tears. Josh had his hand around his throat, making gurgling sounds. Marissa's mouth was opening and closing like a fish out of water. Greg's eyes were bulging as if to pop out of their sockets at any moment. Rehka was the only one who remained calm; she was only waving her hand in front of her wide-open mouth to extinguish the fire inside.

By now, everybody, including the chef, was roaring with laughter.

And Digger? He was enjoying it. He had a big dog-smile on his face as he stared at his six stubborn children, who didn't want to heed his warning. As if to say, "You didn't want to hear it, now feel it."

Minutes later, when the six had recovered enough to speak again, promises of revenge were made.

It would be weeks later when they'd look back and realize that the six days of fun in the sun before the wedding was only the calm before the storm.

Chapter Forty-Two

A TRAITOR?

Beijing, China

Days 7 to 14

Generally speaking, people were free to leave China, those that were privileged enough to get passports; but if one were involved in crime, knew classified information, or was a really important person, it was not so easy to get a passport. Yan met all three requirements to be declined a passport to leave the country in any 'legal' manner. The days of artists making fake passports that could pass human scrutiny were long gone. Nowadays, passports were microchipped. Border control checkpoints had scanners that scanned retinas and fingerprints. And computers checked everything almost instantly. The only way to get a passport that would placate the computers was to get one from the government department that produced them. And for that, one would need to lodge an application or have a contact on the inside.

Gao's organization had no contacts on the inside. In short, the Sun family had to get across the border without passports. China had fourteen international neighbors: Afghanistan, Bhutan, India, Kazakhstan, Kyrgyzstan, Laos, Myanmar, Mongolia, Nepal, North Korea, Pakistan, Russia, Tajikistan, and Vietnam. Considering them all as possible destinations, they decided on Vietnam for a number of reasons but mostly because Gao's organization had a branch close to the border on the way to Hanoi. From Beijing to Hanoi was 1,695 miles, a very long trip, but probably one of the last places the hunters would expect them to go.

Relations between the two countries had been strained ever since China invaded Vietnam in 1979 on the pretenses of supporting China's ally, Cambodia, the alleged maltreatment of Vietnam's ethnic Chinese minority, and the Vietnamese occupation of the Spratly Islands, which they claimed were Chinese property.

And although China was Vietnam's biggest trading partner these days, it didn't stop General Jin's Information Operations and Information Warfare division from spying on Vietnam. As one of Unit 61398's foremost hackers, Yan had often penetrated Vietnamese business and government networks, and in the process, he had collected vast quantities of personal data of Vietnamese IT specialists in both private and government enterprises as well as ethnic Chinese living in Vietnam who were Tuidang members.

Yan studied the data he had and discussed it with Gao and Yong. And again, Yan was stunned by the inexplicable coincide. Gao knew one of the names on the list. A man who owned a big scrapyard in Hanoi, Tan Hui, an ethnic Chinese, whom they were in discussions with to supply them with scrap metal to be recycled in China. He was on Yan's list because he was Tuidang and suspected of having connections to the CIA in Hanoi.

The organization's members knew some tricks about disguises to help them deceive the facial recognition systems, but it was rudimentary, to say the least. In the areas where they lived and operated, they'd started mapping out the locations of CCTV cameras. Country-wide there were 170 million of them, and more were added every day.

Yan had been part of the project teams that developed the software for large parts of the vast surveillance apparatus. With that knowledge and the data he'd copied from Unit 61398's servers a few days before, it took him only two days to develop an app to pinpoint the locations of all CCTV cameras across the country, including the angles at which they were aimed and their blind spots. Gao and the organization's leadership were eternally grateful.

As promised to Gao, Yan also wrote a complete set of detailed instructions about how to secure computers, how to prevent hacking, set up a VPN, and secure communications. Despite all those measures, the overarching rule was that no electronic device could ever be safe. In other words, don't communicate electronically if you could do it in person. He scared the daylights out of them when he told them what the government was capable of and how incredibly lucky, or blessed, they were that other government snoops had not come across them yet.

In the meantime, Yan, Gao, and Yong were working out the details of the escape plan. Per Yan's instructions, they wouldn't dare to put any part of their plan on a computer, let alone communicate via the internet or phone. That slowed everything down, but as difficult and taxing as it was, they knew only fools would rush in where angels fear to tread. The people they had helped to escape in the past didn't have the entire PRC's law enforcement agencies and more than half the country looking for them. But the slow process was not all bad; the longer it took, the less urgent it would become for the police who had their hands full with other pressing matters.

This was also a time for Yan to come to grips with what he was planning to do when he got out. Was he a traitor? The day he went on the run with his family, it was first and foremost to save them. But once he got to the relative safety of Gao's organization, and the initial anxiety subsided somewhat, he also realized that the biggest rescue mission was the people of China. What he understood now that he'd read the full document of more than a thousand pages was that if even only part of the plan was executed, China was going to be in a war. People were going to die by the millions—nuclear annihilation was a reality.

François-Marie Arouet, better known by his nom de plume Voltaire, a French Enlightenment writer, historian, and philosopher famous for his wit, once said, "Common sense is not so common," to which Yan added, "And among the leaders of the PRC, it's nonexistent."

He just couldn't believe that the PRC's most senior people, supposedly intelligent beings, meant to act in the best interests of the people of the country, could be so power-hungry, stupid, and reckless to think the rest of the world would just roll over and let the communists take them over. Humans were classified as homo sapiens, the Latin for intelligent man. Yan opined that there was no intelligence to be found among the PRC leadership. They obviously didn't study history. If they did, they would've found that the annals of history were littered with the accounts of empires brought down by people who would rather die than be oppressed.

The CCP would try to stem the growing tide of internal unrest with harsh measures. They were already doing it, and, in the long run, it would destroy them, but at what cost to the citizens of China?

After days of reflection, he'd become convinced that he was no traitor. He was no hero, either. He was a proud citizen of a beautiful country with good people oppressed by a godless, murderous horde of self-serving ignoramuses. The CCP was what was wrong with China. They had to be ousted. And the red USB stick and the data he'd copied onto his laptop held the key to accomplishing that.

Friendship Pass Border Crossing, China

Day 14

Nine days after knocking on Gao's front door, the Sun family emerged from the back of a heavy-duty truck where they'd been hiding in a makeshift container among a consignment of heavy machinery and equipment necessary to set up a new panel beater shop for Gao's nameless organization. The new shop was set up with the aim of tapping into the scrap metal market in Vietnam and was located only a few miles from the Vietnamese border town of Dong Dang in the Cao Loc District, Lang Son Province. The town was best known for the Friendship Pass Border Crossing, one of the three main terrestrial border crossings with China.

Gao Yong had traveled to Hanoi by plane two days after the Sun family's arrival at their house nine days ago. In

Hanoi, he had met with the Tuidang man, Tan Hui, to discuss two matters: the supply of scrap metal to Gao's recycling business and the escape of the Sun family. The first matter was concluded with a handshake within the hour. The second matter was much more delicate. Yong had to perform the egg dance to not give away too much information yet give Tan enough to understand the importance of getting the Suns, without mentioning their names, into Vietnam. Tan never led on that he had connections to the CIA, but his words, "I've got a friend who I'm sure will be very keen to help," was enough for Yong. That evening, Yong and Tan had dinner at a small restaurant where Tan handed Yong a USB stick.

Back in Beijing, the contents of the USB stick were studied with much interest by Gao, Yong, and Yan. Trying to make a crossing at the Friendship Pass Border Crossing would be foolish, said the presumed CIA agent from Hanoi. They had the best and latest technologies available at the crossing, including thermal scanners and sniffer dogs. However, about five miles to the east of the Friendship Pass Border Crossing, there was a one-mile stretch of border, among the hills and forest, where only infrequent patrols kept the watch. No electronic border control measures such as laser tripwires, drones, etcetera were in operation. They had to make the crossing there. The agent from Hanoi had a helper in Dong Dang who would, starting seven days hence, be at the specified location on the China side of that stretch of the border every morning between 2:00 and 4:00 a.m. for five days in a row. When they reached the location, the agent's man will be there and challenge them with the passphrase, "Which way is east?" to which they had to respond with the phrase, "The direction from where the rain comes."

On the USB stick, accompanying the instructions, was also a high-quality satellite map with the coordinates of the proposed meeting point clearly marked. "Good luck. Hope to see you and your family soon."

Although Yan appreciated the good wishes, he wasn't so sure that luck would play much of a role in getting safely across the border.

Five miles east of the Friendship Pass Border Crossing, China

Day 15

It was 1:30 a.m. when the Sun family, accompanied by Yong and a guide, a local member of the organization who knew the area like the back of his hand, arrived at the rendezvous point. They were tired from the three-mile hike through the dense forest, taking turns to carry Sun Lei on their backs. Ming didn't like it but knew they had no choice; she had to administer a sedative to her little girl to keep her calm and relaxed and, most important of all, quiet during the journey. It worked; Lei had been asleep all the way. Even so, Ming still didn't like it, neither did Yan.

Their guide put them in a good hiding place about one hundred and fifty yards from the spot where they had to meet the agent's man from Dong Dang, which was the ruins of an ancient house about three hundred yards from the border fence, and told them to stay put. He crept forward slowly and quietly until he was about twenty yards from the ruins where he had a good view of the meeting point in the bright light of the full moon. He stayed there until he spotted the lonely figure emerging from the nearby thicket on the other side of the ruins. The guide remained in position and observed the man who was dressed in black from head to toe and had a black scarf around his neck, exactly as per the agent's instructions.

The man looked relaxed. It was a good sign. It meant there were no Chinese or Vietnamese border patrols in the area. The man sat down on one of the low walls, about fifteen yards from where the guide stood motionless behind a tree.

The man looked at his watch and lit a cigarette.

That's our man.

The guide looked at his watch; it was 1:55 a.m., five minutes early. He waited five minutes, got up, and approached the man.

When the guide was about five paces away, the man raised his hand in a stop gesture and said, "Which way is Hanoi?"

The guide stopped in his tracks. *Wrong passphrase!* His heart rate was already over 120, but now it was heading for 200. Yet, somehow, he managed to reply, "The direction from where the rain comes."

The man smiled. "Excellent. Let's get them. We don't have much time before the patrol comes."

The guide half-turned and started in the opposite direction from where the Suns and Yong were hiding. He took one step before his nerves deserted him completely. He pulled his knife out and stormed at the impostor. But it's always a bad idea to bring a knife to a gunfight. The bullet hit him between the eyes just when he took the second step toward the imposter.

The next moment four uniformed and armed border

patrol agents appeared from the trees. The shooter shouted, "They can't be far away. Find them! They're in that direction." He pointed in the direction the guide was heading before he made the stupid move with the knife.

Five miles east of the Friendship Pass Border Crossing, China

Day 15

The hiding place their guide had chosen was perfect, a space between huge rocks, completely overgrown by trees and shrubs. They had to crawl under the branches to get into the space. Unless one knew about its existence and where to look, one would walk past the lair none the wiser. And that's exactly what happened when the border patrol agents passed within three yards of them.

Thank God Lei was still fast asleep.

An hour after they'd heard the single shot and the orders yelled by someone to find them, everything had gone quiet. Their nerves were in tatters. They wanted to get away as quickly and as far away as possible, but they knew the silence could've been a trick to lure them out of hiding. They stayed for another hour before Yong sneaked out and scouted the area. He came back half an hour later and told them the agents were gone, and so was their guide. There was only one of two possibilities, the guide had been killed or wounded. Whichever it was, the agents took his body with them.

Lei began to stir, and Ming had to give her another dose

of sedative; it couldn't be helped. She had to be kept quiet for the next two hours while they walked back to the drop-off point where a vehicle that was supposed to pick Yong and the guide up was waiting.

The border agents would never know how close they came to apprehending the most wanted man in China. But as it were, they didn't even know the fugitives were the Sun family. Their informants on the Vietnam side had kept a watch on the human smuggler from Dong Dang for months, reporting his every move. When they got word that the smuggler was seen in the company of an unknown man from Hanoi earlier in the day, they knew another illegal crossing was probably in the cards.

He was an old man. He broke quickly under torture. But it was embarrassing, not to mention infuriating to know he had outwitted them with his dying breath when he gave them the wrong passphrase.

Chapter Forty-Three

WE CAN ONLY HOPE... AND PRAY

Hanoi, Vietnam

Day 15

Evan Mason was non-declared, meaning he was posing as an innocuous junior attaché of business and commerce working in the U.S. Embassy Hanoi located at No 7 Lang Ha Street, Ba Dinh District, while he was, in fact, a CIA spy. During his three years in Hanoi, he'd built up a vast network of informants, mostly Tuidang members. They were ethnic Chinese living in Vietnam who could easily travel to China to visit family or do business there. During this time, he had helped more than a few Chinese nationals to illegally cross the border from China into Vietnam.

He was expecting news from his messenger, who was the go-between him and the human smuggler in Dong Dang eighty-five miles away. But it wasn't as if he was biting his nails; it was only the first day. There were four more if it didn't pan out earlier this morning. The messenger would only get in touch if the smuggler had made the crossing with the refugees. It kept contact between them to the bare minimum. That's how they'd done it successfully five times in the past.

Mason didn't know much about the defectors. One of his informants, the owner of a scrapyard, Tan Hui, told him his contact, Gao Yong, said they were a family of three; husband, wife, and a four-year-old girl. The husband was apparently a senior programmer working for a cyber warfare division in the PRC military.

The information was third-hand, hearsay evidence, lawyers would call it in a courtroom, and the case would be dismissed. Spies called it information worth looking into and would attempt to verify it. When Mason heard the words 'cyber warfare division,' the first thought that entered his mind was Unit 61398. A defector from them would be a massive intelligence haul. But he had to keep his excitement in check until he met the man and debriefed him. It might all be a ruse.

By 8:00 a.m., he resigned himself to the fact that the crossing didn't happen that morning.

———

Shortly after Yong and the Suns were dropped off at the safehouse Yong and the homeowner were in the latter's car heading for Hanoi.

Tan barely had a chance to take his first sip of tea when Yong walked into his office, ashen-faced and disheveled.

"You look like hell. What's wrong?"

"I need you to get this back to your friend who gave it to

you." Yong handed him the USB stick. "It's critical that you get it to him immediately."

"I'll see to it."

An hour later, Mason read the report on the USB stick and cursed softly as he realized he might have a mole problem. One man was dead or captured because of the mole. For that unknown man's sake, he hoped that he was rather dead than captured. As for his man in Dong Dang, no news was all of a sudden, not good news.

But thank God the defectors were still alive. The report didn't only contain a recount of what had happened at the border earlier that morning, it also contained a brief summary of the importance of the information the defector held in his hands and confirmation that he was indeed a senior programmer at the notorious Unit 61398.

His dilemma was how to get the man and his family out of China while he had a mole who might ruin it all and get more people killed. Fifteen minutes later, he locked himself and the CIA Chief of Station (CoS), Henry Bell, in the embassy's SCIF (Sensitive Compartmented Information Facility). A SCIF was a secured room in which meetings of a secret nature could be conducted.

Tan Hui was their most likely suspect. The man certainly had the opportunity to read the USB drive and tell the Chinese border guards about the planned crossing. But another possible culprit would be the spies in Dong Dang who worked for the Chinese border guards and kept them informed about the activities of known and suspected human smugglers. Illegal border crossings were a big headache for both countries.

It didn't take Mason and Bell long to come up with a solution, at least to find out if Tan was the mole. It wasn't perfect, but it was better than putting the plan on a USB stick and handing it over to their primary suspect.

That night Yong and Tan had dinner at the same place as before, and Tan handed Yong a mobile phone. None of them noticed the man in the vehicle parked across the street taking pictures of them when they left the restaurant. It was Mason wanting to make sure he had a few pictures of Tan's contact, Gao Yong, in case he needed them.

Mong Cai was a city of a little over 100,000 inhabitants in the Quang Ninh Province in northern Vietnam on the border with China. It sat on the southern bank of the Beilun River across from Dongxing city in China's Guangxi Autonomous Region. Mong Cai was about two hundred miles from Hanoi, a little over five hour's drive. That's where Mason was heading. He had two contacts there who might be able to help him.

During the drive to Mong Cai, Mason had time to think about the mole again. This time there was no USB drive to peek at. The mobile phone he'd given Tan to give to Yong was, at first glance, a standard Samsung Galaxy 8 except for a few modifications not noticeable from the outside. It was set up to use a secured military-grade encrypted satellite connection instead of a cellphone tower. It had GPS tracking activated and a CIA bespoke chat app, Lingo, end-to-end secured with the most powerful encryption on the planet. It had only one contact in its address book, PILOT, Evan Mason's codename for the mission randomly assigned by a computer. When the phone was switched on, Mason would immediately receive a notification of the GPS coordinates of the phone. If those coordinates were in Hanoi, where Tan was located, Mason would know the phone was not delivered to its intended recipient, meaning Tan was the mole. If this was the case, Mason would immediately send a message to the phone that would launch a program that would wipe it clean and render it useless. If all went as he hoped and prayed it would, he expected the first GPS coordinates to be received by him later that night, maybe early the next morning. The time didn't matter as long as those coordinates were inside Chinese territory where the intended recipient was located.

It happened shortly after three in the morning. Mason's satellite phone alerted him that the phone had been activated. He sat up in his bed, wiped the sleep out of his eyes, and checked the coordinates, ten miles from the Friendship Pass border crossing inside Chinese territory. He let out a long breath of relief. Tan wasn't the mole. He got out of bed and made himself a big mug of coffee while he waited for a text message on Lingo from BUZZER, the defector's computer-generated mission codename.

Five stressful minutes passed before Mason's Lingo screen came to life.

BUZZER: Nice present.

PILOT: My pleasure.

BUZZER: What's the plan?

PILOT: Working on it. Can you move to Dongxing?

BUZZER: Two minutes.

Mason took a few sips of coffee.

BUZZER: Yes. This afternoon maybe evening.

Mason paused. They were about eighty miles from Dongxing city. Why would it take so long to get there? What he didn't know was that the truck that brought them to the safe house the day before had to be relieved of the tools and equipment it carried and loaded with containers of scrap metal to be shipped to Shanghai out of Dongxing harbor. Among the scrap metal, the Suns' hideaway had to be concealed. He decided not to ask. Besides, he still had to make the necessary arrangements.

PILOT: Excellent. Send a message when you're there.

BUZZER: Will do.

Yan severed the connection, switched the phone off, and put his arms around Ming. "Maybe things will work out this time."

"We can only hope... and pray."

Yan nodded, then turned to Yong and told him what PILOT wanted them to do.

In Mong Cai. Mason had another pressing matter that assured he kept the antacid tablets close by. Disputes over the terrestrial borders between China and Vietnam had been settled with the signing of a treaty in 1999. The maritime borders, however, were still undefined due to ownership disputes over the territorial waters and islands, including the Spratly and Paracel Islands.

It was this dispute which Mason wanted to use to his advantage as he'd done in the past. But, lately, he had been receiving reports that the PRC was getting more and more aggressive with their measures to protect the maritime borders they claimed to be theirs whether they were internationally recognized or not. According to some of the reports, their ships had even fired on foreign vessels on a few occasions.

Chapter Forty-Four

I'M NOT INTERESTED

Mong Cai, Vietnam

Day 16

Mason phoned his contact shortly after six that morning. He was an old man who owned a ramshackle fishing boat, which he and his son operated for commercial purposes and sometimes took out tourists wanting to do line fishing. Mason told the old man that he was in Mong Cai on holiday and wanted to go on a fishing trip that afternoon if possible. The old man hemmed and hawed about losing income but only until Mason offered him a fee, which was about twice as much as they would've earned on their best day fishing.

Mason had used the old man's service once, about a year ago, when a PLA air force colonel who was spying for the CIA was about to have his cover blown and had to get out quickly.

The boat had, unbeknown to both the old man and his son, drifted about a mile into Chinese territorial waters after developing 'engine trouble' while they were trying to fix the engine. The Chinese patrol boat arrived, boarded, and searched the boat but never found the colonel hidden in a coffin-sized space hidden below the floor of the engine compartment scattered with engine parts and tools.

The dinghy with the two-horsepower petrol engine attached astern raised no suspicions; it was used by the old fisherman's son to inspect the nets.

The officer gave them a tongue-lashing and an austere warning that the next time their boat will be confiscated, and they'll be taking their meals on the wrong side of a Chinese prison door for the next year or so.

It was a close shave then, and now Mason was going to ask them to do it again. He hoped that the fee he was going to offer them, enough to buy a new fishing boat and still have a lot of it to spare, would clinch the deal.

Three o'clock that afternoon, the old fisherman started the diesel engine of the boat and navigated carefully out of the berth. The old man's thirty-odd-year-old son busied himself with some of the nets that were in need of repair.

An hour later, the anchor was dropped. Fishing rods came out, and the old man came and sat next to Mason and got right to the point. "If you're here to ask me to go back over the line again, I'm not interested."

Mason retrieved a chewable antacid tablet from his shirt pocket and, while unwrapping it, said, "Oh." He popped the tablet into his mouth, chewed in silence for a while, then said, "By the way, I was going to offer you twenty thousand US dollars. But if you're not interested, then the price doesn't really matter, does it?"

The average monthly income in Vietnam was 4.2

million Vietnamese dong (VND), the equivalent of about $103 USD.

He didn't look at the old man but knew he was busy making calculations: a new boat, new gear, retirement funds... But the old man started shaking his head slowly. "The money you're offering is good. It will change our lives. The problem is it can't be done. The Chinese are fed up with people crossing their sea borders. They've doubled the number of patrol boats over the past year. And they've changed their policies, now they blow offending boats out of the water without warning, and they arrest and jail the survivors. No trials. I won't risk it."

Mason stared out over the water; his brain was working overtime. "Is there any way it could be done without detection?"

"Maybe with a submarine. If you're willing to take the risk of causing a war if you get caught."

Back onshore, Mason called Bell in Hanoi and relayed the conversation he had with the old fisherman. This was a job for a SEAL team. For that, they required approval from the highest authorities. Bell would take it up the chain of command and keep him posted.

At 7:00 p.m. on the dot, Mason got an alert that BUZZER's phone had come online. He checked the GPS coordinates; the phone was less than five miles from where he was on the north side of the Beilun River. *So close yet so far.*

BUZZER: In place. Waiting for instructions.

PILOT: Still working on it. It could take two to three

days. In the meantime, you must stay in hiding. Is this possible?

BUZZER: We have no choice. We're in your hands.

PILOT: I know it must be stressful. We're working as fast as we can. Everything is going to work out fine. I want you to check in every six hours from now. If anything changes on your side, let me know immediately.

BUZZER: Will do.

Chapter Forty-Five

JE LE VEUX

Langley, Virginia, USA

Day 17

It was 3:00 a.m. when Martin Richardson got the call to come into the office. For the past few days, he had been kept well-informed of the matter of the Chinese defector with the codename BUZZER, including the almost disastrous attempt to cross the border at Dong Dang and the decision to try again at Mong Cai.

In the secured meeting room at Langley, he listened to Henry Bell in Hanoi and Bell's superior in Langley, Nathan Parry, and studied the map of Vietnam. "I agree. It's a job for a SEAL team. And I know of such a team that happens to be close to Mong Cai if I can get the necessary authorization. It might spoil a good friend's wedding day, but I'm sure he'll forgive me."

Hạ Long Bay, Vietnam

At that exact moment, 4:00 a.m. in Langley, twelve time zones away at 4:00 p.m., in Ha Long Bay, Vietnam, onboard the *TOMATS*, Felix Mendelssohn's wedding march sounded. The audience rose to their feet. Lucien Laurent, the Prime Minister of France, entered the room with the beaming Christelle Proll, former deputy director of France's DGSE, on his arm. They were followed by Margot Lemaire, a deputy minister in his cabinet, and her four-year-old daughter, Rowena, carrying a basket of flower petals. Following them were Digger and Cupcake. In the front of the room stood an equally happy-looking John Brandt with Rex Dalton by his side. Beside them, a pace back, stood Declan Spencer, the wedding officiant.

Laurent kissed Christelle on both cheeks, leaned over to Brandt, and whispered, "Take good care of her, or I'll send some of my men to bring her back to France."

Brandt smiled. "Don't worry, she'll be treated like a queen." He shook the Prime Minister's hand and held out his arm for Christelle.

When the Prime Minister had taken his seat in the front row, Digger and Cupcake sat down and looked at the couple. They had what dog lovers would swear were smiles on their faces.

When Margot and her uncle Lucien Laurent had received the call from Christelle months ago, they had immediately arranged to pay an official visit to their former colony to coincide with the wedding.

Another notable among the guests was Yaron Aderet, the head of Mossad's largest department, Collections, tasked with all the many aspects of conducting espionage overseas for the state of Israel. He had traveled incognito to be at the wedding of one of his best friends, John Brandt. Aderet took Catia under his wings a few years before when her *katsa*, the Hebrew word for handler, suffered a stroke and had to go on early retirement. He took a quick liking to Catia and became a father figure to her.

Spencer conducted a beautiful ceremony. When John and Christelle took their vows, they did it in French style with the words, "*Je le veux*," which meant, "I want it." There was something about this expression of desire rather than the compliant-sounding 'I do' that felt poetic, romantic, and so quintessentially French, *non*?

After putting the rings on each other's fingers and the traditional, "You may kiss the bride," Spencer concluded, "A wedding is about three Cs—ceremony, commitment, and celebration. You've witnessed the ceremony and commitment; now let the celebrations begin."

When the toasts were made, Spencer and Laurent, in his French-accented English, regaled the guests with a few tales about the newlyweds that had them a little embarrassed at times and their guests roaring with laughter.

When John made his speech, he got his chance for a bit of revenge. "I'm sure you're all curious to know what Prime Minister Laurent whispered into my ear when he shook my hand before the ceremony. Well, he told me to take good care of Christelle, or he'll send some men over to take her back to France. I told him she'll be treated like a queen. When I said that, Mr. Prime Minister, I can assure you I definitely didn't have France's last queen, Marie Antoinette, in mind."

Three hours later, the party was still in full swing when Greg sat down in the empty chair next to Rex and said, "Would you mind if I ask you a confidential question?"

"Here or outside?"

"This is as good a place as any."

"I'm all ears."

Greg tried to explain what was on his mind, but maybe the four glasses of champagne and two glasses of wine he had, had something to do with him not being very structured in the description of the problem he was seeking Rex's advice for.

Rex had a good chuckle. "Well, if I understand you correctly, you want to ask Rehka to marry you. If that's the case, all I can say is it's bloody-well high time. As for my blessing, you have it. However, your problem is her dad. And with that, I can't help you much. You'll have to go to Bilaspur, India, and talk to my good friend, Gyan. I could put in a good word for you. But let me give you a tip; you better learn how to play *chaturanga*. The old coot is an accomplished player, and if you don't pose a good challenge, then forget it, he'll never agree to let you marry his daughter."

Chaturanga was the ancient game that historians believed was the predecessor of the game of kings–chess.

"Did you beat him?" Greg asked.

"Only the last two games of the twenty or so we played; he's very good. But, keep in mind, I never played for Rehka's hand in marriage. He could've felt sorry for me."

"Damn. I don't even play chess."

"All I can do is teach you what I know. But be warned, it's going to be brutal. Rehka is his youngest child and the apple of his eye."

Before Greg could respond, Rex's satellite phone buzzed

with a text message. He looked at the screen; it was Martin Richardson.

Two minutes later, he was in the comms room talking to Richardson on the secured video link.

Fortunately, most everyone on the *TOMATS* had first-hand experience in covert operations and their lousy sense of timing.

Half an hour after the call had ended, the party was over. Lucien Laurent, Margot Lemaire, and Rowena left the yacht in the company of their protection detail. Aderet left in the company of John and Christelle after Brandt tried to argue. "CRC has never conducted an operation without me."

"There's a first time for everything," Rex said. "I'm CEO until your honeymoon is over. You're ordered to leave the yacht with your lovely wife and have a great honeymoon."

Five minutes later, Spencer set course for Mong Cai, seventy nautical miles away. It would take them the best part of five hours to reach their destination.

Chapter Forty-Six

A MOVIE, OF COURSE

En route to Mong Cai, Vietnam

Day 18

As soon as they were en route, the planning started. In the meeting were: from Langley, Martin Richardson and Nathan Parry; from Hanoi, Henry Bell; from Mong Cai, Evan Mason; and from the *TOMATS*, Rex, Catia, Josh, Marissa, Greg, Spencer. Of course, Digger, who never missed a meeting, was already fast asleep in the corner.

On their big screens were maps of the land area around Donxing and Mong Cai, as well as seabed and satellite images, which they studied carefully.

From the outset, it was clear they'd need more human reconnaissance. On the Mong Cai side, that would not be a major problem; Mason and the CRC agents could take care of it. On the Dongxing side, it would be in the hands of

Gao Yong and Tuidang members if he knew any that he could trust.

Broadly speaking, the plan was uncomplicated. Bring the *TOMATS* as close as possible to a rendezvous point while staying well within Vietnamese territorial waters. Launch Nemo and go to the rendezvous point to pick up BUZZER and his family. But the devil was in the details, in particular how to get BUZZER and family to the rendezvous point over a stretch of open water crawling with Chinese patrol boats.

Getting Nemo in place unnoticed wasn't going to be much of a challenge. She was small, silent, and stealthy. US Naval command assured them there were no Chinese subs within 200 miles of their location and the closest warship, more than 400 miles away.

One thing working in their favor was that the Chinese media had stopped talking about the fugitives more than a week ago. It was probably too much of an embarrassment for the government to admit that the traitors had escaped. If they captured or killed them, they would not have passed on the opportunity to splash it all over the news to serve as a warning for anyone else wanting to betray their country.

Mason would meet with the CRC agents in Mong Cai and do the necessary reconnaissance on the Vietnam side. He'd also undertake another fishing trip with his fisherman friend; the man was a fountain of information about the harbor and surrounding areas.

Catia had one concern; how is the little girl going to handle the claustrophobic space in Nemo on top of what must have been a terrible ordeal for the four-year-old the past two weeks.

The *TOMATS* arrived in Mong Cai harbor shortly after 1:00 a.m.

Mong Cai, Vietnam

Day 21

Four days later, it was a perfect day, a cloudless sky and steaming-hot; ideal for time on the beach with family and friends. For the residents of Dongxing, China, there was no better place to spend a day like this than on the famous golden beach of Jingdao Island, about fifteen miles out of the city.

It was 10:00 a.m. when three families, an old couple with what could have been their adult children and three grandchildren ranging in age from three to five, arrived at the beach, which was rapidly becoming crowded by people wanting to have a day of fun and relaxation.

They parked their van and made their way to the beach with their picnic bags and fishing rods. At the water's edge, they took their shoes off and waded into the water carrying the younger children on their shoulders, heading to one of the many small boats bobbing in the shallow surf about fifty yards offshore. The one they were aiming for had a maroon-colored canvas canopy. The group was in high spirits splashing each other with water, laughing, and joking, which made the children squeal with laughter at the adults' antics.

When they reached the boat, the owner helped them aboard, stowed their bags, and issued them with lifejackets. When all passengers were in their seats and had donned their lifejackets, the owner started the two outboard engines and headed out to sea.

Two miles away, on the *TOMATS*, about three-quarters of a mile from the border on the Vietnamese side, Mason got a text message on Lingo.

BUZZER: On our way. All good so far.

Initially, Rex's idea of launching the operation in broad daylight was met with a lot of resistance. However, as he laid out his plan, he finally won them over. And so far, Rex's plan was working like Swiss clockwork. But there was still a lot that had to happen before they could high-five.

The boat with the three families had reached a spot about half a mile away from the border where it dropped anchor. A few minutes later, the fishing rods came out.

Less than half an hour later, one of the women shouted, "Look! That boat is going to run over the border!"

About eight hundred yards away, coming from the Vietnamese side, was a ramshackle old fishing boat heading at full speed toward the border to which it was less than fifty yards away. The next moment two Chinese patrol boats appeared with blaring sirens and someone on a loudhailer shouting a warning at the approaching vessel to stop and turn around.

It didn't.

Everyone from the beaches and on other boats in the area was watching the drama unfold before their eyes. The fishing boat never slowed down. When it crossed the line, one of the patrol boats issued a final warning. The fishing boat steamed ahead. The next moment, both patrol boats opened fire. The large-caliber bullets, every fifth one an incendiary bullet, ripped the dilapidated old boat into pieces and set it ablaze. Within minutes the boat started to sink slowly.

The patrol boats slowly circled the burning wreck

looking for survivors. There were none. What they didn't know was that there was no one on the boat when it crossed the border into China. The patrol boats stayed until all the pieces had disappeared below the water before they turned away.

In the commotion, no one saw the little dinghy with a two-horsepower engine carrying two men on the Vietnamese side of the border, about two miles away from where their fishing boat had gone down. The dinghy was heading for the Vietnamese shore. By the time the fishing boat reached its final resting place at the bottom of the sea, the two men in the dinghy were on land.

And so also did no one notice the three picnic makers on the Chinese side of the border slipping over the side of their boat to disappear one by one into the hatch of the Nemo protruding above the waterline right next to their boat.

BUZZER was the last of his family to go down the hatch. Rex closed it, and the Nemo submerged.

It was an honor to finally meet the brave family that managed to frustrate and embarrass the entire PRC law enforcement apparatus for more than two weeks. It was an emotional moment for the Suns. The four battle-hardened operators of the submarine who had been through hell and back on more than just a few occasions in their lives were deeply moved by the tears streaming down Yan's and Ming's faces. Lei was clinging to her mother, eyes wide shot. Rex and Josh quickly strapped Yan and Ming into their seats, but Lei refused to let go of her mother.

Rex looked at Digger. He sidled up to the little girl and smiled. She gave him one look and said something in Mandarin that Rex didn't catch, but clearly, Digger did. He moved a bit closer and nuzzled her feet. She smiled, let go of her mother, hesitatingly reached out, and started stroking Digger's head gently. Soon after, she told her mother she wanted to sit in her own seat, next to Digger. Catia was right; Digger, she'd insisted, had to be part of the rescue team for this very reason.

The first words Yan said when he was able to speak was a question addressed to Rex in English. "Are you a Christian?"

"Yes, I am."

"Will you tell me everything about your God?"

Rex was not so much surprised as he was curious. People in life-threatening situations often made what soldiers called foxhole promises. But he had the feeling that there was more to it than a promise made in angst. "I'll try my best."

Later, when Yan brought the topic up again, Rex learned that his gut feeling was correct; there *was* a story behind the question—sad, gripping, and deeply inspiring.

The Nemo was hoisted into its berth on the *TOMATS* fifteen minutes later. Thanks to Rex's team, the Suns had made it out of China. Ming's English was halting, and Lei spoke only Mandarin. Out of everyone on the *TOMATS*, only Rex and Catia knew enough Mandarin to converse with the Sun family in their mother tongue. Lei and Digger were inseparable and required no translator; Digger was fluent in all languages known to mankind.

Shortly after the Suns were on board, the *TOMATS* raised anchor and headed back to its berth in the marina at Mong Cai. Mason had a quick errand to run, the final installment of the old fisherman's fee. Ten thousand had already changed hands the day before.

The old man was smiling when Mason handed him the money. He and his son counted it, $15,000 USD. "I'm sure we agreed on twenty," said the old man.

"Ah, sorry, I forgot to mention there would be a five thousand performance bonus if all went well."

The old man smiled. "Thank you very much. I guess it's no use asking you what it is that went so well that I've earned a bonus?"

Mason obviously couldn't share the details of their rescue mission with the old fisherman in which his boat was used as a distraction. He kept a straight face, "It's the camera crew. They were extremely pleased with your performance."

"A camera crew? Do you mean for a movie?"

"Yep. Why? What did you think this was about?"

The old man chuckled. "A movie, of course. You sank my boat for a movie. Have a good day, my friend. Let me know when you want to film the sequel. The movie industry, it seems, pays much better than the fishing industry."

Mason was back on the *TOMATS* an hour later. There was no way he was going to miss BUZZER'S debriefing. Spencer plotted a course for Ha Long Bay but never thought that he'd have to change course soon. Not that it would be a problem; like any good captain, Spencer stocked and fueled the *TOMATS* at every opportunity he got, such as the three days in Mong Cai. They could travel more than 6,000 nautical miles before they had to refuel and replenish.

Late afternoon, the sun almost down, the boat with the

maroon canvas canopy arrived back at the golden beach of Jingdao Island. Their picnic bags were empty, but they were going to have fresh fish for dinner that night. In the semi-darkness, no one at the beach noticed that three fewer people got off the boat than got on in the morning.

Chapter Forty-Seven

72 HOURS

En route to Hạ Long Bay, Vietnam

Day 21 to 23

Mason was as eager as everyone else to hear Sun Yan. Even though they still had to establish the man's bona fides, which could take months as they verified every bit of information he provided to them, it was not going to be an interrogation, rather a friendly questioning.

Spencer and Simona showed Yan and Ming their room. Lei was in the company of Digger, Catia, and Marissa getting the royal tour of the yacht.

In the lounge, while indulging in some refreshments, Rex suggested the Suns get a few hours rest before meeting to talk about the information Yan brought with him.

But Yan shook his head. "Believe me, what I have, you want to get in front of your president without delay."

Catia, Marissa, and Simona invited Ming to join them

on the upper deck, where they could relax on the reclining chairs. Rex, Mason, Greg, and Yan entered the comms room. Digger indicated they'd have to run this one without him—he didn't even look at the door. His new friend still needed his attention.

Martin Richardson, Nathan Parry, and Henry Bell were patched in via secured video links.

Yan started with a brief overview of how the USB drive got into his hands, the killing of his mother, the help he got from Gao Rong and his son Yong.

No one interrupted.

Then he opened his laptop plugged the USB stick in, opened the executive summary of Operation Middle Kingdom, and started translating.

He wasn't joking when he said that they'd want to get this information in front of the President of the United States as soon as possible, if not sooner. But they knew better than to let Yan know what was going through their minds.

When Yan finished the summary, Richardson feigned mild disinterest. "Certainly sounds ominous, on the face of it. Of course, we'll have to verify it before we can present it to our president."

Yan nodded. "The rest of the document is more than a thousand pages. I've read all of it." He unplugged the USB stick and handed it to Rex. "Your translators should be able to produce a machine translation in less than an hour. In the meantime, I can tell you about my work in Unit 61398."

That surprised everyone. Information was this man's bargaining chip, but he had just handed it all to them, and he hadn't uttered a single word about what he wanted in return.

Richardson wanted clarity. "That sounds good. But

before we continue, I think it would be good if we under-stood what your terms are?"

"Terms?"

"Yes, what do you want in exchange for the information?"

"Ah, I see. There's nothing to exchange. The information is yours. You're the only country in the world that can stop this, and I want to help you do it. Although I'd be lying if I didn't tell you that my wife and I would very much like it if you'd allow us to live in your country from now on. However, that's not a condition; it's only a request."

Richardson nodded. "It's not within my power to grant your request, Yan. But I will consider backing it depending on the significance and veracity of your information."

"I understand. I have no doubt about the significance or veracity." For the next hour, Yan gave them an overview of Unit 61398's structure and activities, including high-level details of projects he had worked on and had knowledge of.

Greg interrupted a few times to ask technical questions.

Rex knew Greg well enough to notice that CRC's lead IT specialist, himself among the world's foremost hackers, was gobsmacked.

For years, the PRC's massive cyberwar activities had been the topic of many whitepapers, briefings, and warnings from the US and western intelligence communities, yet, what Yan told them scared them. The only glimmer of hope was Yan's in-depth knowledge of the PRC's computer networks and his equally intimate knowledge about most of the security holes in the US's networks. And his willingness to share it all with the US intelligence community and work with them to plug the holes on the US side while exploiting the holes on the PRC side.

That should get you residence in the US as far as I'm concerned,

Richardson thought just when he got a message that the machine-translated English version of Operation MK was ready.

It would take days to read through it, weeks to study it. But it took them less than an hour of skim-reading to know if only a fraction of this information were true, war with the PRC was a foregone conclusion—a real shooting war, nukes and all.

Richardson adjourned the meeting. He had very urgent calls to make.

Less than an hour later, Spencer plotted a new course that would bring them to within helicopter range of the aircraft carrier USS Ronald Reagan on maneuvers around the Spratly Islands archipelago in the South China Sea 788 nautical miles away.

It was time for everyone to get some sleep.

The next morning the Daltons, Farleys, and Suns were together for breakfast. Lei showed no signs of distress. She was talking non-stop to Digger, who seemed to be regaled by the little girl's stories, which, according to Ming, were what she'd heard from her grandmother. She was still unaware that her grandmother had passed away. It was something that Ming and Yan would have to tell her later when things settled down.

Yan was not long in waiting to remind Rex of his promise the previous day. "I understand there are a lot of things that we'll have to talk about in the days and weeks to come, but would you mind if we talk about the God of the Christians now?"

"Not at all," said Rex. "But I want you to know I'm no

theologian. I can tell you what I believe, and when we get to the US, I will arrange for a clergyman to talk to you."

Yan nodded. "Understood. Ming and I have always believed in the existence of a deity, and more so after our experiences of the last few weeks, but there are so many, it's utterly confusing. Or are they all the same god but known by a different name to different people?"

"I personally don't believe so," said Rex. "The contradictions between religions are too big. My logic dictates that there can't be as many truths as there are religions. In the end, I think only one can be correct. Nevertheless, that's a question that many people have been asking themselves since time immemorial. The thing is, most religions are not very tolerant of other religions. They believe their god or gods, some have more than one, is the only true deity, and everyone else's god or gods are just figments of their imagination. I probably don't have to tell you that people have gone to war, killed millions, and committed the worst possible atrocities in the name of their gods. And that includes Christianity and Islam."

"My mother was a Christian," said Yan. "She had a hard life and very little education, but there's one thing about her that I'll never forget as long as I live; her absolute conviction in the existence of her God. She believed like a child that God and His Son, Jesus, are real and that Jesus died for our sins, and if you believe that, when you die, you go to heaven where you will be with God for eternity. Is that how it works?"

"That's exactly what I believe. You see, among the religions of the world, there is a common theme. They believe that God created everything, including humans. After creation, everyone was in a place and state of peace, tranquility, and happiness and in the presence of God. That place is known by different names, i.e., Paradise, Nirvana, Utopia, Eden, Jannah, and many others. We did something wrong while we were there and got kicked out. And ever since, humanity has been on a quest to get back into that place. But the problem is every religion has a different set of rules as to how we're supposed to get back into paradise.

"All religions, except Christianity, believe that the only way to get back into paradise is through your own efforts. In other words, you have to live a good life and do good deeds, and at the end of your life, you'll be called upon to give an account of what you've done to deserve eternity in paradise. In other words, if your good deeds outweigh the bad ones, you'll gain entry."

"So, what do Christians believe then?"

"We believe that we're saved by the mercy of God, not through our own efforts but because of what we believe. Just like your mother did—God and Jesus are real, that Jesus was crucified for our sins, which means that He was willing to carry the punishment for the sins we committed. Therefore, there's nothing else we have to do to earn a place in paradise. The apostle Paul, one of the most influential authors of the Bible, put it like this: *'It is by grace you have been saved, through faith—and this is not from yourselves, it is the gift of God—not by works, so that no one can boast.'* This means that my salvation doesn't depend on if I have done enough good deeds but on accepting that Jesus died in my place. To be reconciled to God then, I have to confess and acknowledge that I have sinned and then ask God to forgive me my sins because Jesus already paid the penalty for my sins."

Yan was deep in thought. "As simple as that?" he said after a long while.

Rex nodded. "Yes, that's the essence of Christianity. But let me warn you, it's not as if all Christians agree on what it means to have faith. On that topic, there exist thousands of books and as many opinions, hence the many denominations of Christianity. The thing is, it's not easy to agree on what it means to believe in something that you can't experience with your five senses. Paul described it thus; *'Faith is the assurance of things hoped for, the conviction of things not seen.'*"

Yan nodded, deep in thought again.

Catia broke the contemplative silence. "Yan, I get the impression you had some kind of divine experience. Would you mind telling us?"

Yan told them about that day in the park in Beijing, seventeen days ago, when he realized that he had to leave China and came to a conclusion that, humanly speaking, it was all but impossible. How he had prayed to the God of his mother and how, since then, everything had worked out the way it did. The notion that everything could be ascribed to good luck and coincidence just didn't make any sense. As far as he was concerned, there was only one sensible explanation; the God of his mother must've heard his prayers and helped them. Therefore, he and Ming had the desire to know this God.

Rex said, "Many years ago, when struggling with the same questions you have, I read the Gospel of Mark in the Bible, and it put a lot of things in perspective for me."

Thirty-six hours after boarding the *TOMATS*, the Daltons, Farleys, and Suns, as well as Greg and Rehka, were airlifted from the yacht by a helicopter and transported to USS Ronald Reagan. From there, they were flown to Manila, Philippines, and put on a CIA private jet, which brought them to Washington D.C.

A little over seventy-two hours after Rex had closed the hatch of the Nemo behind Yan, the group stepped off the CIA jet inside the secured CIA hanger at Andrews Air Force Base in D.C. Richardson and Nathan Parry were the only people there to meet them. The Suns went with them in a white SUV with tinted windows to a secret location outside Langley. The rest of them caught a taxi to their hotel. Richardson had a meeting scheduled for the next morning at 9:00 a.m. with the DCI, and he wanted Rex to be present.

Chapter Forty-Eight

A STRATEGY OF CONTAINMENT

Langley, Virginia, USA

Day 24

Although they had no way of establishing the authenticity of the MK Plan immediately, Richardson and Parry had agreed that it should be treated as true until proven otherwise. They also agreed that, for now, the existence of the document and how it came into their hands was top secret, to be shared with only a very small group of people, i.e., the DCI, POTUS, and the DNI.

At 9:00 a.m., Rex was in the director's office at Langley with Martin Richardson and Nathan Parry also in attendance. Catia and Digger, accompanied by the Farleys, Greg, and Rehka, had the day to themselves to explore D.C. The Sun family was at the safehouse under the guard of CIA agents.

The position of CIA Director had been for many years,

and still was, a political appointment by the president. Director Howard Lawrence came from old money, born and raised in Boston, a Yale graduate with a baccalaureate in ancient history, spoke three languages besides English. And his family contributed generously to the presidential campaigns of their party. Before being appointed as Director of the CIA, he had held ambassadorial positions in Italy, France, Israel, and the UK. In short, Howard Lawrence was not a spook.

Martin Richardson was. He was 61. He was recruited by the CIA out of the United States Army Special Forces, colloquially known as the 'Green Berets', in 1986 at the age of 28, five years before the official end of the Cold War in 1991. During his tenure, he had seen the Soviet Union go down, the rise of Islamic radicalism, and the rapidly emerging threat from the People's Republic of China.

Richardson and Lawrence had a good working relationship. One of Lawrence's many good traits was his understanding of his strengths and weaknesses. Right from the outset, he made it clear to his deputy directors that he was the PR person of the CIA and expected them to do the spy stuff. Of course, he wanted to know what was going on in his department, but he always deferred to his deputy directors to lead the way when it came to operational matters.

"I had a meeting with the president and Tia Chapman, the DNI, last night," Lawrence started. "As you can imagine, I ruined their day. Nevertheless, they're in agreement we need to treat this document as true and keep everything about it limited to a select group for now. We've decided to include in this group that needs to know Douglas Cole, the Director of the FBI, General Sheldon Morgan, Chairman of the Joint Chiefs of Staff, and General Caiden McKnight, the commander of Cyber Command. The president wants to meet with us at twelve, that's Martin, Rex, and me. He's expecting us to have a high-level plan of action ready by then. So, over to you, Martin."

Richardson started. "I don't have to tell you in our line of work trust is a scarce commodity. Nevertheless, some-times we *have* to trust someone. So the first question we have to answer is, can we trust Sun Yan?"

Parry said, "So far, I've seen nothing that says we shouldn't. But then, spies are trained deceivers. My verdict is trust but verify."

Rex nodded. "Yep. And I suggest that it would be wise not to wait until we have verification to start preparations."

Lawrence nodded.

"Agreed," said Richardson. "The PRC's expansionist ideals and desire to bring the CCP's brand of communism to the rest of the world is no secret. But, presuming the Operation MK document is authentic, this would be the first time we have their playbook in our hands. And we have to act on it, now. I just wish there was a way we could quickly validate this stuff."

"I have two ideas about that," said Rex, "but let's put it aside for a moment and accept the information is real; let's talk about what we want to do with it."

Richardson leaned back in his chair. "Nathan and I've been thinking about that nonstop since before you took the Sun family onboard the *TOMATS*. The family's identity has to be protected at all costs. No one else can know they're in the US or even that they've escaped from China. We have to devise a plan to make them untraceable and unidentifiable. And we have to think of how Yan can work with us without anyone knowing about it.

"We have to do it like the Allies did in World War Two with the Enigma Machine; no one must know we have it, especially the PRC. Compartmentalization and need-to-know. In the CIA, only four people know about the Suns and the document: Howard, Nathan, Evan Mason, and me. Add to that the president and Tia Chapman and soon Douglas Cole as well as Generals Morgan and McKnight. On CRC's side, it's Rex, Josh, and Greg, and your wives if you've told them. The SEALs who participated in the operation know nothing about the document, they only know that they helped a family defecting from China and nothing else, and they'll never talk about it. The Tuidang members who helped the Suns know a bit more, but unless they're tortured, won't talk about it either. In other words, there are already way too many people that know."

"Well, we can't unring those bells," said Rex. "What are your thoughts about preventing Armageddon?"

"We recommend a strategy of containment."

"Like the Cold War?"

"Yep, like the Cold War. Undeclared and brutal as it was, it kept us from annihilating each other with nuclear weapons. No one wants to have a war with the PRC, but this document makes it very clear we're going to have one whether we want it or not. And like my beer, I prefer it cold."

"So do I," said Lawrence, as Rex and Parry joined in.

"Having said that," Richardson continued, "I have to point out that we don't have many people that know how to fight a cold war in our employ anymore. They're either dead or sent on early retirement when the Berlin Wall came down, deemed to be too old to adapt to the challenges of the post-Soviet era. The era of terrorists and religious fanatics. Computers and mobile phones replaced onetime pads, invisible ink, dead letterboxes, and brush-passes—the spy-dictionary now incorporates new words such as e-spying, cyberwarfare, cybersecurity, and cyberattacks. Computer whizkids replaced field agents, and job opportunities for hackers and cybercriminals abound.

"Since nine-eleven, we've spent trillions on building the biggest intelligence enterprise in human history. Eighteen years later, we've created the most cumbrous, most replicated, and possibly most ineffective intelligence apparatus in the world. We generate millions of pages of information every year. We don't have enough people to read them. Out of what we read, we generate more than fifty thousand top-secret reports annually. Only ten percent are read; the rest are simply filed."

"So, may I infer from that you and Nathan have a plan to circumvent this quagmire?" Rex asked.

Richardson laughed. "Yes, you may. We have in mind a small group of experienced Cold War warriors supported by a team of IT aces and a special team of spooks and special operators."

"Bring some of the old guard back... hmm, I like that," said Rex.

"Yep. Starting with John Brandt."

Rex chuckled. "I'd like to be a fly on the wall during *that* conversation. Fair warning though, the Old Man is not amused that you spoiled his wedding."

"Yeah, so I've been told. But apparently, that didn't piss him off half as much as when you ordered him off the yacht."

"Who told you... ah, Spencer, of course."

"Spies never reveal their sources," Richardson chuckled. "Let's hear your ideas about quick fact-checking."

"Okay. Here's what I think," said Rex. "Yan's technical information. We put him in a room with Greg Wade and let him show Greg everything that he claims he knows."

"That can work," said Richardson.

"Agreed," said Lawrence and Parry in chorus.

"Okay, what about the MK document?"

"I haven't read the whole document yet, but I've noticed that there are speeches that their president will be delivering, which will be preceding their various adventures. And we know the exact words the president is going to say, and if his speech is followed by the actions described in the plan, we have our confirmation."

"Agreed," said Richardson. "But, if this whole thing is a ploy, it could be how they set us up to walk into a trap."

"Yes, it could be," said Rex. "However, I've got a gut feeling that this document is real."

"Care to explain?" Lawrence said.

"On the way over from Manila, Josh and I had a long conversation with Yan about how he got the USB drive in his possession. Yan's mother, Jia, was the cleaner of General Lang's offices. It seems that she'd been taking candy out of the bowl on the general's desk every night, which she gave to her granddaughter when she visited. She was illiterate therefore didn't know one of the 'candies' was, in fact, a memory stick.

"I've got no theories about how it ended up in the candy bowl, but I believe Yan when he says that's where she found it. Be that as it may, the interesting part is what the Chinese media reported. According to them, Yan broke into Lang's office and stole a top-secret document. And then, when his mother threatened to report him, he killed her.

"But I think what really happened was when Lang discovered the stick was missing, he realized he was in serious trouble. He couldn't let anyone know he had lost what could very well be the most secret and most important document in the PRC's history. Therefore, to cover his ass, he fed the bogus story to the media. To them, he didn't have to explain what was in the top-secret document. However, to his coconspirators, the marshals, President Liao Qigang, Tao Huan, and the mysterious Zhì Zhě, he would've had to at least give an idea of what was in the 'missing' document. And that's my theory; he didn't tell his buddies it was the MK plan."

Parry said, "That could very well be so. I'd imagine if they knew what Lang had actually lost, he would've been disappeared—"

"Or, they know," Richardson said, "and the document we have has become outdated, and they're now using it to misdirect us. But only time will tell if that's the case."

"Well, if my theory is correct, the conspirators have a weak link in their ranks," said Rex.

"Lang, you mean?"

"Yes."

"Agreed. And I happen to know of a few more," said Richardson. "Weak links, that is."

"I'm listening."

"My source is General Yuan Lee. The guy you sprung out of Shanghai last year. He told us Generals Dai Min and Wan Huang were the marshals involved in his defection, which ultimately led to the ousting of Li Lingxin. Yuan says they blackmailed him. And I'm speculating, just like you did with Lang, that they've forgotten to tell their buddies how they collaborated with the CIA to get Yuan out of the country. If they did, I would've expected Ren Shi to have some knowledge of it. He would've consulted with the two generals as part of his investigation of how Yuan escaped. He didn't. He'd never met them."

Lawrence said, "I can already see your old guards' toes curling when they hear about all of those recruitment prospects. But on the topic of the thirteen conspirators and weak links, who is Zhì Zhě? He's not a marshal, but by the looks of it, he played a significant role in creating this plan."

"I don't think that's his real name," said Rex. "Zhì Zhě is Mandarin for wise man. I think that's a pseudonym, and that's what makes *me* very curious to know who he really is."

Richardson smiled. He must have been thinking how Rex and his team, with the help of Digger, tracked down a man with the pseudonym Dragut a few months ago.

They spent another two hours discussing the setup and launching of Operation Peregrine, named after the powerful peregrine falcon found on most continents, renowned for its speed, reaching over two-hundred miles per hour during its characteristic hunting stoops—the fastest bird in the world.

The spy business was nothing without codes and codenames. Sun Yan was assigned the codename Flat Arrow, and General Lang Jianhong, the codename Deep Mantis. Each of the remaining twelve members of the Operation MK cabal would receive their codenames in due course.

Chapter Forty-Nine

THE SECOND COLD WAR

Oval Office, Washington, D.C., USA

Day 24

Lawrence, Richardson, and Rex were in the waiting room outside the Oval Office fifteen minutes early. FBI director Douglas Cole and Generals Morgan and McKnight arrived a few minutes later, followed by DNI Chapman a minute or so after them. Lawrence introduced Rex to the newcomers as they arrived. It was going to be Rex's second face-to-face with POTUS. The last time they met was about nine months ago when Rex and his team had smuggled General Yuan Lee out of China to the US.

It was a few minutes past 12:00 p.m. when they were shown into the Oval Office.

Morgan, McKnight, and Cole had not been briefed about the intelligence haul from China as yet. Richardson took fifteen minutes to tell them.

Lawrence laid out the high-level strategy discussed earlier at Langley and the recommendation to initiate Operation Peregrine.

Chapman was one of the president's most trusted advisors. She spoke first. "Mr. President, it's no secret, the PRC has been building out its military for the past few decades. They have the most rapidly growing and biggest standing military force in the world. And they're planning to double their stockpile of nuclear warheads in the next ten years, including those designed for ballistic missiles that can reach the US. The only reason they're building their military is to use it to achieve their goal of world domination—the hundred-year plan. If they continue on this path at the current rate, they will replace us as the world's superpower within the next decade. However, now that we have their actual plan in our hands, we might be in a position to stem the tide."

"That's if we can be sure this MK plan is the real thing," said the president. "What can be done to get it vetted as quickly as possible?"

Richardson explained what they had in mind.

"And you think you can trust this Flat Arrow?" The president asked. It was standard operating procedures in the intelligence community not to divulge the real names of assets, and the president understood that very well.

"Mr. President, our approach, for now, is to trust but verify. It will take time to ascertain the authenticity of the document. However, as for his cyberwarfare knowledge, we're planning to put him through the wringer over the course of the next few days and should get a good idea of his trustworthiness."

"Good. Keep us posted on that. I'm interested in the PRC's cyberwarfare capabilities and how we stack up against them. Caidan, I'm aware the PRC is stealing us blind. Ripping our data and intellectual property out of our computers. At times I get the impression we're unable to stop them."

General Caiden McKnight was in command of one of the eleven unified combatant commands of the United States' Department of Defense, responsible for the direction of cyberspace operations, cyberspace capabilities, and cyber expertise.

"Mr. President, there are not many people who could wrap their heads around the scale of China's espionage program. There're not tens of thousands involved; it's hundreds of thousands. Every single day, they're penetrating or attempting to penetrate the computer networks and databases of our private enterprises, government, financial, law enforcement, and military institutions to steal our intel and technology. And they're succeeding. They're doing the same to our allies. The FBI opens a new case against China every ten hours. There is no doubt, Mr. President; China poses a greater national security threat to us than any other nation.

"To answer your question, Mr. President, yes, we can stop them. We're thwarting most of their efforts every day. But the sheer volume of attacks against our IT infrastructure is mindboggling and overwhelming at times. They're launching ever-increasing numbers of cyberattacks against us twenty-four-seven, and sometimes they get through our defenses. Sad as it might be, I have to admit, sir, they're getting the better of us. In other words, no, we can't stop them every time they attack us, and it's getting worse. The PRC's cyber force should be a major worry for us—"

"How did it come to this? I mean, how come we are the

world's technology leaders, but the Chinese can hold us at ransom with their technological capabilities?"

"Sir, since the advent of the internet, the PRC has invested heavily in its cyber force, and they're pouring ever-increasing amounts of time and money into it. For decades they've been studying the internet, looking for vulnerabilities and how to exploit the vulnerabilities in any future conflict with the West.

"In the West, including America, computer science education programs are as good as or better than they are elsewhere. Thousands of well-qualified students graduate every year, but many of them find it hard to get a job, especially when the economy is down. So, many of them end up working in the underworld of cybercrime.

"In China, on the contrary, when computer science students graduate, they have jobs waiting for them in the Ministry of State Security's cyber directorate, or cyberwarfare divisions, or telecommunications, or other government-controlled organizations.

"Thus, over the years, China has become the world leader in everything computer-related, including becoming the world's foremost hackers and software pirates. They also participate in cybercrime, big time. The difference is they're employed by their government to do it. They have government-controlled divisions dedicated to stealing IP, hacking into government networks and private companies' networks, banks, insurance companies, hospitals, police, military, you name it, they collect data on it or copy it and reverse engineer it."

"Are they better than the Russian and old Eastern Bloc cybercriminals we hear so much about?"

"Let me put it this way, sir. Russian cybercriminals will steal your credit card number and empty your bank account; Chinese hackers will shut down the power grid, send warships off course, and make bombers and fighter jets crash into mountainsides. They have botnets consisting of millions of unsuspecting computer owners across the world. The computing power they have is mind-bending. They have server farms spread out across the world, all networked to their main secret hub in China.

"They're planting trojan horses, spyware, e-spies, and viruses in systems and leaving doorways open in networks to access them at a time of their choosing. They're building spyware into the microchips of computers and cellphones and electronic devices that they're manufacturing for their foreign clients. Their clients, and that includes us, are now discovering that competitively priced, the euphemism for cheap, manufactured electronic devices in Chinese factories had a hidden cost all along.

"I can carry on; they're able to penetrate an enemy's power stations, electric grid, and a city's traffic lights. They can take control of satellites and communications systems. They can even switch off the pacemakers and insulin pumps of those that are connected to the IoT, The Internet of Things. IoT is the latest development in the technology space where people have everything in their lives connected to the internet, from their fridges to their sound systems and their medical devices."

The president's face had drained of its color. "Caiden, please tell me we're able to stop them."

"Yes, sir, we are. But it will take time and effort to level the playing field. And we're already on the back foot as it is. If Flat Arrow is indeed a senior employee of Unit 61398, his knowledge would indeed be of immense value to us."

"We could justifiably blame previous administration's lack of action for the current state of affairs, but that's no excuse for the lack of action by this administration," said the president. "It's clear we have to take drastic action. The way I see it, we have to tighten up our cyber defenses, and, at the same time, we have to go on the offensive."

Everyone agreed.

"Sheldon, how prepared are we to go to war with the PRC? And I haste to say, may God forbid it ever comes to that."

General Sheldon Morgan cleared his throat. "Mr. President, in the event of a conventional war without nuclear weapons, the losses on both sides will be of biblical proportions. If we were to bring nuclear weapons into the equation, we're looking at the end of days, Armageddon.

"Nonetheless, military experts here at home and abroad all agree that the US will survive such a conflict. I say survive, not win, because, in such a war, there will be no winners, only survivors. In order to draw their conclusions, military experts analyze and model factors such as how close such a hypothetical conflict will be to mainland China. The further away from the mainland, the less China's chances of success.

"Analyzing the capabilities of our respective land, sea, air, and space warfare capabilities, using nine categories such as air superiority, airspace penetration, anti-surface warfare, cyberwar, etcetera, in a war on the Chinese mainland, the US holds the upper hand in only three of the nine categories. In four of the categories, we are at parity with them, and in two, the Chinese will reign supreme.

"When the war is modeled to take place away from the Chinese mainland, we will hold a major advantage in two categories, a slight advantage in three more, and parity in the remaining four. In the cyberwar category, according to the analysts, we only hold a slight advantage over them, irrespective of where the war takes place. Having said that, please note that the analysis is almost three years old. We've grown in that time, but they've grown more than us.

"The bottom line is, Mr. President, at the moment, we're still in the superior position, but we're rapidly losing ground. Ten years ago, we held major advantages in almost all of the categories, whether the war took place on the mainland of China or not.

"In conclusion, Mr. President, you'll recall that we had a similar conversation during the virus threat about nine months ago when DNI Chapman pointed out the difference between our societies, China's and the Western world's, that is. In the democracies of the West, we don't have the same ability as the communist government of China to rapidly organize and unite our citizens behind a common goal. To a large degree, China is still a revolutionary society; they're a mobilized army, so to speak, ready to march at the drop of a hat. Western democracies are societies geared at functioning in peacetime. To mobilize them to head a major threat takes a lot of effort, money, and time. In other words, the PRC is much better prepared to start a war than we are."

The president nodded slowly. "So, it seems we have to prepare for war while doing our best to prevent it with a Cold War-like strategy of containment?"

Everyone agreed.

"I think we should start to put some diplomatic pressure on them by taking them to task about their ongoing espionage activities on US soil and elsewhere," the president said. "We could start by letting their diplomats know the free ride is over. The time of spying in the United States has passed. From now on, there will be restrictions on them; they'll need to get permission to conduct meetings with any local officials. Let them throw their toys out of their cribs and spit their pacifiers about it; those are the restrictions we've been operating under in China for forty years. It's time to reciprocate in kind."

Chapman and Lawrence started to respond at once. Lawrence stopped and said, "You first, Tia."

She said, "Mr. President, we don't want to do that too quickly and too harshly. We don't want them to get a sniff in the nose that we know what they're up to. In other words, don't rock the boat, not yet."

The president nodded. "I keep forgetting we're at the start of the second Cold War. Okay, let's get Peregrine airborne immediately, if not sooner, and keep me posted."

Chapter Fifty

TO RUN OPERATION PEREGRINE

Langley, Virginia, USA

Day 25

Rex got more than his wish to be a fly on the wall. He was invited to be at the meeting in Richardson's office the next morning.

John and Christelle were on the CRC jet on the way back from their honeymoon when Richardson called and asked him to make a detour to Langley.

Starbucks coffee was served. The secretary left and closed the door before John said, "Before you tell me what I'm doing here, I want to tell you what a wonderful wedding l had until a guy who I thought was a good friend ruined it."

Rex enjoyed the next few minutes as Brandt and Richardson ribbed each other in feigned seriousness. In the end, Richardson conceded that spoiling a man's wedding was more serious, only a little though, than phoning a man in the wee hours of the morning with bad news. The battle-axes were buried when Richardson undertook to make good with a bottle of Brandt's favorite whiskey.

"Okay, now that I have that off my chest, why am I here?" said Brandt.

"To run Operation Peregrine," replied Richardson.

"Right. Of course. How stupid of me. And what exactly is Operation Peregrine?"

Two hours and many questions later, Richardson said, "So, will you take the job?"

"Of course, I want the job but can only accept if Dalton takes over mine at CRC."

They looked at Rex.

He had anticipated Brandt's answer since Richardson told him he was going to ask the Old Man to run the operation. Therefore, he had discussed it with Catia and was not surprised when she was excited about the prospect of living permanently on the Ranch. "I'll stay on."

Brandt looked surprised. Momentarily at a loss for words. Obviously, he expected some pushback from Rex. "No ifs or buts?"

"No. I was thinking of making it a condition that being CEO doesn't mean I can't go on missions. But realized, as CEO, I don't need your permission."

"Good," said Brandt. "As long as you understand that I might give you advice whenever I feel like it."

"I'll be surprised if you don't. And I, of course, have the right to ignore it whenever I feel like it."

Brandt grinned, looked at Richardson, and said, "Okay, it's settled."

"In that case, Operation Peregrine is all yours, John."

Chapter Fifty-One

SAME PLACE AS BEFORE

Langley, Virginia, USA

Day 26

John Brandt had left the CIA in September 1995, four years after the end of the Cold War. In his mid-fifties then, he was one of those deemed 'too old' to acquire the skills required for the new era of spying. They offered him a desk job in accounts, and he told them to shove it and went to his ranch in Arizona to farm cattle like his family had been doing for generations. He knew the CIA was wrong to let the old agents go, and he told them so. He was right. Six years later, on Monday, November 11, 2001, exactly two months after 9/11, the Deputy Director of Operations, the same man who ousted him, wanted to know if he could come and visit Brandt on the Ranch. He arrived the next day and was man enough to apologize. That was the day CRC was born.

Shortly after 8:30 a.m., Richardson swiped his security

card on the electronic reader, a green light lit up. He held his eyes an inch from the lenses of the retina scanner, a green light flashed on the metal revolving gate, and he stepped through. Brandt followed suit.

Catia and Digger, Christelle and Cupcake, Rehka and the Farleys were going to spend another day exploring D.C.

Rex and Greg were at the safehouse with the Sun family.

"Welcome back," said Richardson. "Your return has been more than twenty years overdue. This side of the gate is Operation Peregrine territory. It took a bit of rank-pulling and name-dropping to get this space and some of the staff we want. Three of the team leaders are here, and their teams will join them in the next few hours."

"Good, let's meet them."

Richardson led Brandt into an enormous room divided into four areas with floor-to-ceiling glass partitions. Each area had desks with computers and phones on them. On the walls were big TV screens, electronic world maps, an array of electronic clocks showing the time anywhere in the world, and electronic whiteboards. One of the sidewalls was also glass, behind which was one office, Brandt's, and three meeting rooms. There were two doors in the back wall, one leading to the kitchen area and the other to the bathrooms.

Two women and a man were sitting at a table in one of the meeting rooms talking—the team leaders. Richardson did the introductions. Brandt had studied everyone's files earlier that morning.

Sean Woods, IT team lead. Age thirty-five, married, no children. Five-foot-eight, skinny, dark hair, brown eyes, neatly kept beard, and silver wire-framed glasses. He was one of the smartest IT specialists in the CIA's IT division. He had a master's in computer science from the California

Institute of Technology (Caltech), one of the top science and engineering schools in the United States. Greg and his team were going to work with Sean's team remotely from the Ranch. He would never meet Yan or even know of his existence. Two of Sean's team members were assigned by General Caiden McKnight, the commander of the United States Cyber Command.

Lydia Andrews, FBI assistant director. Age fifty-two, divorced, two adult children, both married but no grand-children yet. She had dark hair with gray streaks dyed in. Maybe it was gray hair with dark streaks dyed in. Five-foot-six, a little overweight but attractive. Her team would get two more FBI senior special agents. Lydia was there as the liaison between the FBI and Operation Peregrine to coordi-nate any domestic operations as the CIA had very limited authority to operate on American soil.

Stacie Barrett, analyst team lead. She was fifty-six, not married. Brandt asked specifically for her. She had worked with CRC on previous missions and proven to be a great asset. Her boss Bryan Shafer was one of those Richardson had to pull rank on to get her assigned to Peregrine. She was a meticulous worker, near anal retentive, an uncanny ability to see connections between seemingly unrelated pieces of information to reveal the whole picture, and a remarkable ability to recollect. Her human relations skills left a bit to be desired, which earned her the nickname M1 or Abrams, a reference to the US M1 Abrams battle tank. She was a straight shooter, not a single bone of political correctness in her body, and she got results.

Her nickname had nothing to do with her looks—she was tall, in good shape, with curly dark brown hair and sparkling brown eyes—in fact, she was quite attractive. She had many male friends and the odd boyfriend every now and then, but her work, two cats, a flower garden, and nature photography kept her contented. A few men at work had tried their luck with her but had none. Her team would be augmented with four senior analysts.

The fourth and missing team leader didn't know about his appointment as yet. Brandt still had to tell him about it.

Bethesda, Maryland, USA

Day 26

It was a short drive from Langley to Bethesda, northwest of D.C. Ollie Campbell was seventy-two. A retired CIA agent, he and his wife had two adult children and five grandchildren. Ollie and Brandt had worked together for the best part of twenty years, much of it on covert operations in the former Soviet Bloc countries. Their last joint operation as field agents was in Dresden in the former East Germany on a mission that succeeded in its goal to retrieve a critical document from a senior East German general but, thanks to the Stasi, ended in tragedy for Ollie.

The Stasi was the state security service of East Germany during the Soviet era. Described as one of the most effective and repressive intelligence and secret police agencies ever to have existed. A well-known world political figure once worked with the Stasi in Dresden. That's according to the German tabloid Bild, who in 2018 published a photo ID card issued on the last day of 1985 by the Stasi offices in Dresden to a young Mr. Vladimir Putin, thirty-three years of age at the time.

Ollie was the driver that picked Brandt up after collecting the documents from a dead drop. Brandt was barely in the car when two Stasi vehicles bore down on them from the front and rear. Ollie kept his cool. He waited until the two cars had parked across the two lanes blocking his way. And he waited until the doors of their cars opened. The moment the Stasi agents put their feet on the ground, Ollie surged forward around the car in front, half of his car on the sidewalk, narrowly missing the Stasi car and sped off. The agents ran for their cars while letting loose with a barrage of gunfire; some of the bullets hit the car but caused no serious damage. Or so it seemed. They were about a mile away when Ollie said in a calm voice as if talking about the weather, "I've been hit. Both legs. You'll have to take over."

He switched the lights off and made a sharp handbrake turn into a side alley, and brought the car to a stop with the handbrake again. He lowered the back of his seat and pulled himself over to the backseat while John moved into the driver's seat. Seconds later, the Stasi vehicles sped past the alley with flashing lights and blaring sirens. Ollie and John were out of the alley in seconds. Half an hour later, they were inside a safe house on the outskirts of Dresden. It took fourteen hours to get him across the border and into a hospital in West Germany where he received the dreadful news, the bullets had caused irreparable damage to his legs. Both had to be amputated above the knee.

The CIA offered him a generous package to take a medical discharge. Ollie refused. "The bullets went through my legs, not my brain. I'm too young to retire," he told the Director.

The Director hinted that Ollie had no say in the matter.

Ollie said, "We'll have to see about that."

A few days later, the president visited Ollie in the hospital to thank him personally and decorate him. Field agents didn't get medals at public ceremonies. When the president came out of the hospital fifteen minutes later than scheduled, he told the director to put Ollie behind a desk in operations.

The director did as he was told. Three months later, Ollie was back at Langley, in operations behind a desk in his wheelchair, which would later be replaced by prosthetics.

What Ollie Campbell had lost in mobility, he more than made up for with his intellect. And ever since, the Stasi and KGB had regretted the day they shot Ollie. The man with no legs, from 4800 miles away, kept their best agents and spymasters running in circles while consuming as much antacid and headache tablets as food.

Brandt arrived right on time for lunch as Ollie's better half, Margaret, had requested. She was an excellent cook, not a skill one would've expected from a family GP who ran a very busy practice all her life, but to her, cooking was a hobby.

She met Brandt at the front door, hugged and kissed him on both cheeks, congratulated him on his wedding, and then whispered in his ear, "I hope you're here to give him something to do. He's driving me crazy. His pet peeve these days is the politicians, and I can't get it through his thick skull that the TV has an on *and* off button."

"If what I smell is your pot roast beef and you have apple pie for dessert, your wish is my command."

Margaret laughed. "I still remember your favorites, John."

Ollie switched the TV off when John and Margaret entered the family room.

After shaking hands, Ollie said, "Take a step back; I

want to see what an ugly old son of a bitch like you has that would've persuaded that stunning French agent to marry you."

John laughed and took a step back.

Ollie looked him up and down and said, "Nah, she needs to pay a visit to a good optometrist."

Margaret was still laughing when she left to check on the food and set the table. Over a glass of red wine, John and Ollie caught up on the things that had happened since they last spoke to each other.

It was only after lunch, with apple pie and coffee in front of them, that Ollie said, "Let's hear it."

"My friend, you will not believe it, but some people at Langley finally came to their senses and realized that the spy game has not actually changed. That computers can't do it all and can't replace real spies. And then they came to the realization that they didn't have any of those left. So they want some of the dinosaurs back to help them fight a new Cold War."

"You're right. I don't believe it. Not even the threat from China stirred them in their sleep. What happened?"

"Discovering what China really has in mind."

Ollie stared at his old friend for a long while. Then he turned his gaze to Margaret. No words were necessary—the approval was in her eyes.

"When do I start?"

"Nine tomorrow morning, same place as before."

Chapter Fifty-Two

LIKE A CONTAINERSHIP

Safehouse, Virginia, USA

Day 26

On the way to the safehouse, Rex told Greg about Operation Peregrine and what was expected of him and Yan for the next twenty-four hours. "Greg, it's critical that you check this guy out. We need to be absolutely one-hundred percent sure he's not pulling the wool over our eyes."

"Understood. The little I've seen so far was impressive."

"Better than you?"

Greg grinned. "I'm the best."

Rex laughed. "That's what I like about you, Greg—your modesty."

Greg chuckled. "Just joking. I don't think in our world there's anyone who can claim that title. No one knows everything. We have areas of expertise, and within that, one could be among the best. This guy is an ace hacker."

"So are you."

"I'm sure we'll get along fine."

The previous day, when Rex visited the Suns, he found them to be taken good care of by the CIA agents guarding them. But it was clear that the Suns were struggling to come to grips with the idea that for all intents and purposes, they had ceased to exist. They knew they would probably never go back to China. They couldn't even contact anyone there. They were nervous and unsure about their future. Rex told them that everything would start to settle down soon, but, unfortunately, they'd have to put up with it for a few more days. Yan had no hesitation in committing to giving his full cooperation to Greg.

Twenty minutes after arriving at the safehouse, Ming and Lei were in the family room watching cartoons, of which it seemed the little girl couldn't get enough. Rex, Greg, and Yan were in the study. Rex had returned Yan's laptop, which they had confiscated with the USB drive and his mobile phone shortly after they'd boarded the *TOMATS*.

It took a few minutes for Greg and Yan to setup and configure a VPN on the internet router before they got into it, and Rex got completely lost in their technobabble.

Greg was following Yan keystroke-by-keystroke as he first showed him all the vulnerabilities in the firewalls of government, law enforcement, and intelligence agencies that he knew of. Greg was making notes on his laptop as they proceeded.

Rex was stunned. Yan didn't have to break into the sacred vaults—he held the keys. In the underground lair of Unit 61398 in Beijing was an entire division of hackers just like Yan. How many more keys did they have, and to what?

And Rex couldn't help but wonder if Yan had left out a few. He could've, and neither he nor Greg or anyone else, for that matter, would know.

Two hours later, Yan was done. "Now, let me take you on a trip inside Unit 61398's servers and my former manager's computer."

Rex and Greg had a good laugh when Yan told them why his manager had earned himself the nickname of Seagull.

First, Yan showed them the information that he had copied onto his laptop twenty-two days ago while sitting on a bench in Beihai Park, Beijing. This consisted mainly of the summary information of the many projects the unit was running plus the configuration of their firewalls and the vulnerabilities, some of which Yan had created that day.

They had hundreds of projects on the go, hacking and spying domestically and internationally—the vast majority of the latter aimed against the USA, and to a lesser extent, its allies.

Next, Yan accessed the unit's servers through one of the keyholes he had created in their firewalls and began showing them the detailed information. To call it a truckload of information would've been an understatement; it was more like a containership—a very large one. And among the information on the servers was also the rest of the details about the holes in the firewalls, which Yan didn't know about or might have forgotten.

That's when Rex decided Yan could be trusted and realized Operation Peregrine had just become understaffed.

Late that afternoon, Greg gave Rex an external hard drive onto which he had copied the information from Yan's laptop and a text document with his notes.

Half an hour later, Brandt signed Rex in at the security

desk outside the revolving gates of the Operation Peregrine control center.

Brandt called Ollie and Sean Woods, the IT team lead, into one of the meeting rooms, introduced them to Rex and asked that he tell them what he had.

Woods had one look at Greg's notes about the vulnerabilities and asked, "Where the hell did you get this?"

"A team of penetration testing experts," Rex said without blinking an eye.

"Okay, we've got our work cut out for us to plug those holes immediately."

"N-o-o-o-o!" roared Brandt and Ollie in chorus.

"What... why not? We can't—" Woods was bewildered.

"Sean, in the old days when we discovered a dead drop, we didn't arrest the people who used it. We watched and followed them. Can't you do that with a hole in a firewall?"

The light went up in Woods's eyes. "Of course, we can. We can even divert them to information we *want* them to see."

"You're a quick study," said Brandt with a small grin. "I want you to make an assessment of each and every hole and what's behind it. Bring that information back, and let's work out a strategy."

Woods left with a big smile on his face.

Brandt called Stacie Barrett in. She and Rex knew each other from previous missions but had never met in person.

An hour later, they'd only skimmed through a fraction of the summaries of the projects on Unit 61398's servers.

"I've never seen anything like this, not even remotely," said Stacie. "It's going to be like shooting fish in a barrel. Except we won't have enough shooters."

"That is a problem we can solve very quickly," said

Brandt as he picked up the phone and dialed Richardson's extension.

⸻

Two days later, the Sun family accompanied by Rex, Catia, and Digger, the Farleys, Greg, and Rehka landed on the Ranch in the CRC jet. According to the Suns' new IDs, they were Zhou Yan (Sean), his wife, Zhou Ming (Millie), and their daughter, Zhou Lei (Linda).

Part III

OPERATION PEREGRINE

Chapter Fifty-Three

A DEFENSIVE BRIEFING

Washington, D.C., USA

Where there's smoke, there's probably fire. The rumors about Senator Lancaster's peccadillos with Jason Crawley proved that notion to be correct when Crawley received a late-night visit from three masked men speaking Chinese-accented English. They didn't have to torture him; he was scared out of his mind. Once they had extracted the information from him, they force-fed him three-quarters of a bottle of Seagram's Seven Crown Blended Whiskey, his favorite drink, before running him over with a car in a side-street with no security cameras, not far from his favorite watering-hole.

Publicly, Senator Lancaster was devastated about the death of her loyal subject; secretly, she was relieved. The stolen vehicle that killed him was found, but the thieves remained unidentified and at large.

Once the MSS agents had discovered the senator's weakness, they knew her seduction was going to be easy.

Powerful people liked to be in charge. All they had to do was to arrange for the right man to show up at the right place and the right time to let her seduce him.

New York, USA

Except for the not so secret three-week fling with the late Jason Crawley, which happened in D.C., Senator Lancaster lived her public life in D.C. and her private life in New York over weekends and holidays. In New York, when preying, she had a few small but stylish hotels she frequented. Management at these establishments knew her well but not as the senior senator of their state. The woman they knew was also extremely attractive, had long dark hair and deep brown eyes, and a body that had men drooling, but no resemblance to their beloved, stunning, blonde senator that decorated their TV screens at least once a week. If the senator would've honored them with a visit, which she would never do, they would surely have recognized her immediately.

Thanks to Jason Crawley, the MSS knew all about Jordyn Lancaster's chameleonic escapades and her propensity for young blond men.

Roger Breeland was a second-generation Norwegian, a blond giant of six foot seven, broad shoulders, narrow hips, blue eyes, a strong jawline, and a friendly smile. He was thirty-three, intelligent, and had looks that made it impossible not to notice him, even in a crowd. All the attributes a male agent specializing in honey-trapping of high-value female targets needed to be successful. That's why he was on MSS's payroll.

It was at once fascinating and sad to watch how this strong woman yielded to their agent so easily. The moment she walked into the small bar, her eyes caught his. He held her gaze for a second or two and returned to his drink, knowing that she was studying him while she took off her coat and handed it to the doorman. There were not many patrons in the room; the stools on either side of him were empty.

"Do you mind if I take this chair?" She pointed to the chair on Breeland's right.

He gave her only a half-glance as he replied, "Go for it."

She faked a shiver and said to the barman, "Johnny, something to heat me up. It's so cold out there; even the politicians have their hands in their own pockets."

The barman smiled, and Breeland started laughing. "Never heard that one. It's good."

She turned and gave him one of her dazzling smiles.

He raised his half-empty beer glass and said, "To the best joke I've heard in a long time."

"Hey, I'm starving. I'm thinking of ordering some fries and nibbles. Care to join me?" she said.

"You must've read my mind. I'll get it."

That was easy. "Okay, but only if you don't expect me to tell more jokes."

"I won't. That one was good enough to cover the food."

And the rest of the night, I hope. "Deal."

An hour later, they were in the just-in-case room, six floors above the bar, which she had booked earlier in the day. The state-of-the-art MSS video and audio equipment hidden in the overhead fire alarm, the four corners of the poster-bed, and the TV facing the bed assured a near-constant view of the senator's face along with all of the more damning angles of the tryst.

Breeland was careful not to touch her hair or do anything that might dislodge her contact lenses; he didn't need to remove those to know who she was, neither would the MSS's facial recognition software.

It was a night the senator would never forget. She had only one desire when she opened her eyes in the bed next to her Nordic sex-god the next morning—she wanted more of the same. A lot more and as often as possible. She told him so over breakfast and was excited when he said, "I'd like nothing better."

What neither Senator Lancaster nor Roger Breeland or the MSS knew was that a very senior and experienced analyst at the CIA, Stacie Barrett, had taken a keen interest in her case since retrieving her project file from Unit 61398's servers a week before.

Washington, D.C., USA

It was Monday morning, shortly after she'd arrived at her office when Senator Lancaster's secretary told her that the Deputy Director of the FBI had requested an urgent meeting with her. She was perplexed; she'd met Dylan Watson a few times at social events but never in an official capacity and couldn't begin to think what the meeting was about.

That the meeting was of a serious nature, she started to realize when Deputy Director Watson entered her office accompanied by Senior Special Agent Lydia Andrews.

Lancaster immediately tried to take charge after the greetings. "Shall we get right into it? I have fifteen minutes before I have to be at a very important meeting."

"I'm afraid this might take a bit longer than that, Senator," said Watson.

"Give it your best shot; otherwise, the first opening I have is Thursday afternoon if you want to reschedule."

"Senator, we're here to give you a defensive security briefing, and it can't wait."

Lancaster had screwed on her trademark iceberg demeanor. "Then brief away, Mr. Deputy Director, but in fifteen minutes, I'm out of here."

"Senator, a little while ago, we received information about a Chinese spy operating here in the US. We immediately obtained a FISA warrant and started watching him—"

"And you think I might know this spy?"

"Yes, we do. His name is Roger Breeland."

There was no trace of shock in her body language except for the sudden dilation of the pupils of her eyes, which both Watson and Andrews noticed.

"Never heard his name." She looked at her watch.

"Maybe not by that name, but you spent the weekend with him at the South House Hotel, Manhattan."

"I don't know what you're talking about. You're wasting my time. This meeting is over." She opened her briefcase and put some documents in it.

Watson nodded at Andrews. She placed her tablet PC on the desk and turned it so the senator could see the four photos on the screen—all of them in her disguise in the company of the tall blond Norwegian.

Lancaster laughed. "That's not me. The man in the photos is not even Asian. Is this some kind of joke?"

"Senator, this is serious. That man in the photos is of Norwegian descent and works as a honeytrap for the PRC's Ministry of State Security, MSS. And the woman in the photos *is* you."

"You've been spying on me! I'll have both of you fired for this!" Her characteristic veneer of being in control of all situations at all times was gone.

"No, Senator, we didn't spy on you; we spied on Breeland, and you turned up."

"And that makes me a Chinese spy, right? Well, I've got news for you. My private life is none of your business. And you'd be well-advised to stay out of it."

"We respect your privacy, Senator. But, unfortunately, when your private life involves a known spy, we have no choice. We *have* to intrude. And we *have* to ask, do you know he's a spy?"

Lancaster's hand was shaking when she picked up the phone and told her secretary to clear her schedule for the rest of the day as she didn't feel well and was going home.

Over the course of the next few months, across the United States, many more prominent people, which included state and federal senators, congressmen and congresswomen, judges, mayors, government officials, and such, had come to the attention of the FBI's counterintelligence division. Some of them had been bribed by the MSS, some had been blackmailed, some hated capitalism, and some didn't even know they were informants for a hostile regime. Some of them received visits from the FBI, were arrested, and charged with espionage. Some received visits and received defensive briefings, just like Senator Lancaster did. And some received no visits; they were watched, very closely.

Chapter Fifty-Four

THE RECRUIT

New York, USA

The defensive briefing of Senator Lancaster by FBI Deputy Director Dylan Watson and Senior Special Agent Lydia Andrews didn't start on a good note, but it ended well. She had her idiosyncrasies and all-consuming ambitions, to be sure, but she was not a traitor. She didn't like the president or his party, but she loved her country.

Learning that Roger Breeland was an MSS agent was a shock. Learning how deep and pervasive the PRC's spy activities in the US were and that she was only one of many high-flyers that they were in the process of ensnaring or already had in their claws was at once incensing and eye-opening. If nothing else, the briefing had served to change her views of the PRC dramatically.

"What do you want me to do, other than punch the bastard in the face?"

Andrews said, "No, don't do that. We have something much more painful in mind."

"I'm listening."

Lancaster was back in New York for the weekend as usual. She met with her 'Nordic god' at a different hotel, in the same disguise. It was every bit as exhilarating as the weekend before. That's what Breeland told her. She didn't correct him. To her, it was repulsive, but despite the MSS's diligent study of her life and habits, they'd never discovered what an accomplished actress she was. And she forgot to tell Roger that their conversations were being recorded and that they were being watched by the FBI.

Back in D.C. on Monday, she met with Watson and Andrews again.

It was on the Saturday night of their third weekend together that Breeland took her out for dinner to a very classy restaurant in Manhattan.

Shortly after being served their dessert, Breeland spotted someone in the restaurant that he apparently knew and waved at the Asian man who was dining alone. The man waved back, and a few minutes later, he came over to their table. Breeland introduced his acquaintance as Song Yuhan, but before he could introduce her, Song bowed ever so slightly and said, "What an honor to finally meet you, Senator Lancaster."

She looked perplexed. "Sorry, you must be mistaken. I'm Elizabeth Kelly."

"No, I'm not mistaken, Senator, and you know it."

She looked at Breeland, then at Song, then at Breeland again. "Is this some kind of joke?"

"No jokes, Senator Lancaster," said Breeland with a big grin.

"Okay, guys, you had your fun. Let's have a nightcap and go home."

Song said, "Roger, will you please excuse us for a few minutes?"

Breeland nodded and left without saying a word. He didn't even look at Lancaster.

Song said, "Senator, I have a proposal, and I suggest you give it some serious consideration."

"Stop right there. Who the hell are you?"

"Song Yuhan, as Roger told you. I am working in the Cultural Office of the Chinese Embassy here in the United States."

"In other words, you're a spy."

"Such bad connotations to that title. No, I'm not a spy; I'm a networker. My job is to promote China-U.S. cultural and tourism exchange and cooperation, promoting mutual understanding, mutual learning, and friendship between our countries."

"Mr. Song cut the bullshit and tell me what you want."

"A partnership—"

"For your benefit, of course."

"If you'd allow me to continue, you'll see it's for our mutual benefit."

Lancaster made no reply. She just stared impassively at Song.

"As chairperson of the Senate Committee on Foreign Relations, you've made very constructive inputs into foreign-policy legislation relating to the PRC. My government appreciates your positive stance about our country very much and would like to repay you in kind."

"Song, don't patronize me. Get to the goddamn point or get out."

"We've been following your career—"

"Diplomatic speak for spying on me."

"We don't spy on our friends. I was about to say, we're impressed with what you've achieved so far, and we want to help you achieve your ultimate goal."

"Right. And I'm to believe you want to do this just because you're so impressed with me?"

"Yes. There's that. But—"

"Ah, there it is; the but."

"Partnerships place responsibilities on all parties involved."

"You've certainly mastered the art of doublespeak. You want a quid pro quo. Right?"

"Yes."

"Well, I'm not interested. This conversation is over." She started to get up.

"Senator, before you go, you might want to have a look at this." Song held his mobile phone so that she could see the video.

Lancaster sat down. She had been forewarned by Watson and Andrews to expect to be confronted with some very compromising material of her trysts with Breeland. But hearing it was one thing, seeing it was another altogether. She was genuinely shocked, embarrassed, and profoundly infuriated—in that order. She wasn't the hit-the-table or breaking-the-crockery type. She pushed the phone back to Song, leaned forward, and with jaw muscles clenched tightly as she battled to maintain her rage, she hissed, "Networker my ass. You're a spy and a blackmailer. Partnership? This is extortion!"

"Those are ugly words, Senator. But if that's what you prefer to call it, so be it. The fact is, you are now working for us."

"And if I refuse?"

"We'll destroy you."

"By leaking this video, and God knows what else you have to the media?"

"Yes. And that'll be the end of your career. Disgrace. Humiliation. Embarrassment. Shame. Is that how you want to be remembered?"

She shook her head slowly. Tears started to well up in her eyes. "No. I'd rather go on early retirement."

"You can, but it will be in disgrace, and then, of course, you'd never be the President of the United States."

"*You* can't guarantee me the presidency."

"You've got no idea what we're capable of, do you? You won't become president this time. But you will either be vice president or secretary of state or have another high-ranking position in the new administration. Come the next election, you'll be the prime candidate."

"You make it sound as if you decide who becomes president."

"No, the voters decide that. We only help them decide who is the best candidate."

She wiped the tears from her eyes with a tissue, sighed, and said, "How is this going to work?"

Song ordered coffee for both of them and, for the next half hour, gave her detailed instructions of what was expected of her and how they'd contact each other in the future.

When Song was finished, Lancaster clapped her hands. Slowly. Sarcastically. "Congratulations, Song, you've just recruited yourself a US senator." She got up, shouldered her handbag, and said, "Tell Breeland I'm licensed to carry a gun. If I ever see him again, I'll shoot him in the face."

In the Operation Peregrine meeting room in Langley,

John Brandt, Ollie Campbell, and Lydia Andrews high-fived.

Song Yuhan had diplomatic immunity, ensuring safe passage, and he was not susceptible to lawsuits or prosecution under his host country's laws, although he could be expelled from the country.

But his deportation was the last thing the Peregrine team had in mind. Song was probably busy sticking feathers in his cap without sparing a moment's thought that he was the one who got recruited.

Chapter Fifty-Five

THE BACKUP PLAN

San Jose, Silicon Valley, USA

According to the project file on the Unit 61398 servers, Penultimate was the MSS's backup plan to get access to JWICS if Zac Macmillan failed. And he did, not for lack of trying, but lack of attention—his psychological affliction.

The Peregrine FBI team had the tabs on him, looking for an opportunity to plant a trojan horse on his computer, which would have enabled them to see what progress he had made with hacking into JWICS. They knew his handler went by the nom de guerre of Michael Feng, a data analyst from Hong Kong, who in reality was Kang Xun, an undercover agent for the MSS. Their plan was to recruit Macmillan and help him finish the 'hack' that would lead the MSS into a labyrinth of JWICS databases containing concocted data, some of it true, some of it half-true, and some of it utterly misleading.

But then everything went south when Macmillan went out for a few drinks one night. There was a beautiful girl in the bar having a good time with her friends. Two males with female companions, she was single.

Across the tables, he caught her eye and raised his glass in a silent toast. She returned the gesture with her near-empty glass. Macmillan called the server over and asked him to give the lovely lady another of whatever she was drinking with compliments from him.

Five minutes later, she came over to his table, sat down opposite him, and thanked him for the drink.

She was an undercover cop. A fact which he only learned much later that night when she showed him her badge and read him his Miranda rights after he'd demonstrated to her how easy it was to hack into her bank's servers with his cellphone and transfer $500 into her account from another client's account.

An hour after the cell door slammed behind him in the San Jose police precinct, he was released into FBI custody.

At this stage, the plan to 'recruit' him was still on track, but when they interviewed him, they changed their minds. Macmillan was in seventh heaven to have so many people so intensely interested in his brilliant work. He told them everything, every hack he'd ever performed, including how much he was paid for it and by whom. Everything he said was true; all of it was on his computer. But Zac Macmillan was a few sandwiches short of a picnic, a mentally sick man. He needed psychiatric treatment, not responsibilities. He was transferred to a behavioral health services facility with beautiful mountain views, where he was kept under guard.

An in-depth study of Macmillan's computer by the Peregrine IT team revealed that he was on the brink of penetrating JWICS. Inarguably, Macmillan was a hacker prodigy. Was it not for the mental issues, he would've been a prime candidate for recruitment.

As it were, with their favorite hacker indisposed, the MSS had to activate their backup plan—Penultimate Pty Ltd. But the MSS's problem was that Jack Ross of Penultimate was a stickler for network security. After all, it was their business to find vulnerabilities in their clients' networks and websites. And they found them. Even when so-called security experts had declared them impenetrable. It would have been bad for Penultimate's business if their own network was hacked. Ross knew that no computer network could be declared absolutely inaccessible, but he made it his job to ensure that Penultimate's was as close as it could get.

Unit 61398 hackers were unable to break into Penultimate's network and couldn't tell the MSS whether Penultimate was indeed conducting pentesting on JWICS or which government networks they were testing. All they had to go on was a slip of the tongue by a friend of Jack Ross on Facebook, hinting that Penultimate worked on government contracts.

Notwithstanding, the MSS was adamant about getting into Penultimate's computers. Even if they didn't find anything about JWICS, they were still keen to find out which government and business systems Penultimate was testing. However, unable to breach the company's firewalls, they decided to send in a team to physically collect the information they wanted.

Sunnyvale, Silicon Valley, USA

According to the FBI, approximately 1.4 million Americans are members of about 33,000 gangs across the country. The 18th Street Gang was the largest gang in California, responsible for at least one robbery or assault per day and linked to homicide, extortion, human smuggling, drug smuggling, and auto theft. They had also infiltrated the U.S. military. It was from this pool of cutthroats that the MSS often hired wetwork crews. Wetwork, the euphemism for violence and killing.

It was 2:15 a.m. when the four men in an SUV turned up in the near-empty parking lot of the strip mall where Penultimate's office was located in a double-story building. In front of the office were three cars. The two identical red Porche Cayennes belonged to Jack Ross and his business partner, and the dark blue Mercedes GLC Coupe to Penultimate's senior programmer. Judging by the cars, Penultimate was doing well. The lights inside the office were on. The rest of the buildings in the mall were dark.

The visitors were oblivious to the FBI's two surveillance drones loitering out of earshot a mile above the car park recording and relaying everything that was happening below to the SWAT team waiting inside the Penultimate office.

Two men in dark clothes with their heads covered by hoodies got out from the backseat of the SUV and approached the front door of the office. One of them fiddled with the lock while the other stood a few yards away, to the side, watching the parking lot and street. Less than a minute later, the man at the lock moved to the wall beside the door and covered his ears. A small but bright flash emanated from the door, followed by a dull thud a split second later. The front doors of the SUV opened, the driver and passenger jumped out and ran to the front door with silenced guns in their hands, entering the building on the heels of their two teammates, who had blown the door lock away.

Sprinting through the reception area, the man in the rear, about five steps behind the rest of his team, suddenly stopped in his tracks. Slowly, he turned back to look behind him. Instead of seeing the door, he was looking down the barrels of two Glock 17M 9mm pistols less than two yards away. He started to raise his gun, wisely changed his mind, dropped the gun, and raised his hands above his head.

Seconds later, several gunshots rang out from somewhere behind him, and then everything went quiet. One of the SWAT team holding him at gunpoint told him to lie down on the floor, face down, hands behind his head. The other stepped forward and slapped handcuffs on him.

Minutes later, four black FBI SUVs were parked in front of the office. The three robbers in the back of the office were dead. They were members of the 18th Street Gang. One of the six SWAT team members covering the rest of the office took a bullet through the left shoulder, and another sustained a flesh wound on his right thigh.

Two ambulances arrived about ten minutes later.

The survivor was a Chinese national who arrived in the USA five days ago on a false passport, posing as Michael Feng, a data analyst from Hong Kong. His real name was Kang Xun, an agent of the MSS and Zac Macmillan's handler. He was also the leader of this band of criminals bent on killing anyone inside Penultimate's office that night and seizing their computers.

Shortly on the heels of the ambulances arrived the police cars with earsplitting sirens and flashing lights. And, of course, the first members of the Fourth Estate with their cameras and questions were not far behind.

The SWAT team leader made a short statement. "It's a sensitive and ongoing operation. Information will be made available in due time." To the barrage of questions hurled at him from the press, the team leader replied tersely, "No comment."

Kang Xun, just like his former colleague, Ren Shi, had made a thorough assessment of his situation on the way to the FBI office. He was facing a long list of charges. The ones that came to mind were entering the country on a false passport, conspiring to commit a crime, breaking and entering, attempted murder, attempted robbery, and maybe espionage. A long time in jail, to be sure. Gut-wrenching, to say the least, but nothing as spine-chilling as being sent back to China.

He tried to make a deal with the FBI interrogators, but they were not in the mood. They wouldn't entertain any of his suggestions until they had the names of each and every one of his assets. And they wanted them within the next hour. They gave him five minutes to decide. He had made up his mind within the first thirty seconds.

Within four hours after Kang started talking, his entire network consisting of five hackers and ten informers were in FBI custody. Over the course of the next few days, more would be arrested as the detainees divulged information to the FBI interrogators.

An official statement was issued by Douglas Cole, the Director of the FBI, at a press conference at four that same afternoon.

Beijing, China

The minister in charge of the MSS, Shen Delan's body was ravaged by waves of ice-cold shivers as he read the news headlines on CNN.

CHINESE SPY RING UNCOVERED.

The news anchor reported that three men were killed in a shootout with the FBI but that the leader of the spy ring was alive and in custody. His name, Kang Xun, a Chinese citizen and agent of the Chinese Ministry of State Security, MSS, and he had been masquerading under the false name Michael Feng, a data analyst from Hong Kong. An unknown number of his collaborators were also in custody.

Shen couldn't help but think about the disappearance of his predecessor, Xuan Bai, after the failure of a similar mission in the USA not too long ago.

He spent a few minutes considering his options and then started typing his letter of resignation. Hopefully, it would appease the president.

Chapter Fifty-Six

THE SOUTH CHINA SEA

Beijing, China

Sir Walter Raleigh, the English adventurer and writer, once noted: "Whosoever commands the sea commands the trade; whosoever commands the trade of the world commands the riches of the world; and consequently, the world itself."

For China to control the world, they had to start by getting control of the South China Sea. A stretch of water, 1.4 million square miles in size, bordered in the north by the shores of South China, in the west by the Indochinese Peninsula, in the east by the islands of Taiwan and the northwestern Philippines, and in the south by Borneo, eastern Sumatra, and the Bangka Belitung Islands. It was linked with the East China Sea via the Taiwan Strait, the Philippine Sea via the Luzon Strait, the Sulu Sea via the straits around Palawan, the Indian Ocean via the Strait of Malacca, and the Java Sea via the Karimata and Bangka Strait. The Gulf of Tonkin and the Gulf of Thailand were both part of the South China Sea.

According to the United Nations Conference on Trade and Development (UNCTAD), the South China Sea carried a third of global shipping, more than USD $3 trillion worth of goods every year. About eighty percent of global trade by volume and seventy percent by value was transported by sea. Sixty percent of maritime trade passed through Asia. Over sixty-four percent of China's maritime trade transited the South China Sea in 2016. During the same period, forty-two percent of Japan's maritime trade and fourteen percent of the US's passed through the South China Sea.

Moreover, besides the maritime trade it carried, below the surface of the South China Sea, were vast untapped oil and natural gas deposits. US estimates put it at 11 billion barrels of oil and 190 trillion cubic feet of natural gas, but a major Chinese government-owned oil company put the figure closer to 125 billion barrels of oil and 500 trillion cubic feet of natural gas, all of it in undiscovered areas. And the cherry on the cake, in the South China Sea, there were rich fishing fields, crucial for the food security of millions in Southeast Asia.

China consumed almost 13 million barrels of oil per day, the world's second-largest consumer of oil, accounting for a little over thirteen percent of the world's total consumption of 97 million barrels per day. China's crude oil imports were about 10 million barrels per day. A source of 125 billion barrels would give them enough oil for 34 years at their current rate of consumption.

There was no doubt, the South China Sea was a region of tremendous economic and geostrategic importance, and everyone knew that. Therefore, China had to control it. It was their first objective.

Since 1947, when the Nationalist government of China, known as the Kuomintang, was still ruling, China had laid claims to large swaths of the South China Sea. It was in 1947 when China introduced a new map showing the Eleven-Dash Line and 286 bits of rock and turf in the South China Sea. Each chunk of rock and reef was named and referred to as the South China Sea Islands or the Spratly Islands. Two years later, in 1949, the nationalists had lost the civil war, and Mao Tse Tungs communists were in charge. But they didn't abandon their claims to the South China Sea; new maps were drawn over time, and the Eleven-Dash Line had eventually become the Nine-Dash Line.

The Spratly Islands were less than two square miles, including 100 or so islets, coral reefs, and sea mounts scattered over an area of nearly 158,300 square miles with no indigenous inhabitants, but scattered garrisons occupied by personnel of several claimant states, which included Taiwan, Malaysia, the Philippines, Vietnam, and Brunei.

The Spratlys offered the ideal positions from which to monitor maritime activity in the South China Sea and the potential to establish naval- and airbases—exactly what China had been doing since 2014 by constructing an airfield on Fiery Cross Reef within the Spratlys whilst continuing its land reclamation activities at other sites.

International law stipulated that every country had the right to claim up to 12 nautical miles from its coast as its territory and can claim an exclusive economic zone extending up to 200 nautical miles for activities like drilling or fishing. China ignored the law. The Nine-Dash Line showed them to claim areas as far as 1,200 miles from the south of Mainland China, and in many instances, less than 200 miles away from the coastal areas of Malaysia, the Philippines, and Vietnam.

China's Nine-Dash Line had been called a revolutionary

approach to sovereign territory. Their controversial claim encompassed nearly ninety percent of the South China Sea and increased China's geographic size by nearly fifty percent.

In 2016, an international tribunal ruled against China's claims, saying it had no legal basis for the extensive claims. That decision was legally binding per international law, but there was no enforcement mechanism. China ignored the ruling and continued building artificial islands and military bases in the South China Sea.

And to add a warning to the seriousness of their claims, from time to time, China undertook extensive military exercises in the South China Sea, cordoning off part of the sea for war games.

Several major sea routes provided entry into the South China Sea; the Sunda Strait, the Lombok Strait, and the Strait of Malacca, among them. The latter was by far the most widely used. It was the shortest and, therefore, most economical passageway between the Pacific and Indian Oceans. Taking control of the South China Sea would have to start by taking control of the three straits: Malacca, Sunda, and Lombok.

The best way to get control of those straits would've been to set up a naval blockade. But in that regard, China had a problem. Although in terms of the number of warships, they had the largest navy in the world, their navy was not as well equipped as that of the US. The US Navy's real edge was in its big-deck aircraft carriers and amphibious assault ships. The US Navy had 11 aircraft carriers of 100,000 tons or more, as well as nine Wasp and America-class amphibious transports. China had two carriers of about 60,000 tons each and was only now building out its first amphibious transport, the Type 075.

China's entire low-end fleet—its force of 137 missile patrol boats and corvettes—didn't even add up to a single American aircraft carrier in tonnage.

The fact that the US Navy had more carriers and much better reconnaissance capabilities meant the idea of a naval blockade of the straits was dead in the water, so to speak.

They had a plan to overcome those limitations. It was all described in the Operation MK plan.

Chapter Fifty-Seven

THE FIRST SPEECH

Beijing, China

It was not President Liao Qigang's first speech since he took office, he had made many, but this was hyped by the media to be the most important. At 7:00 p.m., every day of the week, it was news hour in China. Usually, half a billion people watched it. Tonight, there would be closer to three-quarters of a billion watching China Central Television, the country's most powerful and prolific television program producer. Many millions more in the outer provinces who didn't have TV reception or couldn't afford a TV would be listening in on China National Radio. And China Radio International was going to be broadcasting for the global audience.

At precisely 7:00 p.m., the news anchor came in view, she introduced the president, and the cameras switched to a room with a red carpet and the Chinese flag displayed on a wall-to-wall screen behind the dais where President Liao stood.

Liao looked directly into the cameras. "My fellow citizens, our country is on the threshold of a new chapter in our illustrious history. And I am here to tell you about it. It's not only a message for you on the mainland but also for our citizens in the special administrative regions of Hong Kong and Macau, in Taiwan, and further afield. It's also a message for the rest of the world.

"The time has come for us to start exporting our greatest commodity. The commodity the world needs. Has been in need of for decades—the Chinese brand of socialism. It's Chinese socialism that enabled us to help the world as the disease of capitalism made them sick. We've saved the world when those very capitalist practices caused their economies to collapse and led to the Global Financial Crisis of 2008. It's because of the inadequate capitalistic economic system that they can't afford to take care of themselves anymore. To save them, we took over the production of their medicine, their clothes, their children's toys, their computers, and their cellphones. Our Belt and Road Initiative built their roads and bridges. And we loan them our money because capitalism has left them destitute.

"China has truly been the world's deliverer. And we will continue to be the world's savior. But we're asking of the world today a little gratitude. We're not asking you to pay us back for saving you. We're asking you to stop denying us what's rightfully ours. You know, and we know, China is bigger than just the mainland and administrative regions."

Behind the president, on the big screen, the flag disappeared, and a map of the South China Sea with the Nine-dash line came into view.

"What you see behind me is the South China Sea and the parts of it that have been Chinese territory since time immemorial. Our ownership doesn't date back only to the time of Chairman Mao, as some want you to believe, but long before. The area marked on that map is Chinese sovereign territory. Those waters are ours to fish, to mine, and to develop.

"Only when China has access to all of its territory will there be harmony. And the world will reap the benefits as we develop those resources to their full potential with our skills and expertise.

"We're a peaceful nation, but for far too long, while we've been denied what's rightfully ours, we've been tolerating this injustice. I herewith put on notice every country who has vessels inside our territory delineated by the Nine-dash line; you have twenty-four hours to leave. Twenty-four hours and one minute from now, our navy will start to enforce our sea borders by whatever means deemed necessary.

"Furthermore, although we don't lay claim to the straits of Sunda, Lombok, and Malacca, those passages are of great economic importance not only to China but every country bordering the South China Sea. Our ships and those of others have been plagued by attacks from pirates costing us billions every year. It's clear that Malaysia, Indonesia, Singapore, and Thailand don't have the means to make those waterways safe. We stand ready to share the burden of law enforcement in those waters. We cannot allow lawlessness to continue.

"I wish everyone a good night."

Across the world, as interpreters translated the speech and world leaders started shifting in their chairs and clearing their throats, in the Operation Peregrine command center in Langley, John Brandt picked up his satellite phone and called Rex.

Chapter Fifty-Eight

THE WORLD'S MOST DANGEROUS WATERS

Southeast Asia

It's not the seas around the Horn of Africa and its Somalian pirates peering over the barrels of their Kalashnikovs at their hostages that are labeled as the most dangerous waters in the world; that title belongs to the seas of Southeast Asia. More than 120,000 ships traverse the waterways of Southeast Asia every year, carrying one-third of the world's commerce, including eighty percent of all the oil imported by China and Japan.

And for criminals, these ships offer magnificently rich pickings.

Between 1995 and 2013, forty-one percent of the world's pirate attacks happened in the seas of Southeast Asia. The West Indian Ocean, which includes Somalia, came in at a distant second place with only 28% of the world's pirate attacks, and the waters of West Africa in third place at 18%. During those years, pirates killed 136 mariners in Southeast Asian waters—double the number killed in the waters of the Horn of Africa and more than the combined total killed in the Horn of Africa and West Africa.

A 2010 study by the One Earth Future Foundation estimated that piracy costs the international economy between seven and twelve billion dollars per year. Eighty percent of the attacks are opportunistic, i.e., against anchored ships with thieves stealing equipment and the crews' belongings.

But the monetary value of that kind of freebooting was minuscule compared to the bounty collected by professional pirates who launched large-scale, sophisticated attacks on vessels at sea. In recent years well-armed, well-trained, well-organized criminals had turned their focus to oil tankers on their way to the South China Sea, passing through the narrow Malacca and Singapore Straits. The territory is vast, law enforcement under-resourced, and the profit potential immense.

Such a profitable raid happened on May 28, 2014, when ten armed men boarded the oil tanker Orapin 4 from their speedboats. They locked the crew up below deck, disabled the communications system, and wiped the first and last letters from the name, effectively renaming it to the Rapi. The owners of the tanker in Thailand, failing to make contact, reported the ship missing. But no one had seen it. Four days later, the tanker arrived in its homeport of Sri Racha, Thailand, where the namesake hot sauce was first brewed, minus 3,700 metric tons of fuel that had been siphoned into another vessel. The crew was safe, and the pirates $1.9 million richer.

Usually, an attack such as the one on the Orapin would have received wide coverage in the media; it didn't—probably because it was the sixth such attack in three months.

To siphon oil from a tanker ship while at sea requires a

ship engineer that knows what he's doing, someone with oil-industry experience. Not the type of skills one would expect to encounter among criminal gangs. This is why many of these attacks were executed with the help of insiders, such as the ship's engineer and captain. In days long gone, one could've expected a British vessel to be owned by a British company, flying a British flag, with a British captain and crew. These days, it could be a British-owned ship, sailing under a Maltese flag, with a Thai captain and a Filipino crew.

Such a ship was the Yao Ah Lei. Chinese-owned and built in 2000. She was 749.7 feet long, 105.6 feet wide, and had a draft of 44.3 feet. The draft is the minimum depth of water a ship requires to safely navigate. She was sailing under a Chinese flag with a deadweight of 66,094 tons of crude oil from Saudi Arabia destined for the Port of Shanghai. She had a Thai captain, a Malaysian ship engineer, and a Filipino crew of eight—all in all, a dispensable crew, ship, and cargo.

Not a big tanker by any stretch of the imagination, but she was ideal for what the Operation MK conspirators had in mind. The maximum draft of a vessel that can pass through the Strait, referred to as the Malaccamax, is 82 feet. Any more than that and the ship has to detour a few thousand nautical miles to pass through the Lombok Strait, Makassar Strait, Sibutu Passage, or Mindoro Strait instead.

Shipwrecks, 34 of them, some dating to the 1880s, in that narrow and shallow part of the Strait of Malacca near Singapore, known as the Phillips Channel, and the 94,000 vessels passing through it every year were posing a serious collision hazard. On August 20, 2017, the United States Navy destroyer USS John S. McCain lost ten of its crew in a collision with the merchant ship Alnic MC a short distance east of the strait.

The Yao Ah Lei was well within the dimensions of the Malaccamax and, barring a collision or grounding, able to easily pass through the strait. But the MK planners had a plan to add another shipwreck to the tally.

According to the MK plan, if the president's speech, written for him months ago, included a piece about the piracy problems in the Straits of Malacca, Sunda, and Lombok, it would be the go-ahead for the team of six brigands in two speedboats to move into position and wait for the Yao Ah Lei to arrive at the north entry of the Phillips Channel. At the narrowest point, the channel is only 1.7 miles wide. It's a natural bottleneck with the potential for collisions, grounding, or oil spills.

At the time of Liao Qigang's speech in Beijing, the Yao Ah Lei was five hours away from that narrow point. As soon as she had slowed down to enter the narrow, pirates were going to board the ship, kill the entire crew, rig her with explosives, leave, and set the charges off remotely. The channel would be blocked, and the oil spill and wreckage would take months to clear.

The PRC's planned reaction was going to be one of extreme outrage and immediate action. A PRC-led salvage operation would be launched immediately to clear the channel. PLAN (People's Liberation Army Navy) warships and submarines would be dispatched at the same time to take control of the Straits of Malacca, Sunda, and Lombok and establish a permanent presence so as to protect the PRC's economic interests. And, exactly as the MK plan envisaged, give them control of the South China Sea.

Chapter Fifty-Nine

WHAT'S WRONG?

Strait of Malacca

The marshals believed their plan to take control of the straits was perfect. The cost of losing the Yao Ah Lei, 66,094 tons of crude oil, and the lives of ten non-Chinese citizens were negligible in the overall scheme of things. Besides, those losses would only serve to garner sympathy from the international community. There was, however, one problem with their plan; all of them, except General Lang, were unaware that a copy of the Operation MK had gone missing.

The *TOMATS*, under the command of Declan Spencer, with the usual crew of Special Forces operators and their wives or girlfriends, had been in the Port of Singapore for almost a week. From Langley, the Peregrine team had been tracking the Yao Ah Lei's journey all the way from Saudi Arabia into the Strait of Malacca and southwards to the Phillips Channel. Thanks to the efforts of the IT team and the information streamed from the CIA's satellites and drones, the mission team on the *TOMATS* knew the precise layout of the Yao Ah Lei, as well as the names and faces of the entire crew.

Rex and his usual team of Catia, Digger, Josh, and Marissa had arrived in Singapore two days before President Liao's speech. The day before the speech, the *TOMATS* had left the Port of Singapore on a leisurely cruise up north in the Strait of Malacca. On the way, they'd passed the Yao Ah Lei. Shortly after passing the ship, the *TOMATS* had turned back and followed her, maintaining a gap of about four to five nautical miles.

Liao's speech was word-for-word as it was written in the MK Plan. Three hours after Rex had ended the call with Brandt, Spencer had closed the gap between the *TOMATS* and the Yao Ah Lei to one nautical mile.

When the tanker was an hour away from the narrow, cruising at seven knots per hour, Spencer brought the *TOMATS* to a stop, and the Nemo was launched. Onboard was the pilot and copilot, both US Navy SEALs, Rex, Josh, and four more SEALs.

Digger was not bemused when he discovered that he was not part of the mission team and made it known with growls, yelps, and accusatory looks at Rex. It was only when Catia produced his kong stuffed with peanut butter that he relented. The kong was an odd-shaped toy, part cylinder, part cone, with indentations that made it look like a hard-plastic snowman, with a hole running through it from top to bottom. It was always a joy to see how Digger would lose all dog-dignity as he went into frenzied ecstasy when he saw the kong. It was a special treat, especially when Rex or Catia had stuffed it for him with some delicacy such as dried meat or what Catia called Digger's gelato—peanut butter.

After the Nemo was launched, Spencer let the *TOMATS*

drop back three nautical miles behind the tanker and main-
tained the gap while the Nemo traveling at almost fifteen
knots, twenty-five feet below the surface, closed the gap to
the Yao Ah Lei in less than half an hour.

An hour before the Nemo was launched, Marissa had
launched one of the two mini-helicopter drones they had on
board. These drones were about three times the size of the
drones Rex and Catia used in Jersey City when rescuing
Josh and Marissa. They were more powerful, could stay in
the air for up to one hour before a battery change was
required, and were able to operate up to six miles from their
base.

It was 2:05 a.m. when the first of Rex's team, dark-
cladded and ski-masked, slipped over the aft rails of the Yao
Ah Lei unnoticed. Ten minutes later, all six of them were on
board. Hovering five-hundred feet above them was the
drone controlled by Marissa from the *TOMATS*'s comms
room. Catia was the mission director tonight.

The Nemo had dropped back to about five-hundred feet
behind the ship.

Catia's voice came over the team's molar mics. "Situation unchanged. The captain and first mate are on the
bridge. The engineer is in his cabin, asleep. Two of the crew
are in the kitchen, one is in the engine room, the remaining
four are asleep in the crew cabin."

The first critical part of the mission was to get aboard
unseen. That was achieved without mishap. The next critical part was a bit more challenging. They had to neutralize
the crew quickly and quietly, preventing them from raising
any alarm.

Rex and one SEAL had to take down the captain and
first mate on the bridge. Josh and another were responsible
for the four in the crew's cabin. The remaining SEALs were

responsible for the engineer and his assistant and the two in the kitchen. But the captain and first mate had to be taken down first as they had a commanding view of most parts of the ship from the bridge, and the ship's communications systems were also located there.

The team was armed with Glock 19 pistols with silencers, combat knives, Tazer guns, and special syringes filled with a cocktail of rapid coma- and amnesia-inducing drugs. Hopefully, they'd have no need to use the guns or Tazers.

Rex and Dan, the SEAL who was designated to take over the helm once the captain and first mate were down, arrived at the door leading to the bridge.

Catia said, "The captain is at the wheel; the first mate... hang on, he's heading for the door. Be ready."

Rex signaled to Dan to take the man down when he came out.

The door opened. As the first mate stepped out, Dan threw his right arm around the man's neck, covered his mouth with a gloved hand, and plunged the syringe into his neck.

Rex went through the door onto the bridge at the same time as Dan took the first mate down. The captain was facing straight ahead, headphones over his ears, his back to Rex, unaware of what had just happened behind him.

Rex grinned when he saw the captain's head bobbing up and down to the beat of the music coming from the headphones.

Only a muffled sound escaped from the captain's mouth when Rex's hand slipped over his mouth. He was probably so stunned he didn't even feel the needle sinking into his neck.

Seconds later, Dan was at the wheel of the Yao Ah Lei.

Rex touched the switch on the loop around his neck and said to the rest of the team, "Bridge secured. Over to you."

Seven minutes later, the ten crew members of the Yao Ah Lei were in dreamland, tied up, gagged, and hooded. They had enough drugs in their bodies to keep them asleep for three more hours and wake up with no recollection of what had happened.

One of the SEALs joined Dan on the bridge as the first mate. Although no routine communications were due for the next three hours, they'd left the communications systems switched on.

The six pirates turned up in two speedboats shortly before 3:30 a.m. Marissa's drone had spotted them ten minutes earlier when they'd launched their boats, and Catia had kept Rex and the team updated with their progress.

They pulled up at the stern of the Yao Ah Lei, tied the boats to metal rings, shot two hooked rope-ladders over the rails, and within minutes the first two balaclavad men climbed over the rails and took up positions to help the rest of their team come up the ladders and hoist the bags containing their weapons and explosives up to the deck.

The two men were preoccupied with getting their team-mates and equipment on deck as quickly as possible and never saw the two figures approaching them from behind.

One by one, as the remaining four pirates reached the top of the ladders, they were helped over the rails by men whom they believed were their own team members. Later on, when questioned about the events, all they would remember was that after setting foot on deck, they had no recollection of what had happened.

When the six pirates were all tied up, gagged, and hooded, Rex and the team carried them and their equipment to the dining room.

Dan and his first mate navigated the Yao Ah Lei safely through the narrows of the Phillips Channel and increased the speed to ten knots. Three-quarters of an hour later, they stopped and lowered the anchor. The crew members were checked to make sure they were still unconscious before their restraints and hoods were removed.

The Nemo's sail appeared above the waterline beside the Yao Ah Lei. Ten minutes later, Rex closed the hatch, and the Nemo disappeared below the water.

———————

About half an hour after the Nemo had left, the crew started to regain consciousness; the captain and first mate in their chairs on the bridge, two men on the kitchen floor, the engineer on his bunk in his cabin, his assistant on the floor of the engine room, and four crew members in their bunks in the crew cabin. They all had throbbing headaches but no sensible explanation of what could've caused them or their collective amnesia.

Forty-five minutes later, the Singapore harbor police boarded the Yao Ah Lei and found a very incoherent captain and equally befuddled first mate on the bridge surrounded by the crew in no better mental condition.

To the simple question, "What's wrong?" The answer from the captain was simply, "We don't know."

No, we didn't call you.

No, we didn't drop the anchor, and we have no idea who did.

No, there are no mechanical or technical issues that we're aware of.

However, we found six men on board, and we have no idea who they are or how they happened to be on this ship. We found them tied up, gagged, hooded, and unconscious in the dining room. Apparently, they were armed with guns and backpacks filled with explosives; those we found stacked in a room next to the dining room.

About when and how they'd sailed through the Phillips Channel, the captain and his crew uttered not a single word because they had no recollection of doing so.

A thorough search of the ship by the police showed that she was intact, and every drop of the 66,094 tons of crude oil was still safely in the tanks.

The officer in charge sighed deeply. Twenty years on the force had given him the ability to recognize trouble when he saw it.

Chapter Sixty

NOW YOU'RE TALKING

Beijing, China

In the underground command and control center of Operation MK, General Xia Wei, in charge of the execution of the MK plan, had a different kind of headache altogether. He was a known strategist, planner, and devout student of Sun Tzu, which was why the marshals had picked him from their ranks to lead Operation MK. By now, according to the plan, the Phillips Channel was supposed to be ablaze, the Yao Ah Lei at the bottom of the sea, and the channel completely blocked. In fact, he was expecting the media to be in a frenzy by now. But the satellite feed showed that the Yao Ah Lei had been stationary outside the channel for the past three hours, and although he had been monitoring the ship's communications and could talk to the captain if he wanted to, he wouldn't dare to do it. He had to resign himself to the fact that something had gone wrong and had to get the story through the media and the ship's owners.

The first media report came from The Straits Times, a Singapore-based English-language daily newspaper, acting on an anonymous tip. They called it a failed attempt by pirates to hijack a Chinese oil tanker. Soon the other news outlets picked the story up, and the speculation gained momentum. The most logical explanation of what had happened was also the most popular—the crew of the Yao Ah Lei must've foiled the pirates' plans. Eventually, that's the story that the media settled for as the newsworthiness of the incident started to dwindle.

Fortunately for General Xia and his coconspirators, the pirates couldn't tell the authorities anything about the PRC's involvement. Everything was done through third parties who didn't know anything. The crew also had no idea what was supposed to have happened to them and their ship. In other words, there were no loose ends to tie up. But that did nothing for the enormity of the humiliation of a failed operation.

To General Xia, it never occurred that they had been outwitted by adversaries who had also studied Sun Tzu. And what he had just experienced was a demonstration of Sun Tzu's principle of appearing far to your enemy when in fact, you were near.

In Langley, the Peregrine team was celebrating. John, Ollie, and Richardson were there with them. When there was a moment of quiet, John asked for everyone's attention. "The scoreboard says it's one-nil in our favor. You did a great job. I thank you all for that. Now let's get back to work because this was only the first skirmish in a cold war, which we have to prevent from becoming hot."

Richardson, Ollie, and Stacie Barrett had known Brandt for years. The rest of the Peregrine team still had to experience more of him before they'd know that despite his brusque mannerism, he cared deeply for those under his command.

There were no quibbles from the team; they understood the gravity and magnitude of the threat against their country.

A few minutes later, Brandt had Ollie and Richardson in one of the meeting rooms where Spencer, Rex, Catia, Digger, Josh, and Marissa had dialed in via a secured video link to participate in the post-mission review.

In typical style, Brandt didn't waste much time congratulating Rex and the team. It was a textbook mission. Everything worked out as planned. But don't expect it to happen again. Rex et al. knew John Brandt better than anyone else. Nothing more had to be said.

Apart from successfully containing the PRC's attempt to take control of the Strait of Malacca, the mission also served to confirm that the MK plan in the CIA's possession was the real thing.

"And," said Rex, "my suspicion is confirmed that General Lang didn't tell his comrades he lost his copy of the plan."

"And I suspect our general might be a worried man right now," said Ollie. "So worried that he might consider working for us."

"Now you're talking," said Brandt with a big smile on his face.

Epilogue

About two weeks later, the story was revived in the Singapore media for a few days when it was reported that two of the pirates had decided to confess and become state witnesses in exchange for more lenient sentences. In their confessions, they mentioned that their orders were to kill the crew of the Yao Ah Lei and blow her up with explosives. The papers called it one of the most peculiar acts of piracy they'd ever heard of. Pirates, they said, are in it for the loot. This had the hallmarks of terrorism. Or a false-flag operation, conspiracy theorists postulated.

General Xia winced when he read that and mumbled, "You'll never know how right you are."

The Trustees had been speculating about what happened that night. It didn't take too long to figure out that an unknown group must have boarded the ship and overpowered the crew and pirates. One theory was that it could've been a rival gang. But why didn't they steal anything from the ship? Another theory, more plausible than the first, was that the Singapore Security and Intelligence Division could've had a hand in it. But then they must've had prior intelligence about the operation. How? They could've been watching the pirates and were ready with a task force of special operators who boarded the ship, neutralized everyone, and called the Singapore police to do the mop-up.

General Lang had his own theory but didn't share it with the others. He *knew* the only way that operation could've been pulled off was by someone who had insight into the MK plan. That meant Sun Yan must have escaped from China, which meant the document was in the hands of a law enforcement and/or intelligence agency; by the looks of it, the Singapore Security and Intelligence Division and/or the Singapore Police Force. He shivered at the thought that it could be, probably already was, in the hands of the CIA. Singapore and the United States had good relations. There existed a Free Trade Agreement between the two countries. More than 30,000 Americans lived in Singapore, and he had no doubt that the two countries shared intelligence with each other.

The more Lang thought about his dilemma, the more he realized that it was too late to put the genie back in the bottle. His options were few. Tell his comrades. For that, he would be executed. Suicide. For that, he didn't have the guts. Defect. For that, he had the resolve. It was better than being dead. But it had to be planned very carefully, or he would end up dead anyway.

A FREE Novella from JC Ryan

vinci-books.com/no-doubt-free

Even paradise has shadows...

When a beautiful woman is found stabbed to death on the tranquil island of Olib, police quickly blame her boyfriend. But, Digger, a big black Dutch Shepherd, a trained military dog, and his alpha, Rex Dalton, a former black ops specialist, know the police were mistaken.

Fact and Fiction

About China's ambitions to become the paramount global power, there is a growing body of evidence. China experts say that the PRC government is indeed aiming for global power as it seeks to upend the American-led international system and create a world order of its own.

Visitors to the great state of Arizona will search in vain for the CRC Ranch. It doesn't exist.

My sincerest apologies to the management of the nonexistent One Tree Hill hotel in Manhattan, New York, for abducting two fictional characters, Josh and Marissa Farley, from their establishment.

I also apologize to the management of the nonexistent South House Hotel, Manhattan, New York, for conducting a fictitious honey trap operation on their premises.

The information about the Underground Great Wall of China contained in this story is, to the best of my knowledge, accurate. So is the existence of Unit 61398, a division of the People's Liberation Army (PLA), the alleged source of Chinese computer hacking attacks. The unit is, however, stationed in Pudong, Shanghai, not in the Underground Great Wall.

The existence of and information about the Tuidang (Quit the Party) movement in China, as described in the story, are, to the best of my knowledge, accurate.

The information about the persecution of religious groups in China, specifically Christians, and Muslims, is, to the best of my knowledge, accurate.

The information about the existence of fake social media accounts and automated bots that control them is, to the best of my knowledge, accurate.

Although the Nemo is purely my imagination, I used information about mini-submarines, aka midget-submarines to construct it.

The molar mics used by Rex and his team for communication throughout this story are real. More information is available on Sonitus Technologies's website.

Next in the Rex Dalton K9 Thrillers Series

vinci-books.com/the-abyss

With famine looming and tensions rising, Rex Dalton must act fast to prevent catastrophe.

Rex Dalton embarks on a covert operation to prevent a catastrophic war between the US and China. As tensions escalate and a devastating famine grips China, Rex races against time to recruit a high-ranking general, navigating a treacherous landscape of espionage and deceit. Failure is not an option.

Turn the page for a free preview…

The Abyss: Prologue

Zhongnanhai, Beijing, China

Ever since taking office, President Liao Qigang's sleeping habits had become erratic. Stress had been his ever-present companion, stalking him every waking moment, and nightmares haunted his dreams. On a good night, he'd get six hours of sleep, but those were few and far between. Most nights, he would get four to five hours, and then there were the nights when he got no sleep at all—like tonight. The prospect of invading Taiwan and the international repercussions, including the likelihood of war with America and its allies, weighed heavily on him as he waited for the call from General Xia, who was in charge of the operation.

And if the threat of war was not enough to keep Liao in a constant state of despondency, the reports about severe flooding in the Kwei Zhou area in the southwestern part of the country were making a generous contribution to his acute dyspepsia.

The benefit of state-controlled media is that the state

determines what information is released to the public. The flood was labeled as 'lots of rain.' The number of people displaced was quoted as half a million, while the actual number was about three times that. The number of dead, which was actually more than 100,000, was reported to be 40,000.

Even so, the president couldn't dare to visit the stricken area because that would make it look as if there really had been a major disaster.

Though that kind of disingenuous reporting helped keep the populace's stress and anxiety levels down, it did nothing for the president's.

Liao felt the knot in his stomach as he looked at the information about the threatening disaster posed by the overflowing of the Three Gorges Dam. The City of Wuhan had already been flooded. Two major lakes on both sides of the Yangtze River functioned as natural draining reservoirs for excessive water flowing down the river. The Por Yang Hu Lake on the northern side of the Yangtze, normally about 3,000 square miles, had in three days grown to more than 4,000 square miles. If the Three Gorges Dam gave way, 450 million, one-third of China's total population, would be negatively impacted, and as many as 45 million people would either die or suffer from severe health issues.

He took a long deep breath and let it out slowly and noisily.

At the break of dawn, with no call from Xia and no breaking news out of Taiwan on any of the news channels, he knew the operation must've run into some kind of problem.

He felt relief washing over him. China would not be going to war today. "But there are things worse than war— famine. I can only hope that we will never fall over that cliff into the hellish abyss of food insecurity and starvation," he mumbled softly.

He took a hot shower and put on a clean suit, then ordered his favorite breakfast of congee (rice porridge), pancakes with eggs, and a pot of tea.

By 8:00 a.m., when Mao Xinya, the Minister of Agriculture and Rural Affairs, entered his office, Liao felt almost rejuvenated.

It was with no small measure of trepidation that Mao Xinya arrived at Zhongnanhai. Messengers bearing bad news were not usually at peril for merely conveying the message. But Mao Xinya was no ordinary messenger; he was the Minister of Agriculture and Rural Affairs, a position he had held for more than a decade.

In the world's fourth-largest and most populous country, his responsibilities were vast: agriculture and environmental issues relating to agriculture, fishery, consumer affairs, animal husbandry, horticulture, animal welfare, foodstuffs, hunting and game management, as well as higher education and research in the field of agricultural sciences.

To be concise, Mao Xinya carried the ultimate responsibility for the production of the food that the 1.4 billion citizens of China put on their tables every day.

For almost four weeks, Mao and his advisors worked meticulously and slept very little to collect and verify data, analyzed same, made projections, and wrote their conclusions down in a report—the fount of Mao's disquiet—currently in his briefcase.

During the Great Chinese Famine of 1959 to 1961, thirty million had starved to death. In addition, miscarriages due to malnutrition and abortions because there was no food for babies, claimed another thirty million.

Mao was about to tell the President that the country was facing another famine—this one would make the Great Famine pale in comparison.

Bringing Professor Lei Hai, senior agronomist and grain specialist, to answer the technical questions he was bound to be asked provided little comfort.

Whether the fact that he was distantly related to the great Chairman Mao Tse-tung would count in his favor, he would know shortly.

The Abyss: Chapter One

FIRST DAY ON THE JOB

CIA Headquarters, Langley, Virginia, USA

It was Monday morning shortly before eight when John pulled up in his designated parking space at Langley. He switched the engine off and looked at his wife, Christelle. "This is it, your first day on the job. Excited?"

She smiled and nodded. "Just like old times." Christelle was a tall woman with an athletic build, green eyes, and blond hair that didn't come out of a bottle—she was a head-turner. She was formally dressed in a charcoal pantsuit. Attentiveness and intelligence radiated from her persona.

John chuckled. "Yep, except now we're up against the Chinese communists instead of the Russians, we're forty years older, and we have a service dog to watch over us."

Said service dog was in the backseat. Her name was Cupcake, a seven-month-old, short-haired, brindle-colored Dutch Shepherd. She was a gift to them from Rex and

Catia when John got out of the hospital after brain surgery five months ago.

"I don't feel forty years older. I barely feel forty."

"And you don't look a day older," said John with a big smile.

"Flattery will get you everywhere, my dear."

John stood at six-foot-two in his socks. A handsome man with gray hair and hazel eyes, stately comportment, and in excellent shape for someone of seventy-four years.

Christelle, a former deputy director of the DGSE, the French equivalent of the American CIA, had worked with John on a few joint missions in their younger days during the Cold War. There was a romantic spark between them back then, but the Atlantic Ocean and work had put an end to it. More than thirty years after their last joint mission, they caught up again. The old flame was rekindled, and two months after Christelle's retirement, she and John were married.

They had plans to settle on the Ranch, a 20,000-acre property in Yavapai County, in the western part of Arizona, CRC'S headquarters and training facility. However, they had to change their plans when they were on their way back to the Ranch after their honeymoon in Vietnam. Richardson contacted Brandt and asked him to divert the flight and come to Langley to discuss a very urgent matter. The pressing issue was the Operation Middle Kingdom Plan.

Since then, John and Christelle had been living in an apartment fifteen minutes' drive from CIA headquarters.

It had been nearly three months since the defection of Flat Arrow, the codename for a senior computer programmer working for China's foremost military hacking outfit, Unit 61398, a subdivision of the Information Operations and Information Warfare division, the cyberwarfare arm of the People's Liberation Army (PLA).

The insider knowledge about Unit 61398's activities brought over by Flat Arrow was a significant haul for the US intelligence community. It helped them to identify and rectify the vulnerabilities in their own computer networks, and it enabled them to exploit the vulnerabilities in the PRC's networks.

But it was the details of Operation Middle Kingdom, delivered by Flat Arrow, that shook the foundations of the US intelligence community.

Soon dubbed the MK Plan, it was the blueprint conceived by a top-secret power group, who called themselves the Trustees, which included the Chinese President and ten senior generals from the People's Liberation Army (PLA) to dethrone America as the world's only superpower and achieve Mao Tse-tung's hundred-year plan—the entire world under Chinese communist rule by 2049—twenty-five years ahead of time.

There was no ambiguity in the MK Plan—China was on the verge of instigating a series of actions that would bring them into direct conflict with most of their neighbors and the USA. It was equally clear that unless China was dissuaded from its chosen course, a world war was inevitable.

Within days of receiving the MK Plan, the CIA had obtained presidential authorization to launch Operation Peregrine, a Cold War-like strategy aimed at containing China's expansionist ideals and prevent an all-out war, which would, without doubt, see the use of nuclear weapons.

After reading the MK Plan, Martin Richardson, the deputy director in charge of CIA operations, persuaded

John Brandt to take control of Operation Peregrine. John was a veteran of the Cold War who left the CIA in 1995. Six years later, in 2001, after the 9/11 attacks, he had established CRC (Crisis Response Consultancy), a private military contractor specializing in black operations on behalf of the CIA and other US security agencies.

Christelle opened the rear passenger door for Cupcake, took her leash, and hooked her arm into her husband's as they approached the front entrance of the George Bush Center for Intelligence colloquially known as the CIA Headquarters.

For the past three months, since John took charge of Operation Peregrine, despite being newlyweds, Christelle hadn't seen much of him. She and Cupcake had visited every noteworthy, and some not so noteworthy, statue, museum, and historical and contemporary building in the Langley and DC areas, including the White House and the Capitol Building.

After a lifetime in the spy business, she knew what was at stake, and intelligence officers seldom had the luxury of nine-to-five shifts. She supported and encouraged John, and she never complained, but that didn't prevent her from getting bored and a little frustrated with her dreary daily routine and lack of intellectual stimulation.

John took notice and had been thinking about a solution when he got home one night and found her working on a large petit point tapestry. She might as well have said, "John, I've had enough of museums and statues and art galleries." The next morning John spoke to Richardson.

Richardson took the matter to Howard Lawrence, the director of the CIA. Lawrence thought it was a matter for the Commander in Chief to decide. Therefore, he went to see the president, whose response was, "Bloody hell. You've got a senior Cold War veteran, a former deputy director of the DGSE, no less, sitting around idle, making tapestries, and keeping a dog company?"

"I'm afraid so, sir. I'd like her to join the Peregrine team, but we don't have any precedents for it."

"Well, if I understand you correctly, she's been working on joint missions with us since the Cold War and on another handful of missions over the past few years. And she knows as much about Peregrine as her husband knows. In other words, there's no trust issue?"

"None at all, sir."

"So, what's the holdup? Put her to work already. And if your French counterpart has any issues, let me know, I'll give their president a call. I presume the French hate the idea of a Chinese flag flying over France just as much as we hate the idea of it flying over America."

It was Friday afternoon, and John went home early to take his lovely wife out for dinner.

At the restaurant that evening, after placing their orders, it didn't take long before Christelle said, "John, you've got something on your mind. I'd like to hear it."

He managed to keep an impassive composure. "Well, I've got a vacancy on the Peregrine team, and I'm at a loss as to whom I should recruit."

"What's the job description?"

"I need someone with Cold War experience."

"Okay, but what specialty?"

"Strategic thinking, planning, managing agents and such—"

"And you don't know anyone like that?"

John shook his head. "The thing is, it must be a woman; she must be over sixty-five, and she must be very beautiful—"

Christelle leaned forward, "What's—"

John interjected, "Oh, and she must also be French and the former deputy director of the DGSE—"

"John!" Christelle had the most beautiful smile. "How did you pull that off?"

"Howard Lawrence got the president's permission—"

"You mean the President of the United States?"

"Uh-huh."

"But what about the DGSE? My terms of employment stated that I can't work for another country's intelligence service without explicit permission from the director—"

John held his hand up. "Don't worry, Lawrence called him. He says it was an easy sell once he gave your former boss a summary overview of the MK Plan. He agreed on the proviso that we share information pertaining to France with them."

"When do I start?"

"Monday morning."

"We'll have to get someone to take care of Cupcake while we're at work—"

John chuckled. "She's part of the deal. Her job description is to provide aid and comfort to you and me and anyone else on the team who might need it."

Christelle's face was beaming, and her eyes were sparkling.

And twelve time zones away, the Chinese intelligence agencies were totally unaware of the formidable former spymaster who had joined the ranks of their adversaries.

Grab your copy...
vinci-books.com/the-abyss

About the Author

JC Ryan is a bestselling author renowned for his intricate espionage, archaeological thrillers, and conspiracy mysteries. With over 30 acclaimed novels, including the popular Rex Dalton K9 Thrillers, Rossler Foundation Mysteries, and Carter Devereux Mystery Thrillers, Ryan has captivated readers around the globe.

Drawing from his diverse professional background—as a military officer, lawyer, and IT manager—Ryan creates compelling narratives that skillfully blend historical accuracy with thrilling adventure. He is celebrated as a master storyteller, known for crafting riveting plots, meticulous historical details, and engaging, multidimensional characters. Ryan's meticulous research lends authenticity and depth to each story, immersing readers in richly constructed worlds filled with intrigue, suspense, and adventure.

Fans of David Baldacci, Lee Child's Jack Reacher, Tom Clancy's Jack Ryan, Nelson DeMille's John Corey, Vince Flynn's Mitch Rapp, Mark Greaney's Gray Man, Gregg Hurwitz's Orphan X, Robert Ludlum's Jason Bourne, Daniel Silva's Gabriel Allon, Brad Taylor's Pike Logan, Brad Thor's Scot Harvath, James Rollins' Sigma Force, Steve Berry's Cotton Malone, and Dan Brown's Robert Langdon will find JC Ryan's novels equally compelling and unforgettable.

When not writing, Ryan enjoys spending time with his college sweetheart, whom he married in 1978. They are proud parents of two daughters, have two sons-in-law, and are grandparents to two grandchildren.